EVIL STAR

BOOK TWO OF
THE GATEKEEPERS

ANTHONY HOROWITZ

Evil Star

Anthony Horowitz
AR B.L.: 4.7
Points: 13.0   MG

SCHOLASTIC INC.
New York Toronto London Auckland Sydney
Mexico City New Delhi Hong Kong Buenos Aires

ISBN-13: 978-0-545-00334-6
ISBN-10: 0-545-00334-2

12 11 10 9 8 7 6 5 4 3 2 1   7 8 9 10 11/0

Printed in the U.S.A.   40
This edition first printing, January 2007

Text design by Steve Scott
Text was set in New Baskerville.

The old man's eyes burned red, reflecting the last flames of the fire. The sun had already begun to set behind the mountains, and the shadows were closing in. Far away, a huge bird — a condor — wheeled round in a lazy circle before plunging back down to earth. And then everything was still. The night was just a breath away.

"He will come," the old man said. He spoke in a strange language, known to very few people in the world. "We have no need to send for him. He will come anyway."

Supporting himself on a walking stick carved from the branch of a tree, he got to his feet and made his way to the edge of the stone terrace where he had been sitting. From here he could look down into a canyon that seemed to fall away forever, a fault line in the planet that had given way perhaps a million years ago. For a minute he was silent. There were a dozen men behind him, waiting for him to speak. None of them dared interrupt him while he stood there, deep in thought.

At last he turned back.

"The boy is on the other side of the world," he said. "He is fourteen years old."

One of the men stirred uneasily. He knew it was wrong to ask questions, but he couldn't stop himself. "Are we just going to wait for him?" he demanded. "We have so little time. And even if he does come, how can he help us? A child!"

1

"You don't understand, Atoc," the old man replied. If he was angry, he didn't show it. He knew that Atoc was only twenty years old, barely more than a child himself, at least in the elder's mind. "The boy has power. He still has no idea who he is or how strong he has become. He will come here and he will arrive in time. His power will bring him to us."

"Who is this boy?" someone else asked.

The old man looked again at the sun. It seemed to be sitting, perfectly balanced, on the highest mountain peak. The mountain was called Mandango . . . the Sleeping God.

"His name is Matthew Freeman," he said. "He is one of the five."

ONE
Big Wheel

There was something wrong about the house in Eastfield Terrace. Something unpleasant.

All the houses on the street were more or less identical: red brick, Victorian, with two bedrooms on the first floor and a bay window on either the left or the right of the front door. Some had satellite dishes. Some had window boxes filled with brightly colored flowers. But looking down from the top of the hill, one house stood out immediately. Number twenty-seven no longer belonged there. It was as if it had caught some sort of disease and needed to be taken away.

The front garden was full of junk and the garbage can beside the gate was overflowing, surrounded by plastic garbage bags that the owners had been unable to stuff inside. This wasn't uncommon in Eastfield Terrace. The net curtains were permanently drawn across the front windows and, as far as anyone could tell, the lights were never turned on. But even this wasn't particularly strange. What was unusual was the way the house smelled. For weeks now, there had been a rotten, sewage smell that seemed at first to be coming from a blocked pipe but which had rapidly gotten worse until people had begun to cross the street to avoid it. Whatever was causing it seemed to be affecting the entire place. The grass on the front lawn was beginning to die. The flowers had wilted and then been choked up by weeds. The color seemed to be draining out of the very bricks.

The neighbors had tried to complain. They had knocked on the front door, but nobody had come. They had telephoned, but nobody had answered. Finally, the borough council at the Ipswich Civic Center had been called . . . but of course it would be weeks before any action was taken.

The house wasn't empty. That much they knew. They had occasionally seen the owner, Gwenda Davis, pacing back and forth inside. Once — more than a week ago — she had been seen scurrying home from the shops. And every evening the television was turned on.

Gwenda Davis was well known on the street. She had lived there for much of her adult life, first on her own and then with her boyfriend, Brian Conran, who had worked occasionally as a milkman. But what had really set the neighbors talking was the time, six years ago, when she had inexplicably adopted an eight-year-old boy and brought him home to live with her. Everyone agreed that she and Brian were not exactly ideal parents. He drank. The two of them argued. And, according to local gossip, they hardly knew the boy whose own parents had died in a car accident.

Nobody was very surprised when the whole thing went wrong. It wasn't really the boy's fault. Matthew Freeman had been nice enough when he arrived, but a bit of time spent with Gwenda and Brian had soon had an effect. He had started missing school. He'd been hanging out with the wrong crowd, known for a whole range of petty crimes.

4

Inevitably he had gotten into trouble with the police. During a robbery at a local warehouse, just around the corner from Ipswich Station, a security guard had nearly died, and Matthew had been dragged out with blood on his hands. As punishment, he'd been sent away on some sort of fostering program. He had a new foster mother, somewhere in Yorkshire. And good riddance to bad rubbish. That was the general view.

All this had happened three months ago. Since then, Gwenda had gradually disappeared from sight. And as for Brian, no one had seen him for weeks. The house was silent and neglected. Everyone agreed that soon something would have to be done.

And now it was half past seven in the first week of June. The days were stretching out, holding on for as long as they could. The people in Eastfield Terrace were hot and tired. Tempers were getting short. And the smell was as bad as ever.

Gwenda was in the kitchen, making supper for herself. She had never been a very attractive woman, small and dowdy with dull eyes and pinched lips that never smiled. But in the weeks since Matt's departure, she had rapidly declined. Her hair was unbrushed and wild. She was wearing a shapeless flowery dress and a cardigan which, like her, hadn't been washed for some time. She had developed a nervous twitch and was constantly rubbing her arms as if she were cold or perhaps afraid of something.

"Do you want anything?" she called out in a thin, high-pitched voice.

Brian was waiting for her in the sitting room, but she

knew he wouldn't eat anything. She had preferred it when he'd had his job down at the milk depot, but he'd been sacked after he'd gotten into a fight with one of the managers. That had happened just after Matt had been sent away. Now he'd lost his appetite, too.

Gwenda looked at her watch. It was almost time for *Big Wheel*, her favorite television program of the week. In fact, thanks to cable, she could see *Big Wheel* every night. But Thursdays were special. On Thursday, there was a brand-new program — not a repeat.

Gwenda was addicted to *Big Wheel*. She loved the bright lights of the studio, the mystery prizes, the contestants who might win a million pounds if they got enough questions right and dared to spin the wheel. Best of all, she loved the host — Rex McKenna — with his permanent suntan, his jokes, his perfect white smile. Rex was about fifty years old, but his hair was still jet-black, his eyes still glimmered, and there was a spring in his step that made him seem much younger. He had been on the show for as long as Gwenda could remember, and although he hosted two other quiz programs as well as a dancing competition on the BBC, it was on *Big Wheel* that Gwenda liked him best.

"Is it on yet?" she called out from the kitchen.

There was no reply from Brian. He hadn't been talking very much lately, either.

She reached into a cupboard and took out a can of beans. It wasn't exactly what you'd call a feast, but it'd been a while since either of them had earned any money, and she was beginning to feel the pinch. She looked around the kitchen for a clean plate but there wasn't one. Every surface was covered with dirty crockery. A tower of soiled plates and bowls rose out of the sink. Gwenda decided she would eat the beans out of the tin. She plunged her hand into the brown, filthy water and somehow managed to find a fork. She wiped some of the grease off on her dress and hurried out of the room.

The lights were out in the living room, but the glow of the television was enough to show the way. It also showed the mess that the room had become. There were old newspapers scattered across the carpet, overflowing ashtrays, more dirty plates, old socks, and underpants. Brian was sitting on a sofa that had looked ugly and secondhand the moment it had left the shop. There was a nasty stain on the nylon cover. Ignoring it, Gwenda sat down next to him.

The smell, which had been bad throughout the house, was worse in here. Gwenda ignored that, too.

It seemed to her that things had gone from bad to worse since Matt had left. She didn't quite know why. It wasn't as if she had actually liked him. On the contrary, she had always known there was something weird about the boy. Hadn't he dreamed his mother and father were going to die the night before the accident had actually happened? She had only taken him in because Brian had persuaded her — and of course, he'd only wanted to get his hands on the money that Matt's parents had left him. The trouble was, the money had gone all too quickly. And then Matt had gone, too, taken away by the police as a juvenile delinquent. All she'd been left with was the blame.

It wasn't her fault. She'd looked after him. She'd never forget the way the police looked at her, as if she were the one who'd committed the crime. She wished now that Matt had never come into her life. Everything had gone wrong because of Matt.

"And now, on ITV, it's time once again to take your chances and spin . . . the Big Wheel!"

Gwenda settled back as the *Big Wheel* theme tune began. Fifty-pound notes twisted and spun across the screen. The audience applauded. And there was Rex McKenna walking down the flashing staircase with a pretty girl holding on to each arm, dressed in a bright, sequined jacket, waving and smiling, happy as always to be back.

"Good evening, everyone!" he called out. "Who knows who's going to win big-time tonight?" He paused and winked straight at the camera. "Only the wheel knows!"

The audience went wild as if they were hearing the words for the first time. But of course Rex always began the show the same way. *"Only the wheel knows!"* was his catchphrase, although Gwenda wasn't quite sure if it was true. The wheel was just a big piece of wood and plastic. How could it know anything?

Rex came to a halt and the applause died down. Gwenda was staring at the screen in a kind of trance. She had already forgotten her baked beans. Somewhere in the back of her mind, she wondered how it was that the television still worked when the electricity in the house had been turned off two weeks ago because she hadn't paid the bill. But the back of her mind was a very long way away and it didn't really matter. It was a blessing. How would she get through the nights without *Big Wheel*?

"Welcome to another show where the spin of the wheel could mean a million pounds in your pocket or a return ticket home with absolutely nothing!" Rex explained. "And what a busy week I've had. My wife woke me up at six o'clock yesterday morning to remind me to put the alarm on. The alarm went off at seven and it still hasn't come back!"

The audience roared with laughter. Gwenda laughed, too.

"But we've got a great show for you tonight. And in a minute we're going to meet the three lucky contestants who are competing for tonight's big prizes. But remember: If you want to get your hands on a cool million, what do you have to do?"

"You have to spin to win!" the audience yelled.

Brian said nothing. It was beginning to annoy Gwenda, the way he just sat there.

"But before we can get started," Rex went on, "I want to have a quick word with a very special lady, a real favorite of mine. . . ." He stepped closer to the camera, and as his face filled the screen, it seemed to Gwenda that he was looking directly at her.

"Hello, Gwenda," he said.

"Hello, Rex," Gwenda whispered. It was difficult for her to believe that he was actually talking to her. It always was.

"And how are you tonight, my love?"

"I'm all right. . . ." She bit her lip and folded her hands in her lap.

"Well, listen, my darling. I wonder if you've given any more thought to what we were talking about. Matt Freeman. That guttersnipe. That little creep. Have you decided what you're going to do about him?"

Rex McKenna had started talking to Gwenda two months ago. At the beginning, it had puzzled her. How could he interrupt the show (watched by ten million people) just to speak to her? Somehow he even managed to do it in the repeats — and that couldn't be possible, because some of them had been recorded years ago. At first, it had worried her. When she'd told Brian about it, he'd laughed in her face and said she was going mad. Well, Rex had soon put her straight about Brian. And now she didn't worry about it anymore. It was bizarre but it was happening. The truth was, she was flattered. She adored Rex McKenna and it seemed he was equally fond of her.

"Matt Freeman made a fool out of you," Rex went on. "He came into your house and he ruined your relationship with Brian. Then he got into trouble and everybody said it was your fault. Now look at you! No money. No job. You're a mess, Gwenda. . . ."

"It's not my fault," Gwenda muttered.

"I know it's not your fault, old love," Rex replied. For a moment the camera cut away and Gwenda could see the studio audience getting restless, waiting for the show to begin. "You looked after the boy. You treated him like a son. But he's pushed off without so much as a by-your-leave. No gratitude, of course. Kids these days! He's full of himself now — and you should hear the things he says about you! I've been thinking about it and I have to say . . . I believe the boy ought to be punished."

"Punished . . ." Gwenda muttered the word with a sense of dread.

"Just like you punished Brian for being so rude to you." Rex shook his head. Maybe it was a trick of the studio lighting, but he seemed almost to be reaching out of the television set, about to climb into the room. "The fact of

10

the matter is that Matt is a very nasty piece of work," he went on. "Everywhere he goes, he causes trouble. You remember what happened to his parents."

"They died."

"It was his fault. He could have saved them. And there are other things you don't know about. He recently upset some very good friends of mine. In fact he more than upset them. He killed them. Can you believe that? He killed all of them. If you ask me, there's no question about it. He needs to be punished very severely indeed."

"I don't know where he is," Gwenda said.

"I can tell you that. He goes to a school called Forrest Hill. It's in Yorkshire, just outside the city of York. That's not so far away."

"What do you want me to do?" Gwenda asked. Her mouth was dry. The can of beans had tilted forward in her hands and cold tomato sauce was dripping into her lap.

"You like me, don't you, Gwenda?" The television host gave her one of his special smiles. There were little wrinkles in the corners of his eyes. "You want to help me. You know what has to be done."

Gwenda nodded. For some reason she had begun to cry. She wondered if this would be the last time Rex McKenna would talk to her. She would go to York and she wouldn't come back.

"You go there on the train and you find him and you make sure that he never hurts anyone again. You owe it to yourself. You owe it to everyone. What do you say?"

Gwenda couldn't speak. She nodded a second time. The tears were flowing faster.

Rex backed away. "Ladies and gentlemen, let's hear it

11

for Gwenda Davis. She's a lovely lady and she deserves a big round of applause."

The audience agreed. They clapped and cheered until Gwenda left the room and went upstairs.

Brian remained where he was, sitting on the sofa, his legs slightly apart, his mouth hanging open. He had been like that ever since Gwenda had stuck the kitchen knife into his chest. It was still there, jutting out of the bloody rag that had once been his shirt. Rex had told her to do that, too. Brian had laughed at her. He had said she was mad. She'd had to teach him a lesson he wouldn't forget.

A few minutes later, Gwenda left the house. She'd meant to pack, but in the end she hadn't been able to find anything worth taking, apart from the ax that she once used to chop wood. She'd slipped that into the handbag that dangled from her arm.

Gwenda locked the door behind her and walked away. She knew exactly where she was heading: Forrest Hill, a school in Yorkshire. She was going to see her nephew, Matt Freeman, again.

He would certainly be surprised.

TWO
The New Boy

It was the same dream as always.

Matt Freeman was standing on a tower of black rock that seemed to have sprouted out of the ground like something poisonous. He was high up, alone, surrounded on all sides by a sea as dead as anything he had ever seen. The waves rolled in like oil, and although the wind was howling all around him and the sea spray stung his eyes, he felt nothing . . . not even the cold. Somehow he knew that this was a place where the sun never rose or set. He wondered if he had died.

He turned and looked toward the shoreline, knowing that he would see the other four waiting for him, separated by a stretch of water half a mile wide and many miles deep. They were always there. Three boys and a girl, each about his age, waiting for him to make the crossing and join them.

But this time it was different. One of the boys had somehow found a vessel to carry him across the water. It was a long, narrow, flimsy boat made of reeds that had been woven together with a prow rising up at the front, shaped like the head of a wildcat. Matt could see the waves battering it, trying to send it back. But the boy was rowing with strong, rhythmic strokes. He was cutting across the water, getting closer by the minute. Now Matt could make out some of his features: brown skin, dark eyes, black, very straight hair hanging down to his neck. He was wearing torn jeans and a loose shirt with a hole in one of the elbows.

Matt felt a surge of hope. In a few minutes the boat would reach the island. If he could just find a way down, he would at last be able to escape. He ran to the edge of the tower and that was when he saw it, reflected in the inky surface of the water. A bird of some sort. Its shape rippled, distorted by the waves, and he was unable to make out what it was. It seemed to have enormous wings, white feathers, and a long, snakelike neck. A swan! Apart from the three boys and the girl, it was the only living thing that Matt had seen in this nightmare world. He looked up, expecting it to skim overhead on its way inland.

The swan was huge, the size of a plane. Matt screamed out a warning. The creature was hideous, its eyes blazing yellow, its claws reaching down to grab hold of the water, pulling it up like a curtain behind it. At that moment, its bright orange beak opened and it let out an earsplitting cry. There was an answering crash of thunder, and Matt was beaten to his knees as it flew overhead, wind pounding at him, the sound of its shriek exploding in his ears. The curtain of water fell, a tidal wave that smothered the tower, the shore, the entire sea. As Matt felt it crash down on him, he opened his mouth to scream . . .

. . . and woke up, gasping for breath, in bed, in his little attic room with the first light of dawn seeping in through the open window.

Matt did what he always did when his day began like

this. First he checked the time on the clock next to his bed: half past six. Then he looked around, reassuring himself that he was in his bedroom, on the third floor of the flat in York where he had been living for the past five weeks. One by one, he ticked the items off. There were his school books, piled up on the desk. His uniform was hung over the back of a chair. His eyes traveled over the posters on the wall: a couple of Arsenal players and a film poster from *War of the Worlds*. His PlayStation was on the floor in the corner. The room was a mess. But it was *his* room. It was exactly how it should be. Everything was all right. He was back.

He lay in bed for the next thirty minutes, half awake and half asleep, listening to the early morning traffic that started with the milk truck wheezing past the front door and gradually built up with delivery vans and buses setting out on the school run. At seven o'clock, he heard Richard's alarm go off in the room downstairs. Richard Cole was the journalist who owned the flat. Matt heard him get out of bed and pad into the bathroom. There was a hiss of water as the shower came on. It told Matt that it was time he started getting ready, too. He threw back the covers and got out of bed.

For a moment, he caught sight of himself in the full-length mirror that stood in the corner of the room. A fourteen-year-old boy wearing a gray T-shirt and boxers. Black hair. He had always cut it short, but recently he had allowed it to grow and it was untidy, with no part. Blue eyes. Matt was in good shape, with square shoulders and well-defined muscles. He was growing fast. Richard had been careful to buy him school clothes that were one size up, but

15

as he reached out and pulled on his pants, Matt reflected that it wouldn't be long before they would be too small.

Half an hour later, dressed for school and carrying a bagload of books, he came into the kitchen. Richard was already there, stacking up the dishes that had been left out the night before. He looked as if he hadn't had any sleep at all. His clothes were crumpled and although he'd been in the shower, he hadn't shaved. His fair hair was still wet and his eyes were half closed.

"What do you want for breakfast?" he asked.

"What is there?"

Richard swallowed a yawn. "Well, there's no bread and no eggs." He opened a cupboard and looked inside. "We've got some cornflakes but that's not much use."

"Don't we have any milk?"

Richard took a carton of milk out of the fridge, sniffed it, and dumped it in the sink. "It's off," he announced. He held up his hands in a gesture of apology. "I know. I know. I said I'd get some. But I forgot."

"It doesn't matter."

"Of course it matters." Richard sounded genuinely angry with himself. "I'm meant to be looking after you. . . ."

Matt sat down at the table. "It's not your fault," he said. "It's mine."

"Matt . . ." Richard began.

"No. We might as well admit it. This isn't really working, is it?"

"That's not true."

"It is true. You don't really want me here. The truth is, you don't even want to stay in York. I don't mind, Richard.

If I were you, I wouldn't want to have someone like me hanging around, either."

Richard looked at his watch. "We can't talk about this now," he said. "You're going to be late for school."

"I don't want to go to school," Matt replied. "I've been thinking about it." He took a deep breath. "I want to go back to another family on the LEAF Project."

Richard stared. "Are you crazy?"

LEAF stood for Liberty and Education Achieved through Fostering. It was a government program that had been designed for delinquents, and Matt had been part of it when he and Richard had met.

"I just think it would be easier," Matt said.

"The last time you joined the LEAF Project, they sent you to a coven of witches. What do you think it'll be next time? Vampires, perhaps. Or maybe you'll end up with a family of cannibals."

"Maybe I'll get an ordinary family that'll look after me."

"I can look after you."

"You can't even look after yourself!" Matt hadn't meant to say it, but the words had just slipped out. "You're working in Leeds now," he went on. "You're always in the car. That's why there's never any food in the house. And you're worn out! You're only staying here because of me. It's not fair."

It was true. Richard had lost his job at *The Greater Malling Gazette* but after a few weeks he had managed to find work on another newspaper, *The Gipton Echo*, just outside Leeds. It wasn't much better. He was still writing about local businesses. The day before, he'd reported about a new fish restaurant, a garbage disposal plant, and a geriatric hospital that had been threatened with closure. *Chips, tips, and hips,* as he put it. Matt knew that Richard was working on a book about their adventures together — including the events that had led to the destruction of the nuclear power station known as Omega One and the disappearance of an entire Yorkshire village. But he hadn't been able to sell the story to the press. Why should publishers be any different?

"I don't want to talk about this now," Richard said. "It's too early. Let's meet up later. I won't be in late — for once — and we can go out for dinner if you like. Or I can get takeout."

"Yeah. All right. Whatever." Matt gathered up his books.

He still doubted he could bring Richard anything more than trouble.

●   ●   ●

Forrest Hill was a private school in the middle of nowhere, halfway between York and Harrogate. And although Matt hadn't said as much, it was the main reason he had begun to think about leaving the north of England. He hated it there, and although the summer holidays weren't far away, he wasn't sure he could wait that long.

From the outside, it was attractive enough. There was a quadrangle, an old courtyard with arches and outside staircases — and next to it a chapel complete with stained glass and gargoyles. Some parts of the school were three hundred years old and looked it, but in recent times the governors had managed to attract more money and had invested it in new buildings. There was a theater, a science department, and a barn-size library on two floors, as well as tennis courts, a swimming pool, and playing fields. Everything was situated, as Forrest Hill's name suggested, in what was a basin in the countryside with the roads sloping steeply down from all directions. The first time Matt had seen it, he had thought he was being driven into a university campus. It was only when he saw the boys, aged thirteen to eighteen, walking between classes in their fancy blue jackets and gray trousers that he realized that it was just a secondary school.

It was certainly a world apart from St. Edmund's, the comprehensive school he had gone to in Ipswich. Matt didn't know where to begin when he compared the two. Everything was so neat and tidy here. There was no graffiti, no smell of chips, no flaking paint and goalposts with the net hanging in rags. There must have been a thousand books in the library, and all the computers in the technology center were state-of-the-art. Even the uniform made a huge difference. Putting it on for the first time, Matt felt as if something had been taken away from him. The jacket weighed down on his shoulders and cut underneath his arms. The tie with its green and gray stripes was ridiculous. He didn't want to be a businessman, so why was he dressing up as one? When he looked in the mirror, it was as if he were seeing someone else.

It wasn't Richard who had come up with the idea of sending him here. The Nexus — the mysterious organization that had taken over his life — had suggested it. Matt had done almost no work for two years. He was behind in every subject. Sending him to a new school in the middle of the summer term would cause problems wherever he went. But a private school wouldn't ask too many questions and might be able to look after his special needs. The Nexus was paying.

It seemed like a good idea. But it had gone wrong almost from the start.

Most of the teachers at Forrest Hill were all right, but it was the ones who weren't who really made themselves felt. It seemed to take Matt only days to make permanent enemies with Mr. King, who taught English, and Mr. O'Shaughnessy, who doubled as French teacher and assistant headmaster. Both these men were in their thirties but behaved like they were much older. On the first day, Mr. King had given Matt a dressing-down for chewing gum in the quadrangle. On the second, it had been Mr. O'Shaughnessy who had given him a high-pitched, ten-minute lecture for an untucked shirt. After that, both of them seemed to have taken every opportunity they could to pick on him.

Still, the teachers were nothing compared with the other boys at the school. Matt was a survivor. There had been some real bullies at St. Edmund's, including one or two who seemed to take a real pleasure in picking on anyone who was small, hardworking, or just different from them. He had known it would take time to make friends in a new school, especially now that he was moving into the private sector. But even so, he had been surprised by how few of them had been prepared to give him a chance.

Of course, they all knew each other. The other fourteen-year-olds at Forrest Hill were at the end of their second year and they'd already made their friendships. A pattern of life had been established. As a newcomer, Matt knew that he was intruding. Worse than that, he had come from a completely different world. Very few of the boys were snobs, but they were still suspicious about him. One boy in particular seemed determined to give him a hard time.

His name was Gavin Taylor. He was in most of the same classes as Matt. And he controlled their entire grade.

Taylor wasn't physically big. He was slim with a turned-up nose and blond, slightly greasy hair that hung down to his collar. He made a point of ensuring that his tie was never straight, slouching around with his hands in his pockets and an attitude that warned everyone — staff or student — to keep his distance. There was an arrogance to him that Matt could feel a hundred yards away. It was said that he was one of the richest boys in the school. His father had a company selling secondhand cars on the Internet throughout Britain. And Taylor had four or five friends who *were* big. They followed him round the school like bit-part villains in a Quentin Tarantino film.

It was Taylor who had decided that Matt was bad news. It wasn't what he knew about the new arrival that offended him. It was what he didn't. Matt had come out of nowhere at the end of the school year. He hadn't been to a prep school and he wouldn't explain why he had left his comprehensive, what had happened to his parents, or what he had been doing for the past two months. Taylor had taunted and teased Matt for the first few weeks, trying to make him drop his guard. The fact that Matt wasn't scared of him and refused to tell him anything only angered him all the more.

But then something happened that made the whole

situation infinitely worse. Somehow, Taylor overheard the school secretary talking on the phone in her office and learned that Matt had been in trouble with the police. He'd spent time in a Secure Children's Home or something similar. And he had no money. Some sort of charity, an organization in London, had picked up the tab to send him here. Within minutes, the story had spread all around the school, and from that moment, Matt had been doomed. He was the new boy. The charity case. A loser. He wasn't part of the school and never would be.

Maybe there were boys there who would have been more generous . . . but they were too scared of Gavin Taylor. So Matt found himself virtually friendless. He hadn't told Richard any of this — Matt had never been the sort of person to complain out loud. When his parents had died, when he had been sent to live with Gwenda Davis, even when he had been working as a virtual slave at Hive Hall, he had tried to build a wall around himself. But each day was becoming harder to endure. He was certain that sooner or later something would snap.

As usual, the bus dropped him off at half past eight. The day always began with an assembly in the chapel, a hymn sung tunelessly by six hundred and fifty schoolboys who were only half awake, and a brief address from the head or one of the teachers. Matt kept his head down. He thought about what he had said to Richard that morning. He really was determined to go. He'd had enough.

The first two lessons weren't too bad. The math and history teachers were young and sympathetic and didn't allow the other boys in the class to pick on him. Matt spent the morning break in the library, trying to catch up with his homework. After that, he had forty-five minutes with the special-needs teacher who was trying to help him with his spelling and grammar. The last lesson before lunch was English, and Mr. King was in a bad mood.

"Freeman, will you please stand up!"

Matt got warily to his feet. Out of the corner of his eye, he saw Taylor nudge another boy and grin. He made sure his own face gave nothing away.

Mr. King walked toward him. The English teacher was beginning to lose his hair. He combed the ginger strands from one side of his head to the other, but the bald curve of his skull still showed through. He was holding a dog-eared copy of *Oliver Twist*. This was the book they had been reading in class. He also had a pile of exercise books.

"Did you read the chapters that I set you in *Oliver Twist?*" he asked.

"I tried to," Matt said. He liked the characters in the story, but he found some of the language old-fashioned and difficult to follow. Why did Charles Dickens have to use so much description?

"You tried to?" Mr. King sneered at him. "I think what you mean is, you didn't."

"I did —" Matt began.

"Don't interrupt me, Freeman. Your essay was the worst in the class. You scored a pathetic two out of twenty. You can't even spell *Fagin* correctly! *F-A-Y-G-I-N!* There is no *Y* in *Fagin*, Freeman. If you'd read the chapters, you'd know that."

Taylor guffawed. Despite himself, Matt felt his cheeks glowing red.

"You will read the chapters again and you will do the test again, and in the future, I'd prefer it if you didn't lie to

23

me. Now sit down." He threw Matt's exercise book onto the desk as if it were something he had found in the gutter.

The lesson dragged on until the lunchtime bell. There were games that afternoon and at least Matt should have enjoyed that. He was fit and fast on his feet. But he was never part of the team on the sports field, either. They were playing cricket this term and Matt hadn't been surprised when he was sent to field at deep cover, as far away from everyone else as possible.

The school ate lunch in one of the school's modern buildings. There was a self-service buffet with a choice of hot or cold food, and fifty long tables arranged in lines beneath an ugly, modern chandelier. The boys were allowed to sit where they wanted to, but normally each year stuck together. The clatter of knives and forks and the clamor of so many voices echoed all around.

Matt was hungry. He had been late for the school bus and hadn't had time to buy anything at McDonald's. And there hadn't been much to eat in Richard's flat the night before. The food was the one thing at Forrest Hill that he did like, and he helped himself to a healthy lunch of ham, salad, ice cream, and fruit juice. Carrying his tray, he looked for somewhere to sit. After five weeks at the school, he had lost hope of anyone inviting him to join them.

He saw an empty space and made for it. With the tray in front of him, he didn't see the foot that was stretched out in his path. The next thing he knew, he had been tripped. Helplessly, he pitched forward. The tray, two plates, a glass, his knife, fork, and spoon left his hands and hit the floor with a deafening crash. Matt followed them. Unable to stop himself, he fell on top of what was meant to be his lunch. The entire room fell silent. Even before he looked up, Matt knew that everyone was staring.

It hadn't been Taylor who had tripped him up. It was one of Taylor's friends. But Matt had no doubt that it had been Taylor's idea. He could see him, a few tables away, standing up with a glass in one hand, a stupid smile spreading across his face. Matt got to his knees. Ice cream was dripping from his shirt. He was surrounded by pieces of salad, kneeling in a puddle of fruit juice.

And then Taylor laughed.

It was a cue for the rest of the school to join in. It seemed to Matt that just about the entire room — the entire school — was laughing at him. He saw Mr. O'Shaughnessy making his way toward him. Why did the assistant headmaster have to be on lunch duty that day?

"Why do you have to be so clumsy, Freeman?" Mr. O'Shaughnessy asked. The words seemed to be coming from a long way away. They echoed in Matt's ears. "Are you all right?"

Taylor was pointing at him.

Matt looked up. He could feel the anger coursing through him — and not just anger. Something else. He couldn't have stopped it, even if he had tried to. It was as if he had become a channel. There were flames flowing through him. He could actually smell the burning.

The chandelier exploded.

It was an ugly thing, a tangle of steel arms and lightbulbs that some architect must have thought would suit the room. And it was directly over Gavin Taylor. Now, as Matt stared, the bulbs shattered, one after another, each bursting apart with the sound of a pistol shot. Glass showered down,

25

smashing onto the tables. Taylor looked up and cried out as a piece of glass hit him in the face. More glass rained down on him. A few wisps of smoke rose up to the ceiling. Nobody was laughing anymore. The entire room was silent.

Then the glass that Taylor was holding exploded, too. It simply blew itself apart in his hand. Taylor cried out. His palm had been cut open. He looked at Matt, then at his hand. His mouth opened but it seemed to take him forever to find the words.

"It was him!" he screamed. "He did it!"

He was pointing at Matt. His whole body was trembling.

The assistant headmaster stared helplessly. He looked bewildered, unsure what to do. This sort of thing had never happened before. It was way outside his experience.

"It was him!" Taylor insisted.

"Don't be ridiculous," Mr. O'Shaughnessy said. "I saw what happened. Freeman was nowhere near you."

Gavin Taylor had gone pale. It might have been the pain, the sight of his own blood welling out of the cut in his hand. But Matt knew that it was more than that. Gavin was terrified.

Mr. O'Shaughnessy tried to take charge. "Someone get the matron," he snapped. "And we'd better clear the room. There's glass everywhere. . . ."

People were already moving. They didn't know what had happened. They just wanted to get out of the dining hall before the whole ceiling came down. They seemed to have forgotten Matt for the moment . . . but if any of them had looked for him, they would have seen that he was already gone.

THREE
A Second Gate

The streets were beginning to empty by the time Matt got home. The summer months were fast approaching and more tourists were arriving every day. The queues around the Viking museum and The Minster were getting longer. The medieval walls were more crowded. Soon there would be more people visiting York than actually living there, or so it would seem. From city to tourist attraction. It was a process that was repeated every year.

Matt stood in the narrow, cobbled street called the Shambles and looked up at the flat located three floors above a souvenir shop. He had been happy here for a while. Living with Richard was odd — the journalist was more than ten years older than him — but after all they had been through together in Lesser Malling, it had sort of worked. They needed each other. Richard knew that Matt could provide him with the newspaper story that would make him famous. Matt had nowhere else to go. The flat was just about big enough for the two of them, and usually they were both out all day. On weekends they went hiking, swimming, go-karting . . . whatever. Matt tried to think of Richard as a big brother.

But during the past weeks he had become increasingly

uncomfortable. Richard *wasn't* his brother. The two of them had only met by chance and as the memories of their shared nightmare faded, there seemed to be less and less reason for them still to be living together. Matt liked Richard. But there wasn't going to be any Pulitzer Prize–winning scoop, and the simple truth was that he was in the way. That was why he had suggested going back to the LEAF Project. Despite what Richard had said, an ordinary family somewhere in the country couldn't be so bad. He surely wasn't going to end up with a Jayne Deverill a second time.

Matt wondered if the school had phoned Richard and told him what had happened. There was no reason why they should. Despite Gavin's accusations, none of the teachers seriously believed he had been responsible for the explosion in the dining hall. But Matt knew differently. He had felt the power flowing through him. It was the same power that had stopped the knife and snapped the cords when he had been a prisoner, tied down in Omega One. But this time there had been one difference. It had been directed at someone his own age. Gavin wasn't his enemy. He was just a stupid kid.

He couldn't stay at Forrest Hill. Not now. Another taunt from Gavin, another bad morning with Mr. King and his English class, and who could say what might happen? All his life, Matt had known he was different. He had been aware of something inside him . . . this power . . . whatever it was. Sometimes, when he'd gone to movies like *Spider-Man* or *X-Men*, he'd wondered what it might be like to be a superhero, saving the world. But that wasn't him. His power was useless to him because he didn't know how to use it.

Worse than that, it was out of control. Once again he saw the blood oozing out of Gavin's hand, saw the terror in his face. He could have torn the chandelier out of the ceiling. He could have crushed the other boy, buried him under a ton of twisted metal and broken glass. It had almost happened. He had to leave, go far away, before it happened again.

There was a movement behind the first-floor window, and Matt saw Richard, standing with his back to the street. That was strange. The journalist had said he wouldn't be late, but even so, he was never home before seven o'clock. The editor of *The Gipton Echo* liked to keep him in the office just in case something happened — although it very seldom did. Richard was talking to someone. That was unusual, too. They didn't often have visitors.

Matt let himself in and climbed up the stairs that ran past the souvenir shop. As he went, he heard a woman's voice. It was one he recognized . . . and it filled him with dread.

"There's a meeting in London," she was saying. "Three days from now. We just want you to be there."

"You don't want me. You want Matt."

"We want both of you."

Matt put down his school bag, opened the door to the main living room, and went in.

Susan Ashwood, the blind woman he had met in Manchester, was sitting in a chair, her back very straight, her hands folded in front of her. Her face was pale, made more so by her short, black hair and unforgiving black glasses. A white stick rested against her chair — but she hadn't come alone. Matt also knew the slim, olive-skinned man who was standing opposite her. His name was Fabian.

He was the younger of the two, perhaps in his early thirties, and Matt had also met him before. It was he who had first suggested that Matt continue living with Richard and who had managed to get him a place at Forrest Hill. As usual, Fabian was smartly dressed, this time in a pale gray suit and tie. He was sitting down with one leg crossed over the other. Everything about him was very neat.

Both Fabian and Susan Ashwood were members of the secret organization that called itself the Nexus. As they had made clear from the start, their role was to help Matt and to protect him. Even so, he wasn't particularly happy to see either of them here. He knew they could only be bringing bad news.

Miss Ashwood had heard him come in. "Matt," she said.

"What's going on?" Matt asked immediately.

Richard moved away from the window. "They want you," he said.

"I heard. Why?"

"How are you, Matt? How's the new school?" Fabian smiled nervously. He was trying to sound friendly, but Matt knew the atmosphere was anything but.

"School's great," Matt said without enthusiasm.

"You're looking well."

"I'm fine." Matt sat down on the arm of a sofa. "Why are you here, Mr. Fabian?" he asked. "What do you want me for?"

"I think you know." Fabian paused as if unsure how to continue. Even though he'd changed Matt's life, Matt knew very little about him . . . or about anyone else in the Nexus.

"The first time I came here, I warned you," Fabian went

on. "I told you that we believed there might be a second gate. You destroyed the first one, the stone circle in the woods outside Lesser Malling. But the second one is on the other side of the world. It's in my country. In Peru."

"Where in Peru?" Richard asked.

"We don't know," Fabian answered.

"What does the gate look like?" Richard followed up.

"We don't know that, either. We hoped that after what happened here in Yorkshire, we would have time to find out more. Unfortunately, we were wrong."

"The second gate is about to open," Susan Ashwood said. There was no doubt at all in her voice.

"I suppose you've been told this," Richard said.

"Yes."

"By ghosts."

"Yes." Susan Ashwood was a medium. She claimed that she was in contact with the spirit world. "You still don't believe me?" she continued. "After what you've been through, after everything you've seen, I'm frankly amazed. You didn't listen to me last time. This time you must. It's as if winter has come in the spirit world. Everything is cold and dark, and I hear the whispers of a growing fear. Something is happening that I don't understand. But I know what it signifies. A second gate is about to open, and once again we have to stop it if we don't want the Old Ones to return. We want Matt to come to London. Only he has the power to prevent it."

"Matt's in school," Richard protested. "He can't just get on a train and take a week off. . . ."

Matt looked out the window. Soon it would start to

get dark. Shadows had already fallen over the Shambles and the streetlamps had come on. Richard reached out and turned the lights on inside, too. Light and dark. Always fighting each other.

"I don't understand," Matt said. "You don't even know where this gate is. Why do you think I can help you?"

"We're not the only ones looking for it," Susan Ashwood replied. "There has been a strange development, Matt. You would doubtless call it a coincidence, but I think it's more than that. I think it was *meant* to happen."

She nodded at Fabian, who produced a DVD. "Can I play you this?" he asked.

Richard waved a hand at the television. "Be my guest."

Fabian fed the video into the player and turned the television on. Matt found himself watching a news report. "We recorded this last week," Fabian said.

The DVD began with a shot of a leather-bound book, lying on a table. It was obviously very old. A hand reached forward and began to turn the pages, showing them to be thick and uneven, covered with writing and intricate drawings that had been made with an ink pen or perhaps even a quill. Matt had seen something very like it at school. The history teacher had brought in pictures of a fifteenth-century book of poetry rescued from some castle. The letters had been drawn so carefully that each one was a miniature artwork. Many of the pages in the book were the same.

"Some people are already describing it as the find of a lifetime," the commentator explained. "It was written by St. Joseph of Cordoba, a Spanish monk who traveled with Pizarro to Peru in 1532 and witnessed the destruction of the Inca empire. St. Joseph later came to be known as the Mad Monk of Cordoba. His diary, bound in leather and gold, may explain why."

The camera moved in closer on the pages. Matt could make out some of the words — but they were all in Spanish and meant nothing to him.

"The diary contains many remarkable predictions," the voice continued. "Although it was written almost five hundred years ago, it describes in detail the coming of motor cars, computers, and even space satellites. On one of the later pages, it manages to predict some sort of Internet, working inside the church."

Now the television program cut to a picture of a Spanish town and what looked like a huge fortress with a soaring bell tower, surrounded by narrow streets and markets.

"The diary was found in the Spanish city of Cordoba. It is believed that it had been buried in the courtyard of the tenth-century mosque known as the Mezquita and must have been unearthed during excavations. It passed into private hands and may have been sold many times before it was discovered in a market by an English antiques dealer, William Morton."

Morton was in his fifties, plump, with silver hair and cheeks that had been burned by the sun. He was the sort of man who looked as if he enjoyed life.

"I knew at once what it was," he said. His accent was very English, very upper class. "Joseph of Cordoba was an interesting chap. He traveled with Pizarro and the conquistadors when they invaded Peru. While he was out there, he stumbled onto some sort of alternative history. Devils and

33

demons . . . that sort of thing. And he wrote down every-thing he knew in here." He held up the diary. "There are plenty of people out there who said that the diary didn't exist," he went on. "For that matter, there are people who think that Joseph himself didn't exist! Well, it looks as if I've proved them wrong."

"You're planning to sell the diary," the commenta-tor said.

"Yes, that's right. And I have to tell you that I've already had one or two quite interesting offers. A certain busi-nessman in South America — I'm not mentioning any names! — has already made an opening bid in excess of half a million pounds. And there are some people in London who seem very keen to meet me. It looks as if I may have an auction on my hands. . . ." He licked his lips with relish.

The camera cut back to the diary. More pages were being turned.

"If anyone can untangle the strange riddles, the often illegible handwriting, and the many scribbles, the diary could reveal a completely new mythology," the voice con-cluded. "St. Joseph had his own, very peculiar view of the world, and although some think he was mad, others call him a visionary and a genius. One thing is sure. William Morton has struck it lucky, and for him the book is quite literally pure gold."

The pages were still turning. Fabian froze the image. Matt gasped.

At the very end of the film, the camera had rested on one page with handwriting — hundreds of tiny words com-pressed into narrow lines — at the top and the bottom. But in the middle there was a white space and a strange symbol. Matt recognized it at once.

He had seen it at Raven's Gate. It had been cut into the stone on which he had almost been killed. It was the sign of the Old Ones.

"You see?" Fabian said. He left the image frozen on the screen.

"We believe the diary will tell us the location of the second gate," Susan Ashwood said. "It may also tell us when, and how, it is supposed to open. But as you've heard, we aren't the only ones interested in it."

"A businessman in South America . . ." Matt remembered what the report had said. "Do you know who he is?"

"We don't even know which country he lives in — and William Morton isn't saying anything." Fabian scowled.

"You're the people who he said wanted to meet him in London," Richard said.

"Yes, Mr. Cole. We contacted Mr. Morton the moment he went public with what he'd found."

"We *have* to have the diary," Ashwood said. "We have to find the second gate and either destroy it or make sure it never opens. Unfortunately, as you heard, we're not alone. This 'businessman,' whoever he is, got in there ahead of us. Since that video was made, he has quadrupled his offer. He's now offering to pay two million pounds."

"But you can pay more," Richard said. "You've got lots of money."

"We told Morton that the last time we spoke to him,"

Fabian explained. "We said he could more or less name any price he liked. But it's no longer a question of money."

"He's afraid," Susan Ashwood said. "At first, we didn't understand why. It seemed to us that he was being threatened by whoever he was dealing with in South America. They'd shaken hands on a price and he wasn't allowed to speak to anyone else. But then we realized it was something more than that."

She paused.

"He'd read the diary," Matt guessed.

"Exactly. He had the diary for the best part of a month and in that time he read it and understood enough of it to comprehend just what it was he had on his hands. Right now he's in London. We don't know where, because he won't tell us. He has a house in Putney — but he's not there. As a matter of fact, there was a fire a few days ago. We assume it's connected. We don't know for certain. All we know is that William Morton has gone into hiding."

"How do you contact him?" Richard asked.

"We don't. He calls us. He has a cell phone. We've tried to trace the calls, but it's no good. Until yesterday, all we knew was that he was going to sell the diary to the businessman and we weren't even going to meet. But then, yesterday, he telephoned us again. I happened to take the call." Ashwood turned to Matt. "And I mentioned you."

"Me?" Matt didn't know what to say. "He's never met me. . . . "

"No. But he knows about the five. Don't you see? He must have read about them in the diary. The fact that you're one of them, Matt . . . he couldn't believe it when we told him. But we managed to intrigue him, and he agreed, at last, to meet us. He made one condition."

"He wants me to be there," Matt said.

Ashwood nodded. "He wants to meet with you first, alone. He's given us a place and time. On Thursday, three days from now."

"We're just asking you for one day of your time," Fabian said. "If Morton sees you and believes you are who we say you are, maybe then he'll sell us the diary. Maybe he'll give it away. I honestly believe that he wishes now that he had never found it. He wants to be rid of it. We just have to give him an excuse, a good reason to hand the diary to us." He gestured at Matt. "*You* are the reason. All you have to do is meet him. Nothing more."

There was a long silence. At last, Matt spoke.

"You keep on saying that I'm one of the five. And maybe you're right. I don't really understand any of it, but I know what happened at Raven's Gate." For a moment it all came back to him, and he knew he was saying the right thing. "I don't want to get involved. I had enough the first time. Right now I just want to get on with my life, and I want to be left alone. You say it's just one meeting in London, but I know it won't happen that way. Once I get started, I won't be able to stop. Something else will happen and then something after that. I'm sorry. You can find Morton without me. Why don't you just offer him more money? That seems to be all he wants."

"Matt —" Susan Ashwood began.

"I'm sorry, Miss Ashwood. You can manage without me. You're going to have to. Because I don't want to know."

37

Richard stood up. "I'm afraid that's it," he said.

"You're only here because of the Nexus," Fabian snapped — and suddenly he was angry. His eyes were darker than ever. "We pay for your school. We have made it possible for you to stay here. Maybe we should think again."

"We can manage without you —" Now Richard was getting angry, too.

"It doesn't matter!" Susan Ashwood got stiffly to her feet. "Fabian is wrong to threaten you. We came here with a request, and you have given us your answer. As you say, we must manage without you." She reached out and Fabian gave her his arm. "But there is one thing I will add." She turned her empty eyes on Matt and for a moment she sounded genuinely sad. "You have made a decision . . . but you may have less choice than you think. You can try to ignore who you are, but you may not be able to for much longer. You are central to what is happening, Matt. You and four others. I think it will find you before too long."

She nudged Fabian, and the two of them left together. Richard waited until he heard the front door close, then he sank back into a chair.

"Well, I'm glad they've gone," he said. "And I think you're absolutely right, by the way. What nerve! Trying to drag you back into all that. Well, it's not going to happen. They can get lost."

Matt said nothing.

"You must be hungry," Richard went on. "I managed to look into a supermarket on the way over. There are three bags of food in the kitchen. What do you fancy for dinner?"

It took Matt a few moments to absorb what he had just heard. Richard had been shopping? It had to be a first. Now he remembered his surprise when he had arrived at the flat, seeing Richard there at all. "What's happened?" he asked. "How come you're home so early?"

Richard shrugged. "Well, I was thinking about what you said this morning. About you and me. And I realized you were right. I can't look after you when I'm traveling back and forth to Leeds all the time. So I threw the job in. . . ."

"What?" Matt knew how much the job meant to Richard. He wasn't quite sure what to say.

"I just don't want you to go back to the LEAF Project," Richard continued. "I said I'd look after you and that's what I'm going to do. I can always find a job in York." The thought made Richard sigh. "Anyway, you're lucky I was here tonight. Did you really want to be left alone with Mr. and Mrs. Creepy?"

"Do you really think it was okay to say no?" Matt asked.

"Of course it was. If you didn't want to go, then why should you? It's your choice, Matt. You must do what you want."

"That's not what she said."

"She was wrong. You're safe here. Nothing's going to happen while you're in York except — possibly — food poisoning. I'm cooking tonight!"

•   •   •

Seventy miles away, on the M1 motorway, a man named Harry Shepherd was just coming out of a service station. He had started earlier in the day at Felixstowe and was on

39

his way to Sheffield. As darkness had fallen, he had stopped for a bite and a cup of tea. He was only allowed to drive a certain distance without a break. And he liked this service station. There was a waitress he always chatted with. He was thinking of asking her out.

It was getting dark as he drove out, and it had begun to rain. He could see the streaks of water lighting up as they slanted across his headlamps. He slammed the engine into second gear, preparing to rejoin the motorway — and that was when he saw her, standing on the slip road, one thumb out. The universal symbol of the hitchhiker.

It wasn't something he saw very often these days. Hitchhiking was considered too dangerous. Nobody in his right mind would get into a car or a truck with a stranger. Not with so many weirdos around. And here was something else that was odd. The hitchhiker was a woman. She looked middle-aged, too. She was wrapped up in a coat that wasn't doing much to protect her from the rain. Her hair was dragging over her collar, and he could see the water running down the sides of her cheeks. Harry felt sorry for her. Somehow she reminded him of his mother, who was living on her own in a bed-sit in Dublin. On an impulse, he took his foot off the accelerator and pressed the brake. The woman ran forward.

Henry knew he was breaking every regulation in the book. He wasn't allowed to give lifts. Especially when he was carrying fuel. But something had persuaded him. An impulse. He couldn't really explain it.

Gwenda Davis saw the petrol tanker as it slowed down. The motorway lights reflected off the great silver cylinder with the word SHELL in bright yellow letters. She should

40

have been farther north by now. It had definitely been a mistake leaving Eastfield Terrace without any money, and she had almost given up trying to hitchhike. She knew she had let Rex McKenna down. She hoped he wouldn't be angry with her.

But now her luck had changed. She wiped the rain out of her eyes and ran forward to the passenger door. It was a big step up but she managed it, her handbag swinging from her arm. The driver was a man in his thirties. He had fair hair and a silly schoolboy smile. He was wearing overalls with the Shell logo on his chest.

"Where are you going, love?" he asked.

"North," Gwenda said.

"A bit late to be out on your own."

"Where are you heading?"

"Sheffield."

"Thanks for stopping." Gwenda closed the door. "I thought I was going to be there all night."

"Well . . . put your seat belt on." The man smiled at her. "My name's Harry."

"Mine's Gwenda."

Gwenda did as she was told. But she made sure that the seat belt didn't restrict her movements. She had her handbag next to her with the ax handle sticking out of it. She'd decided she was going to use it as soon as they slowed down. It would be so easy to swing it into the side of Harry's head. She had never driven a petrol tanker before, but she was sure she would be able to manage it. Rex McKenna would help her.

Over two thousand gallons of petrol might come in handy, too.

FOUR
Fire Alarm

Matt went back to school the next day with a sense of dread.

None of the adults would blame him for what had happened the day before, but the boys might have a different view. He had been there. He was weird. He was involved. It occurred to Matt that he had probably given them yet more rope to hang him with.

And he was right. The moment he stepped onto the school bus, he knew that things — which had always been bad — were now set to get much worse. The bus was just about full, but somehow the one empty seat always happened to be next to him. As he walked up the central aisle, the whispers began. Everyone was staring at him, then looking away when he tried to meet their eyes. As the doors hissed shut and the bus began to move, something hit him on the side of the head. It was only a rubber band fired from the back, but the message was clear. Matt was tempted to stop the bus, to get off and go home. He could get Richard to phone in and say he was sick. He resisted the idea. That would be giving in. Why should he let these stuck-up kids with their stupid prejudices win?

The dining hall was closed for the day. Lunch would be served on temporary tables set up in the gym while electricians repaired the damage and tried to work out what had caused it. The rumor was that there had been some sort of massive short circuit in the system. It had caused a power surge and that was what had made the chandelier explode. As for Gavin Taylor (who had needed three stitches and had come to school with his right hand completely bandaged), it seemed that he had broken the glass he was holding himself. It was a perfectly natural reaction to the chaos that had been happening just above his head.

That was what the boys at Forrest Hill were told. The head teacher, a gray-haired man called Mr. Simmons, even mentioned it at morning assembly in the chapel. The teachers, sitting in their pews at the very back, nodded wisely. But of course a school has its own knowledge, its own intelligence. Everyone understood that what had happened must have had something to do with Matt, even if nobody knew — or wanted to say — exactly what it was.

They sang another hymn. Mr. Simmons was a religious man and liked to think that the rest of the school was, too. There were a few announcements. Then the doors were opened and everyone flooded out.

"Hey, weirdo!" Gavin Taylor had been sitting just a few places away from Matt and stopped him on the other side of the door. His blond hair was cleaner than usual. It occurred to Matt that they might have insisted on washing it when he was at the hospital.

"What do you want?" Matt demanded.

"I just want you to know that you might as well get out of this school. Why don't you go back to your friends in prison? Nobody wants you here."

"I wasn't in prison," Matt said. "And it's none of your business anyway."

"I saw your file." Matt could tell this was a bluff, but Gavin taunted him nonetheless. "You're weird and you're a crook and you shouldn't be here."

A few other boys had stopped, sensing a fight. There were five minutes until the first lesson but it would be worth being late to see the two of them slugging it out.

Matt wasn't sure how to react. Part of him wanted to lash out at the other boy, but he knew that was exactly what Gavin wanted. One punch and he would go running off to a teacher with his bandaged hand. Matt would be in even more trouble.

"Why don't you just get lost, Gavin?" he said. And then, before he could stop himself: "Or would you like me to rip open your other hand, too?"

It was a stupid thing to say. Matt remembered what he'd been thinking as he walked home only the day before. The idea that he could actually use his powers to hurt someone his own age horrified him. So what was he doing making threats like this? Gavin was right. He *was* weird. A freak.

He tried to backtrack. "I didn't mean to hurt you," he said. "And what I said just now, I didn't mean that, either. I didn't ask to come to this school."

"Well, now we're asking you to leave," Gavin replied.

Despite himself, Matt was beginning to get angry again.

He stopped.

He could smell burning.

He didn't need to look around. He knew there was nothing on fire . . .

. . . and if he closed his eyes he could see a sudden flare

44

of yellow, a tea pot shaped like a teddy bear, his mother's dress on the morning she was killed. . . .

And he knew it meant something was about to happen. That was what he had learned at Raven's Gate. The smell of burning was important. So were the brief flashes of memory. There had been a teapot shaped like a teddy bear in the kitchen that morning, six years ago. The morning his parents had been killed. His mother had burned the toast. Somehow, the memories acted as a trigger. They were a signal that everything was about to change.

But why was it happening now? Everything was under control. He wasn't in any danger. There were no chains he needed to smash, no door to be blown open. He forced himself to ignore it and was relieved when the smell faded away.

He looked up and saw that Gavin was staring at him. There were half a dozen other boys grouped around, too. How long had he been standing there, frozen like some sort of idiot? One or two of the boys were smirking. Matt struggled to speak. But he had nothing more to say.

"Loser," Gavin muttered, and walked away.

The other boys went with him, leaving Matt standing on his own outside the chapel door. It was half past nine. The first lessons of the day had begun.

•   •   •

Thirty miles away, the police had closed an entire street, sealing each end with blue-and-white tape and the usual signs: POLICE — DO NOT CROSS.

The unconscious man had been discovered by a milkman. He had been lying on the pavement about a hundred meters away from a Shell garage. The paramedics had arrived and they had quickly established that he had been hit once with a blunt instrument . . . possibly a hammer or a crowbar. His skull was fractured . . . but the good news was that he was going to live. He'd sustained other injuries, too, and the police suspected that he might have been a passenger in some sort of truck. Perhaps he had been pushed out while the vehicle was moving at full speed.

It had been easy to identify him. There was a wallet in his back pocket, complete with cash and credit cards. The fact that it hadn't been taken had automatically ruled out theft as a motive. His wife in Felixstowe had been woken up and was being taken at high speed to the emergency ward at the hospital where he was being treated. From her, the police had learned that Harry Shepherd was a driver for Shell petrol and should have been delivering over two thousand gallons of fuel to the garage.

Once the police knew what Harry Shepherd had been driving, they also realized what was missing: the tanker itself. They immediately contacted Shell's office at Felixstowe and circulated the registration number of the vehicle to all units.

The petrol in the tanker was worth many thousands of pounds. Was this why the driver had been knocked out? The police hoped so, because simple theft was something they could handle. It was certainly a lot less worrying than the alternative.

But the thought was still there. This might, after all, be a quite different sort of crime. Suppose the tanker had been taken by terrorists. The local police put a call through to London, and the decision was made to keep what had

46

happened out of the news. There was no reason yet to start a panic. As they searched the roads up and down Yorkshire, the police remained tight-lipped. But they all knew: Over two thousand gallons of petrol could create a *very* large bonfire.

They didn't want to admit they were afraid.

●　　●　　●

For Matt, the morning only got worse.

He arrived five minutes late for his first lesson, stumbling into the classroom while the teacher — Miss Ford — was in full flow.

"I'm sorry I'm late, Miss —"

"Why are you late, Matthew?"

How could he explain? How could he tell her that he'd had some sort of premonition outside the school chapel that had left him paralyzed, uncertain what to do?

"I forgot my bag," he said. It was a lie. But it was simpler than the truth.

"Well, I'm afraid I'm going to have to put you in the detention book." Miss Ford sighed. "Now, will you please take your seat?"

Matt's desk was right at the back of the classroom. Although he kept his eyes fixed on the floor, he felt everyone watching him as he took his place. Miss Ford was one of the better teachers at Forrest Hill. She was plain and old-fashioned, which somehow suited her since she taught history. She had been kind to Matt and had tried to help him fill in the gaps in his knowledge. For his part, Matt had done his best to catch up, reading extra books after school.

They were studying the Second World War and he found it more interesting than medieval kings or endless lists of dates. It might be history, but it still mattered now.

Even so, he was unable to concentrate today. Miss Ford was telling them about Dunkirk, May 1940. Matt tried to follow what she was saying but he couldn't make the words link up. She seemed a long way away. It was becoming very warm in the classroom.

". . . the army was cut off and it seemed to many people in England that the war was already lost. . . ."

Matt looked out the window. Once again he became aware of the sharp, acrid, burning smell.

And that was when he saw it, floating through the air, making no sound. It was some sort of truck. There was a figure hunched behind the wheel, but the sunlight was reflecting off the windscreen and he couldn't make it out. Like a great beast, the truck soared toward the school, plummeting out of the sky. Its headlamps were its eyes. The radiator grille was a gaping mouth. The tanker seemed to stretch into the distance, a huge, gleaming silver cylinder on twelve thick tires. Closer and closer it came. Now it filled up the whole window and was about to smash through . . .

"Matthew? What is it?"

Everyone was looking at him. Again. Miss Ford had stopped whatever she was saying and was looking at him with a mixture of impatience and concern.

"Nothing, Miss Ford."

"Well, stop staring out the window and try to concentrate. As I was saying, many people thought that Dunkirk was a miracle. . . ."

Matt waited a few moments, then glanced out the

window again. The classroom looked across to the sports center, a solid, brick building on the other side of a field, separated from the main part of the school by a single road which rose steeply and then continued back toward York. There was no traffic. It was a beautiful day. Matt pressed a hand against his forehead. When he drew it away, there was sweat on his palm. What was wrong with him? What was going on?

Somehow he managed to stumble through history and then physics and PE. But the last lesson of the morning just had to be English with Mr. King. They were reading *Macbeth*, and Matt found Shakespeare's language difficult enough at the best of times. Today it meant nothing to him — and Mr. King seemed to have a built-in radar that allowed him to hone in on anyone who wasn't paying attention. It only took him a few minutes before he pounced on Matt.

"Am I boring you, Freeman?" he asked with an unpleasant sneer.

"No, sir."

"Then perhaps you can tell me what I was just saying about the three weird sisters?"

Matt shook his head. He might as well admit it. "I'm sorry, sir. I wasn't listening."

"Then come and see me at the end of the lesson." Mr. King brushed a strand of ginger hair out of his eyes. "The weird sisters tell Macbeth his future," he went on. "And of course he believes them. In Shakespeare's time, many people still believed in witchcraft and black magic. . . ."

The end of the lesson took forever to arrive and when it finally came, Matt didn't hang around to receive whatever

49

punishment Mr. King had in mind. It seemed to be getting hotter and hotter in the school. The glass in the windows was magnifying the sun, dazzling him. The walls seemed to be bending and shimmering in the heat. But he knew that he was only imagining it. This was early summer . . . the beginning of June. Looking around him, he could see that none of the other boys was feeling anything.

There was a fifteen-minute break before the entire school would cross the road and go into the sports center for lunch. Once again Matt thought about calling Richard and asking him to help. Cell phones weren't allowed at Forrest Hill but there were three pay phones on the other side of the quad.

"Matthew . . . ?"

He turned round and saw Miss Ford walking toward him, on her way to the staff room.

"Mr. King is looking for you," she said.

Of course, he would be. Matt had defied him. That would mean more trouble than ever.

"I wanted to tell you that your last essay was a real improvement," Miss Ford went on. She was looking at Matt a little sadly. Now she frowned. "Are you feeling ill?" she asked. "You don't look very well."

"I'm okay."

"Well, maybe you should go and see the nurse." She had said enough. Even the teachers at Forrest Hill didn't want to be seen spending too much time with Matt. She brushed past him and continued on her way.

And that was when Matt made his decision. He wasn't going to see the nurse, a thin, scowling woman who seemed to treat any suggestion of illness as a personal insult. Nor was he going to call Richard. It was time to leave Forrest Hill. Today. The other boys had made it perfectly clear to him from the start that he didn't belong. Well, maybe they were right. What was he doing in a private school in the middle of Yorkshire? The only thing that he had in common with the rest of them was the uniform he was forced to wear.

There was a garbage can in the corridor, just outside the staff room. Matt had been holding a pile of books, but now, without even thinking about it, he threw them all in. *Macbeth*. Math. A GCSE Guide to the Second World War. Then he took off his tie and threw that in, too. He felt better already.

He turned round and began to walk.

•　•　•

Gwenda Davis had stopped at the top of the hill. She knew what she had to do but she still couldn't quite bring herself to do it. Gwenda had never liked pain. If she so much as cut her finger, she'd have to sit down for half an hour and smoke several cigarettes before she was ready to move. And she was fairly sure that her death was going to hurt very much indeed.

Could she really do it? The school was spread out in front of her. She could see it through the windscreen. It looked like a very posh place, very different from the comprehensive she had sent Matt to when he lived with her. She couldn't imagine him going to a place like this. It wasn't like him at all.

There were a whole load of old buildings grouped around a church — but she knew that she wouldn't find Matt there. He was going to be in the big brick building next to the football field. There would be lots and lots of boys in there with him. It was a shame, really, that so many of them would have to die. The more she thought about it, the more she wondered if this was a good idea. It wasn't too late. So far she had only killed one person — Brian. At the last minute, she had decided to hit the driver of the petrol tanker with the flat end, rather than the blade, of the ax. He'd seemed a friendly sort of person. She hadn't even really wanted to fracture his skull.

The police would never catch up with her anyway. She could just get out of the petrol tanker and walk away. Maybe that's what she ought to do.

On an impulse, she reached out and turned on the radio. It was one o'clock. The news would be on and she would find out if the driver had been found yet. But strangely enough, nothing came out of the speaker. She knew the radio was on. There was a faint hiss. But nobody was talking.

And then she heard a single word.

"Gwenda . . ."

It was coming out of the radio, out of the dashboard. She knew who it was and she was so glad to hear him. But at the same time, she felt ashamed of herself. How could she have had second thoughts?

"What are you doing, just sitting there?" Rex McKenna asked.

"I don't know. . . ." Gwenda muttered.

"You weren't thinking of walking away, were you, you

naughty girl?" It made Gwenda tingle when he talked like that. She had seen him do it on the television. Sometimes he treated adults like children. It was part of his act.

"I don't want to die," she said.

"Of course you don't, Gwenda. Nor do I. Nor does anybody. But sometimes, you know, it just has to happen. Sometimes you don't have any choice."

"Don't I have any choice?" Gwenda asked. A single tear trickled down her cheek. She caught sight of herself in the rearview mirror, but it only told her what she already knew. She was looking very old and dirty. There was dried blood on her coat. Her skin had no color at all.

"Not really, my love," Rex answered. "It's a bit like the Big Wheel in a way. You spin the wheel, and your number comes up. There's not much you can do about it." He sighed. "Your whole life was a bit of a waste of time, if you want the honest truth. But at least you've been given the chance to do something important now. We need this boy killed. And you're the one who's been chosen to do it. So off you go! And don't worry — it'll all be over very soon."

Gwenda could imagine Rex McKenna winking at her. She could hear it in his voice.

The radio had gone silent again but there was nothing more to be said. Gwenda turned the engine on, pressed her foot on the accelerator, then slammed the gear into first.

● ● ●

Matt was on his way out. He could see the double doors at the end of the corridor with notice boards on both sides, lining the way. There were boys everywhere, getting ready

53

to go for lunch. For once they didn't notice him. Nor had anyone seen him dump his books. He felt a sense of elation. No matter what happened, he would be glad to leave Forrest Hill behind him.

And then Matt smelled it again. The burning. And at exactly the same moment, the doors burst open. As he stared in horror, a river of flame rushed in toward him, rolling down the corridor, peeling away the walls, scorching everything in its path. There were two boys standing there and suddenly they were black skeletons, X-rays of themselves as they had been seconds before. It was as if Hell had come to Forrest Hill. Matt saw a dozen more boys swallowed up instantly, too quickly even for them to cry out. Then the fire reached him and he flinched, closing his eyes, waiting for his own death.

But there was no flame.

When Matt opened his eyes again, everything was exactly as it had been before. It was two minutes to one. Morning lessons had ended. The students were on their way to lunch. He had simply imagined it.

Except that he knew. It wasn't his imagination.

He couldn't just walk out of the school. The fire hadn't happened . . . but it was about to. That was what he had been sensing from the moment he had arrived that day.

He looked around him. A bell sounded. The lunch bell. It told him what he had to do. He took three steps down the corridor and found a fire alarm, set behind a glass panel and mounted on the wall. He used his elbow to smash the glass, then pressed the alarm button with his thumb.

At once, much louder bells sounded throughout the school. People stopped what they were doing and began to

54

look at each other, half smiling, wondering what was going on. They knew the sound of the fire alarm. There had been fire drills often enough. But it was as if no one wanted to make the first move, afraid of looking foolish.

"There's a fire!" Matt shouted. "Move!"

One or two boys began to make their way past him, walking away from the double doors and back toward the other side of the school. The main assembly point was a football field next to the chapel. As soon as the first few had started moving, others followed. Matt heard doors opening and slamming. People were asking questions, but the alarm was so loud that Matt couldn't make out any words.

Then Mr. O'Shaughnessy appeared. The assistant headmaster was looking flustered. His face, never cheerful at the best of times, was thunderous. There were pinpricks of red in his normally pallid cheeks. He saw Matt standing next to the fire alarm. His eyes moved and took in the broken glass.

"Freeman!" he exclaimed. He had to shout to make himself heard. "Did you do that?"

"Yes."

"You set off the alarm?"

"Yes."

"Where's the fire?"

Matt said nothing.

Mr. O'Shaughnessy took his silence as an admission of guilt. "If you've done this as a prank, you will be in serious trouble!" he boomed. And then, an afterthought that was so bizarre it almost made Matt want to laugh, he added, "Why aren't you wearing your tie?"

"I think you should get out of the school" was Matt's only reply.

There was nothing to be done. The alarm could be switched off only in the bursar's office, and only with the approval of the fire brigade. Mr. O'Shaughnessy grabbed Matt by the arm, and the two of them followed the other boys out of the school. In minutes, all the buildings were empty. On the other side of the main road, the dinner ladies had spilled out of the sports center. The few boys who had arrived for lunch early were with them. They crossed the road and joined the rest of the students.

The entire school had congregated on the football field. The teachers were with them, trying to get them into some sort of order. Even the cafeteria workers had come over to see what all the fuss was about. Everyone was looking for the flames, or at least a little smoke, but already it was being whispered that the alarm had been set off as a joke and that Matthew Freeman was to blame. The headmaster had also arrived. He was a short, solid-looking man, built like a rugby player and known as the Bulldog. He saw his assistant, who was standing next to Matt, and came striding over.

"Do you know what's going on?" he demanded.

"I'm afraid I do, Headmaster," O'Shaughnessy replied. "I'm afraid it's a false alarm."

"Well, I'm glad of that!"

"Of course." O'Shaughnessy nodded. "But this boy set the alarm off on purpose. His name is Freeman and . . ."

But the headmaster wasn't listening anymore. He was staring past Mr. O'Shaughnessy. Slowly, Matt turned round to see what was happening. Mr. O'Shaughnessy did the same.

They were just in time to see the tanker come careening down the hill. They knew at once that something was

56

wrong. It was zigzagging across the road, seemingly out of control. But Matt could just make out the figure — a woman with mad eyes and straggling hair — sitting in the driver's seat. He recognized her at the same moment that he realized she knew exactly what she was doing, that she had come especially for him.

Gwenda Davis had her eyes fixed on the sports center where, according to Rex McKenna, the entire school would be having lunch. The petrol tanker was now facing away from the football field. As Matt watched, it left the road, plowed through a bush, and began to roll across the playing fields on the other side of the road. Matt saw the tires cutting up the turf. The tanker had to be doing seventy or eighty miles an hour. Its engine was roaring. Gwenda had her foot clamped down on the accelerator, and the steep slope of the hill was adding to her speed.

Some of the other boys had seen it, too. Faces turned. Hands pointed. There could be no doubt what was about to happen.

The tanker smashed into the wall of the sports center and continued right through it. Its window smashed and Gwenda was killed instantly, thrown into the brickwork even as it shattered all around her. With its engine screaming, the tanker continued, disappearing from sight, swallowed up by the building. There was a moment's pause. Then it exploded. A fireball erupted into the sky, hurling hundreds of tiles in every direction. It rose up, higher and higher, carrying with it a huge fist of black smoke that threatened to punch out the very clouds. Matt put a hand up to protect his face. Even at this distance, he could feel the fantastic heat of the thousands of gallons of petrol as they ignited.

57

Flames splashed out of the wrecked building, falling crazily onto the grass, the trees, the road, the edges of the main school, setting everything alight. It was like a war zone. The entire place seemed to be on fire.

Matt knew that he had cheated death by minutes. And if the whole school had been in the sports center, if they had been queuing up for lunch as they should have been, hundreds of children would have died.

The headmaster was thinking the same thing. "My God!" he croaked. "If we had been in there . . . !"

"He knew!" Mr. O'Shaughnessy let go of Matt and backed away. "He knew before it happened," he whispered. "Freeman knew."

The headmaster looked at him, his eyes wide.

Matt hesitated. He didn't want to stay here a minute longer. In the distance, he could already hear sirens.

He walked away. Six hundred and fifty boys stepped out of his way, forming a corridor to allow him to pass. Among them, Matt saw Gavin Taylor. For just a brief instant, their eyes met. The other boy was crying. Matt didn't know why.

Nobody said anything as he passed between them. Matt no longer cared what they thought of him.

One thing was certain: He would never see any of them again.

FIVE
The Diary

"You don't have to do this," Richard said.

It was the first time he had spoken since the train had pulled out of York on its way to London. Matt was sitting opposite him, his head buried in a book that he had bought at the station. The book was meant to be funny but Matt couldn't even bring himself to smile. For the last hour he had been skipping from paragraph to paragraph but the story simply wouldn't let him in.

"Matt . . . ?" Richard began again.

Matt snapped the book shut. "You saw what happened at Forrest Hill," he said. "It was Gwenda! She'd come to kill me and she'd have killed everyone else in the school if I hadn't warned them."

"But you did warn them. You saved their lives."

"Yes. And they all came running up to thank me for it." Matt stared out the window, taking in the rushing countryside. Raindrops crawled slowly across the glass, moving from left to right. "I can't go back," he said. "They don't want me there. And I've got nowhere else to go. Miss Ashwood was right. Raven's Gate wasn't the end of it. I don't think it is ever going to end."

Two days had passed since the destruction of the school.

The blazing petrol had spread from the gymnasium to the old buildings, and by the time the fire brigade had arrived, there hadn't been very much left. By then, Matt had returned to the flat in York, joining a shocked Richard, who had already heard the first reports on the midday news.

The school did their best to keep Matt out of the newspapers — and fortunately, nobody yet knew the identity of the madwoman who had been driving the petrol tanker. But there had been too many witnesses, too many boys willing to talk. And by the following morning, all the headlines were screaming the same impossible story:

BOY FORESEES SCHOOL CATASTROPHE
PRECOGNITION BOY SAVES SCHOOL
DID FORREST HILL BOY SEE FUTURE?

At least nobody had a photograph of Matt apart from one muddy, almost unrecognizable image that had been taken on a cell phone. By the time the first editions came out, Richard and Matt were already gone. Richard had spoken with Susan Ashwood on the phone and she had arranged a "safe house" for them in Leeds — an empty flat where they had stayed overnight. While they were there, Matt had agreed to travel to London to meet the Nexus, just as they had asked. Looking back, it seemed to him that there had been something inevitable about it.

"It was meant to happen. It was planned. . . ."

Susan Ashwood had said that, too. She had been talking about the discovery of the Spanish monk's diary. But she could just as easily have been talking about him. It was

60

beginning to seem to Matt that his every move was being dictated for him. It didn't matter what he wanted. Someone, somewhere, had other ideas.

"Maybe it'll work out okay," Richard said. "All you've got to do is meet this guy, William Morton. Get him to hand over the diary and then you and I can go back to York or somewhere and start over again."

"You really think it will be as easy as that?" Matt asked.

Richard shrugged. "Nothing's ever easy where you're concerned," he said. "But at the end of the day, Matt, you're still in control. Whatever they ask, you only have to say no."

• • •

A taxi had been sent to meet them at the station and took them to a hotel in Farringdon. Matt hardly knew London. The first time he had been here, he had been under police escort, whisked in and out of an office with barely enough time to smell the air. Farringdon was an old part of the city which seemed to slip further back in time as the evening drew on. There were dark alleyways and cobbled streets and even, in places, gas lamps. If an air raid siren had suddenly split the air, Matt wouldn't have been surprised. It was the London he had seen in films that took place during World War II.

The hotel was small and so discreet that it didn't even have a name on the front door. Richard and Matt both had rooms on the third floor — paid for, of course, by the Nexus. After they'd unpacked, they took the tiny, rickety elevator back to the ground floor and had an early supper together in the dining room. They were still eating when Mr. Fabian appeared, this time in a dark suit with black, brightly polished shoes.

"Good evening," he said. "I have been asked to take you to the meeting. But you must finish your meal first. We have plenty of time. Do you mind if I join you?"

He drew up a chair and sat down.

"Is it far from here?" Richard asked.

"No. A short walk." Fabian was in a good mood. He seemed to have forgotten the way their last meeting had ended.

"Can I ask you something?" Richard asked.

"Please. Go ahead."

"I know nothing about you. I mean, you once told me you lived in Lima. . . ."

"In fact I live in Barranco. It's a suburb of Lima."

"But what do you do? How did you get chosen by the Nexus? Do you have a wife or any children?"

Fabian had raised a finger to his lips at the mention of the Nexus, but there was nobody else in the room and he relaxed. "I will answer your questions," he said. "No, I am not married. Not yet, anyway. As to my work, I'm a writer. I have written many books about my country, its history, its archaeology. That was how I came into contact with the Nexus. I was a good friend of Professor Dravid before he was killed. It was he who recruited me."

Richard and Matt finished eating. A waiter came into the room to clear away the plates.

"If you're ready . . ." Fabian began.

"Lead the way!" Richard said.

They left the hotel and went down the street, walking for about five minutes until they arrived at a plain, black door set between a real estate agency and a café. Fabian had a key and unlocked the door, leading them through a cramped hallway and up a flight of stairs. The second floor was more modern than the rest of the building, with glass doors and security cameras. Matt had thought they were entering a private house, but the upper level was more like an office. The carpet was thick. The doors were closed. Everything felt silent and secretive.

"It's through here." Fabian gestured with a hand and, as if by magic, one of the doors slid open. On the other side was a room with an elongated table and eleven people sitting together in silence, waiting for them. Fabian went in and sat down next to Susan Ashwood. That left two empty chairs.

One for Matt. One for Richard.

"Please, come in." Matt wasn't sure who had spoken. All he was aware of was that everyone was looking at him. Matt felt himself beginning to blush. He didn't like being the center of attention at the best of times, but this was definitely weird. They were staring at him as if he were a film star. He felt that at any moment they were going to break into applause.

Richard walked in. Matt followed and the door closed behind them.

So this was the Nexus! Matt knew only what Fabian had once told him. The Nexus was a secret, worldwide organization that existed only to fight the Old Ones. Its members included representatives from government, police, church, and business — but they were here independently,

63

presumably at their own expense. Not that the cost would matter. The Nexus had all the money it needed. What it didn't have — yet — was him.

Quickly, Matt weighed up the twelve people sitting around the table. Now that Fabian had joined them, there were eight men and four women. Two of the men were black. One looked Chinese. Their ages ranged from about thirty to seventy. The oldest person in the room was wearing a clerical collar and a crucifix — some sort of priest. They were all smartly dressed. He could imagine them sitting at the theater together, or perhaps the opera. They shared the same sort of seriousness. None of them was smiling.

The room itself was long and narrow, with only one window giving a view of the street. The glass was tinted so that nobody outside could look in. The furniture was quietly expensive but there were no paintings or ornaments, just some maps and a number of clocks showing different times. Matt dropped into the nearest chair, trying to avoid eye contact. But not Richard. He was still standing by the door, looking around him in amazement.

"I know you!" he said. He pointed to a grim-faced man sitting with a straight back and an immaculately cut suit. "You're a policeman. Tarrant. Isn't that your name? You're very senior. New Scotland Yard. I've seen you on television." He turned to the woman who was next to him, expensively dressed, with reddish hair that was surely dyed. "And you're Natalie Johnson."

Even Matt knew that name. He had seen it often enough in the newspapers. She was often called the female Bill

Gates. She had made her fortune in computers and was one of the richest women in the world.

"Let's not bother with names, Mr. Cole," she said. She had an American accent. "Please take a seat and we can get started."

Richard sat down next to Matt. It was difficult to be sure who was in charge. Miss Ashwood was at the head of the table, but there was no obvious leader. It also occurred to Matt that someone in the room must be new. Fabian had told him that there were twelve members of the Nexus and sure enough there were twelve men and women here. But Professor Dravid had once been a member of the organization, too, and he had died. Presumably, he had been replaced.

"We are very grateful to you for coming to London, Matt," another man began. His accent was Australian. He was more casually dressed than the others, with an open-neck shirt and rolled-up sleeves. He was about forty and had the pale skin and bloodshot eyes of a man who had spent too many hours on long-distance planes. "We know you don't want to be here and we wouldn't have asked you if there was any other way."

"You must let us protect you," Susan Ashwood said. Her hands were resting on the table but her fists were clenched. "You were nearly killed at Forrest Hill. That can't happen. We are here only to help you."

"I thought it was Matt who was meant to be helping *you*," Richard said.

"We've got to help each other," the Australian went on. "There's a whole lot of things we don't know, but this much is certain. Things are going to get bad. Worse than you can imagine. The reason that the twelve of us are here tonight is because we want to do something about it."

"About what? What are you talking about?" Richard asked.

"A third world war," Ashwood said. "Worse than the two wars that preceded it. Governments out of control. Destruction and death all across the planet. We don't know exactly what form the future will take, Mr. Cole. But we think even now that we can prevent it from happening."

"With your help." The priest, a bishop, nodded at Matt.

"Look, let's get one thing straight," Richard said. "Matt and I don't want to know about death and destruction. We're not interested in world wars. The only help we need is to find somewhere else to live because, right now, Yorkshire doesn't seem to be an option and we don't have anyone else we can turn to."

"The petrol tanker that drove into your school . . . ?" The policeman had spoken. He left the question hanging in the air.

"It was driven by my aunt," Matt said. "Gwenda Davis. I saw her behind the wheel." He shivered. He had known it was her even as his every sense told him it was impossible. He had never liked her, not in all the years he had known her. But she had never been a monster. Not until the end.

"Your aunt?" the Australian muttered.

"Yes."

The information caused a stir in the room. The twelve members of the Nexus muttered briefly to each other, and Matt saw Fabian write something down.

"She didn't know what she was doing," Susan Ashwood said. "To steal a petrol tanker and somehow find her way to your school . . . she couldn't have done it on her own."

"The Old Ones," Fabian muttered in a low voice.

Ashwood nodded. "Of course. They helped her. They influenced her. Maybe they forced her. But undoubtedly they were behind it."

"All right," Richard cut in. "You want us to go and meet this man . . . William Morton. Matt's agreed to that. But I'm telling you now, if it means putting him in any more danger . . ."

"That's the last thing we'd want," Natalie Johnson said. She leaned forward, her long hair falling over her eyes. She must have been about fifty years old, but she had spent a lot of money making herself look younger. "All right, Richard — you don't mind if I call you that, do you? Let's give it to you straight. We need Matt to meet with this guy William Morton tomorrow afternoon at twelve o'clock because it's the only way we can get him to hand over the diary. But Matt is more important than the diary. Right now, if he really is who we think he is, he's just about the most important kid in the world."

"You've told Morton that Matt is one of the five," Richard said. He was speaking slowly, working it out as he went. "And Morton wants to meet him to see if it's true. But how's he going to do that? Is Matt going to have to see into the future or blow something up to prove it?"

"We don't know," the American replied. "Remember: Morton's read the diary; we haven't. He may know more than we do."

"All we know is that he's afraid," Susan Ashwood cut in. "He's afraid of the man he was dealing with in South America. And he's afraid of what he's read in the diary itself. William Morton has realized he's stumbled into something bigger and darker than anything he's experienced in his life, and he's looking for a way out."

"Where does he want to meet me?" Matt asked.

"At first he wouldn't tell us." This time it was a Frenchman who had picked up the story. He was slim and gray-haired and looked like an expensive lawyer. "He speaks to us only with his mobile phone and he gives us no idea where he can be found. But now he has mentioned a church in the city, not so far from here."

"St. Meredith's in Cannon Street," Ashwood said.

"He will be there at twelve o'clock tomorrow. He will meet with you alone. . . ."

"Matt's not going in there on his own," Richard said.

"He tells us that he will be watching out for the boy," the Frenchman continued. "We have not described to him what Matt looks like but it is unlikely that there will be any other fourteen-year-old adolescents near the church at that time. The deal is very simple: If Matt is not alone, Monsieur Morton will disappear. We will never see him again. And whoever it is that he has been dealing with in South America will have the diary."

"Why this church?" Richard asked. "It seems to be a strange place to meet. Why not a restaurant or a café or something like that?"

"Morton insisted," Johnson said. "I guess we'll find out the answer to that when Matt gets there."

"Maybe the church is mentioned in the diary," the bishop suggested. "As it happens, St. Meredith's is one of the oldest churches in the country. In fact, there's been a church on the site since the Middle Ages."

"And how can we be sure Matt will be safe there? For all we know, this mysterious South American businessman or whoever he is could have already got to Morton. This could all be a trap."

"Leave that to me," the policeman said. Richard had been right. His name was Tarrant and he was an assistant commissioner, one of the highest-ranking officers in London. "I'll have access to the security cameras all around Cannon Street. We can't go into the church, but I'll make sure there are a hundred officers in the immediate area. One word from me and they'll move in."

"But I still don't understand what happens," Matt said. "This man — William Morton — meets me. Maybe he asks me some questions. But what then? Is he going to give me the diary?"

"He's said he'll sell it to us if he believes in you," Natalie Johnson replied. "He's not *giving* it to anyone! He still wants his money."

There was a pause.

Richard turned to Matt. "Do you want to go?" he asked.

Matt shook his head. "No, I don't," he said. He glanced around the table. Everyone was staring at him. He could see his own face reflected in the black glasses that covered Susan Ashwood's eyes. "But I will," he went on, "if you'll give me something in return."

"What do you want?" the Australian asked.

69

"You people have a lot of influence. You stopped Richard getting his article published in the newspapers. So maybe you can get him a job, here in London."

"Matt . . ." Richard began.

"That's what you always wanted," Matt said. "And I want to go to an ordinary school. I'm not going back to Forrest Hill. I want you to promise me that if you get the diary, you'll leave me alone."

"I'm not sure we can promise that," Fabian said. "You're part of all this, Matt. Don't you see that?"

"But if we can leave you out of this, we will," Susan Ashwood cut in. "We don't like this any more than you do, Matt. We never wanted to bring you here."

Matt believed her. "All right," he said.

A decision had been made, but even now Matt wasn't convinced that he'd been the one who'd made it. Much later that night, as he lay in his bed on the third floor of the hotel, he told himself that soon it would all be over. He'd meet with Morton. He'd get the diary. And that would be the end of it.

But somehow he didn't believe it.

Everything that had happened in the last few days had been done against his wishes. And what happened next would be the same. There was no way out for him. He had to get used to it. There were strange forces all around him and they were never going to let him go.

•   •   •

Ten thousand miles away, a man was approaching his desk.

It was the middle of the afternoon in the town of Ica, just south of the Peruvian capital of Lima. Peru was five hours behind Britain. The sun was shining brilliantly, and as the room was open to the elements, with a tiled floor that stretched past a row of pillars into the courtyard, the entire room was flooded with light. High above, a fan turned slowly, not actually cooling anything but giving the illusion that it might. The man could hear the gentle sound of water splashing. An old fountain played in the court-yard. A few chickens pecked at the gravel. There were flowers everywhere and their scent hung heavy in the air.

The man was fifty-seven years old, dressed in a white linen suit that hung off him in such a way that it might still have been in the wardrobe. He moved slowly and with dif-ficulty, reaching out with his hands to find his chair and to lower himself into it.

He was horribly deformed.

He was unnaturally tall — well over six feet — but what gave him his extra height was his head, which was twice as long as it should have been. The head was huge, its eyes so high up that on anyone else they would have been in the middle of the forehead. He had a few tufts of hair that were really no color at all, but mainly he was bald, with liver spots all over his skin. His nose extended all the way down to his mouth, which was too small in relation to everything else. A child's mouth in an adult face. A muscle twitched in the side of his neck as he moved. The neck was obviously strug-gling to hold up such a great weight.

The man's name was Diego Salamanda. He was the chair-man of one of the largest companies in South America. Salamanda News International had built an empire with newspapers and magazines, television stations, hotels, and telecommunications. Some people claimed that SNI owned Peru. And Diego Salamanda was the sole owner, the chairman, and the single stockholder of SNI.

His head had been stretched quite deliberately. It was a practice from more than a thousand years before. Some of the ancient tribes of Peru had selected newly born babies whom they believed to be "special" and had forced them to live with their head sandwiched between two wooden planks. This was what caused the abnormal growth. It was supposed to be an honor. Salamanda's parents had known that their baby was special. So they had done the same to him.

And he was grateful for it.

They had caused him pain. They had made him hideous. They had prevented him from ever enjoying a normal human relationship. But they had been right. They had recognized his talents the very day he was born.

The telephone rang. Still moving slowly, Salamanda reached out and took the receiver. It looked slightly ridiculous, far too small, as he held it against his ear.

"Yes." He didn't need to give his name. This was a private number. Only a handful of people had it. They would know who they were calling.

"It's at twelve o'clock tomorrow," the voice at the other end said. "He's going to be at a church in London. St. Meredith's."

"Very good." Both of them were speaking in English. It was the language that Salamanda used for all his business.

"What do you want me to do?" the voice asked.

"You have done enough, my friend. And you will be rewarded. Now you can leave it to me."

"What will you do?"

Salamanda paused. An ugly light shimmered in his strangely colorless eyes. He didn't like being asked questions. But he was in a generous mood. "I will take the diary and kill Mr. Morton," he replied.

"And the boy?"

"If the boy is there, then of course I will kill him, too."

SIX
St. Meredith's

The church was near Shoreditch, in an ugly part of London that really wasn't like London at all. At school, Matt had learned about the Blitz, when German bombers had destroyed great chunks of the city, particularly in the East End. What the teachers hadn't told him was that the blank spaces and rubble had been replaced with modern, concrete office blocks, multilevel parking garages, cheap, tacky shops and — cutting between them — wide, anonymous highways that carried an endless stream of traffic with a lot of noise but not a great deal of speed.

He had been brought here by taxi, dropped off at the end of Market Street, which in fact turned out to be a grubby lane running between a pub and a launderette. The church stood at the bottom end, looking sad and out of place. It had been bombed, too. A new steeple had been added at some time in the last twenty years and it didn't quite match the stone pillars and arched doorways below. St. Meredith's was surprisingly large and at one time must have been quite grand, standing at the center of a thriving community. But the community had moved on and the church looked exactly as it was — abandoned. It no longer had any reason to exist.

Once again, Matt wondered why the bookseller, William Morton, had chosen this place for their meeting. At least they would have no difficulty recognizing each other. There were few people around — and certainly no sign of the hundred armed police officers that the assistant commissioner had promised. As he made his way down the lane, a door of the pub opened and a bearded man with a broken nose stepped unsteadily out. It was only twelve o'clock, but he was already drunk. Or perhaps he was still hung over from the night before. Matt quickened his pace. There was a cell phone in his pocket, and Richard was only a few minutes away if he needed help. Matt wasn't afraid. He just wanted to get this over with and go back to ordinary life.

He walked up to the front door, wondering if he would even be able to get in. The door was very solid and somehow gave the impression of being locked. Matt reached out and lifted the handle. Cold and heavy in his hand, it turned reluctantly, with a creaking sound. The door swung open and Matt stepped forward, passing from bright daylight to a strange, shadow-filled interior. The sun was shut out. The sound of the traffic disappeared. Matt had left the door open but it swung closed behind him. The boom of the wood hitting the frame echoed through the empty space.

He was standing at the end of the nave, which stretched out to an altar some distance away. There were no electric lights in the church, and the stained-glass windows were either too dusty or too darkly colored to let in any light. But there were about a thousand candles illuminating the way forward, flickering together in little crowds, gathered round the chapels and alcoves that lined the sides of the building. As Matt's eyes got used to the gloom, he made out various figures, old men and women kneeling in the pews or hunched up in front of the tombstones, dressed in black and looking like ghosts that had somehow drifted up from the catacombs below.

He swallowed. He was liking this less and less, and he wished now that he had insisted on Richard coming with him. The journalist had wanted to, but Fabian and the other members of the Nexus had dissuaded him. Matt was to enter alone. That was what they had agreed with William Morton and if they broke faith, they might never see him again.

Matt looked around him, but there was no sign of the bookseller. He remembered the face he had seen on the video. At least he would know what Morton looked like when he chose to reveal himself. Where was he? Hiding somewhere in the shadows, perhaps, checking that Matt was alone. If someone had come with him, there were plenty of other ways out of the church. Morton could slip away without ever being seen.

Matt continued down toward the altar, passing a carved wooden pulpit shaped like an eagle. The priest would address the congregation from above its outspread wings. The walls of the church were lined with paintings. A saint shot full of arrows. Another broken on a wheel. A crucifixion. Why did religion have to be so dark and cruel?

As he arrived at the apse, just in front of the altar where the east and west formed a cross, a man stood up and gestured to him. The man had been sitting in a pew, his head half hidden in his hands. Matt recognized him at once. Overweight, with silver hair in tufts on either side of a round, bald head. Ruddy cheeks and small, watery eyes. The man was wearing a crumpled suit and no tie. There was a package, wrapped in brown paper, in his hand.

"Matthew Freeman?" he asked.

"I'm Matt." Matt never used his full name.

"You know who I am?"

"William Morton."

Matt could see at once that the bookseller was a very different man from the one he had seen in the television interview. Something had cut through his arrogance and self-regard. Both physically and mentally he seemed to have shrunk. Now that they were closer, Matt could see that he hadn't shaved. Silver stubble was spreading across his cheeks and down to his neck. And he hadn't changed his clothes in days. He smelled bad. He was sweating.

"You're very young." Morton blinked a couple of times. "You're just a child."

"What were you expecting?" Matt didn't try to keep the annoyance out of his voice. He didn't like being called a child. He still didn't know what this was all about.

"They didn't tell you?" Morton asked.

"They told me you had a book. A diary . . ." Matt glanced at the brown paper package and Morton drew it closer to him, holding it more tightly. "Is that it?"

Morton didn't answer.

"They said you wanted to meet me," Matt went on. "They want to buy it from you."

"I know what they want!" Morton glanced left and right. Suddenly he was suspicious. "You came here alone?" he hissed.

"Yes."

"Come this way. . . ."

Before Matt could say anything, Morton scurried along the line of the pews and began to move down the side of the church, leaving the other worshippers behind. Matt followed slowly. It occurred to him that the bookseller might be a little mad. But at the same time he knew it was worse than that. He thought back to the farmer, Tom Burgess, who had spoken to him outside the nuclear reactor at Lesser Malling and who had later died. He had been just the same. As he walked into the darkness in the farthest corner of the church, Matt realized that William Morton was scared out of his wits.

Morton waited until Matt had arrived, then began to speak, the words tumbling over each other in a soft gabble. There was nobody else around in this part of the church. Presumably that was why he had chosen it.

"I should never have bought the diary," he said. "But I knew what it was, you see. I'd heard of the Old Ones. I knew a little of their history . . . not very much, of course. Nobody knew very much. But when I saw the diary in an antique shop in Cordoba, I recognized it immediately. There were people who said it didn't even exist. And many more who thought that the author — St. Joseph of Cordoba — was mad. The Mad Monk. That's what they called him.

"And there it was! Incredibly. Waiting for me to pick it up. The only written history of the Old Ones. Raven's Gate. And the five!" As he spoke this last word, his eyes widened and he stared at Matt. "It was all there," he went on. "The beginning of the world, our world. The first great war. It was only won by a trick. . . ."

"Is that the diary, there?" Matt asked a second time. This was all moving too quickly for him.

"I thought it would be worth a fortune!" Morton whispered. "It's what every bookseller dreams of . . . finding a first edition or the only copy of a book that has been lost to the world. And this was much, much more than that. I went on television and I told everyone what I had in my hands. I boasted — and that was the biggest mistake I could have made."

"Why?"

"Because . . ."

Somewhere in the church, someone dropped a hymn book. It fell to the floor with a thunderous echo, and Morton's head whipped round as if a shot had been fired. Matt could see the sinews bulging on the side of his neck. The bookseller looked as if he were on the edge of a heart attack. He waited a moment until everything was silent again.

"I should have been more careful," Morton continued, speaking in a whisper. "I should have read the diary first. Maybe then I would have understood."

"Understood what?"

"It's evil!" Morton took out a handkerchief and wiped it across his brow. "Have you ever read a horror story, Matt? One that you can't get out of your mind? One that stays and torments you when you want to go to sleep? The diary is like that, only worse. It speaks of creatures that'll come into this world, of events that will take place. I don't understand it all. But what I do understand won't leave me alone. I can't sleep. I can't eat. My life has been turned upside down."

"Then why don't you just sell it? You've been offered millions of pounds."

"And you think I'll live to enjoy a penny of it?" Morton laughed briefly. "Since I read the diary, I've had nightmares. Horrible nightmares. And then I wake up and I think they're all over, but they're not. Because they're real. The shadows that I have seen, reaching out for me, aren't just in my imagination. Look!"

He pulled back a sleeve and Matt winced. It looked as if Morton had tried to cut his wrists. There were half a dozen mauve lines, recent wounds, crisscrossing each other about an inch away from his hand.

"You did that?" Matt asked.

"Maybe I did. Maybe I didn't. I don't remember! I wake up in the morning and they're just there. Blood on the sheets! Cuts and bruises. I'm in pain. . . ." He rubbed his eyes, fighting for control. "And that's not all. Oh, no! I don't see things properly anymore. Ever since I read the book, all I see are the shadows and the darkness. People walking in the street are dead to me. Even the animals, the dogs and the cats . . . they look at me as if they're going to leap out and . . ."

Once again, he was forced to stop.

"And things happen," he continued. "Just now! Coming here today. A car nearly ran me down. It was as if the driver hadn't seen me — or *had* seen me and didn't care. Do you think I'm going mad? Well, ask yourself what happened to my house. It burned down. I was there. The fire just started, all on its own. It came from nowhere! The doors slammed shut. The telephones stopped working. Do you see what I'm saying? Do you *understand*? The house wanted to kill me. It wanted me dead."

Matt knew that at least part of this was true. The Nexus had already told him about the fire.

"I am a condemned man," Morton said. "I have the diary. I've read all its secrets. And now it won't let me live."

"Then why don't you just get rid of it?" Matt persisted.

Morton nodded. "I've thought of destroying it. Of course I have. But there's the money!" He licked his lips and it was then that Matt saw the true horror of Morton's predicament. He was being torn apart between fear and greed. It was a constant battle and it was destroying him. "Two million pounds! It's more than I've ever earned. I can't just throw it away. How would I be able to live with myself? No! I'll sell it. That's what I am. A bookseller. I'll sell it and I'll take the money and then it'll leave me alone."

"You have to sell it to us," Matt said.

"I know. I know. That's why I agreed to meet you. Four boys and a girl. They're in the diary. You're one of them. One of the five."

"Everyone calls me that," Matt interrupted. "But I don't even know what it means. Ever since I got tangled up in all this, I've been trying to find a way out. I'm sorry, Mr. Morton. I know you want me to prove something to you. But I can't."

Morton shook his head, refusing to believe what Matt had just told him. "I know about the first gate," he said.

"Raven's Gate."

"There's a second gate. It's all in here. . . ."

"Then give it to me." Suddenly Matt was tired. "If you really want to get rid of the diary and I'm the only person you'll give it to, that's fine. Give it to me. You'll get your money. And then maybe we can both go home and forget all about it."

Morton nodded, and for a brief moment Matt thought it was all over. He'd hand over the package, and he and Richard would be on the next train to . . . wherever. But, of course, it wasn't going to be as easy as that.

"I have to be sure you are who you say you are," Morton rasped. "You have to prove it to me!"

Matt's head swam. "I've already told you. I can't do that."

"Yes, you can!" Morton was gripping the book so tightly that his fingers had turned white. He looked quickly around the church, once again making sure they weren't overheard. "Do you see the door?" he asked.

"What door?"

"There!" Morton twitched his head and Matt looked past him to a strange, wooden door set in the stone wall. What was strange about it? It took him a few moments to work it out. It was too small, about half the size of all the other doors in the church. He assumed it must lead out into the street. It was set underneath a stained-glass window with gloomy paintings on either side. Looking more closely, he saw that there was something carved into the wood. A symbol. A pentagram. A star with five points.

"What about it?" Matt asked.

"It's why I chose this place to meet. It's in the diary."

"That's not possible." Matt tried to work it out. The diary had been written in the sixteenth century, four hundred years ago. Parts of this church were older. Parts of it were quite modern. Either way, how could the monk have known about the existence of a single door?

"Of course it's not possible," Morton agreed. "But that doesn't matter. I want you to go through the door and I want you to bring me something from the other side. It doesn't matter what it is. Whatever you choose will prove to me that you are . . . who they say you are."

"What's on the other side?"

"You tell me. Bring me whatever you find. I'll wait for you here."

"Why don't you come with me?"

"You really do know nothing," Morton said. Suddenly his voice was urgent again. "We don't have time to argue. Do as I say. Do it now. Or I'll leave and you'll never hear from me again."

Matt sighed. He didn't understand any of it. But there was no point in answering back. He wanted this to be over. This was the only way. He glanced one last time at the bookseller, then went over to the door. Slowly he reached out, his hand resting on the iron handle. It was only now that it occurred to him that although the door was too small for the church, it was perfectly in proportion with his own height.

It had been built for a child.

He turned the handle. Opened the door. And stepped through.

While Matt and William Morton had been talking, neither of them had heard the front door of the church open again. Nor had they seen the man who had come in. He was dirty, dressed in rags, with a beard and a broken nose. Matt had noticed him in Cannon Street when he had come out of the pub, pretending to be drunk.

The man stood for a moment, allowing his eyes to become used to the gloom, then moved down toward the apse. It didn't take him long to find the bookseller. Morton was standing next to a half-size door, shifting his ample weight from one foot to the other as if he were waiting to go into the dentist. There was a square parcel, wrapped in brown paper, held in his hand.

The diary . . .

It seemed that the boy had gone. But the boy wasn't important. The man with the broken nose had been paid to kill Morton and take the book. If the boy was there, he would die, too. But he wasn't and the man was secretly pleased. Killing children was occasionally necessary but always unpleasant.

He reached into the pocket of his raincoat and took something out. The knife was only about ten centimeters long, but that didn't matter. The man knew how to use it. He could kill with a knife half that size.

The man noticed the altar ahead of him and briefly crossed himself, using the blade of the knife. The point touched his head, his chest, both his shoulders.

Then, with a smile, he continued on his way.

• • •

It was too hot.

That was Matt's first thought. When he had gone into the church, it had been a normal London summer's day. That is, it had been sunny but cool, and most people had been glad it wasn't raining. He had only been in the church for a few minutes, but in that time the sun seemed to have intensified. And the sky was the wrong color. It was an intense, Mediterranean blue. All the clouds had disappeared.

And that wasn't the only thing that was wrong.

Matt hadn't been sure what he would find on the other side of the door. He had been half expecting to step back out into Cannon Street. Instead he was in a cloister, a covered walkway forming a square around a courtyard with a fountain in the middle. Well, there was nothing surprising about that. Lots of churches had cloisters. It was where the priests went to walk and to think about their next sermon or whatever.

But this cloister was completely different from the church. It looked older — and more beautiful. The pillars holding up the arches were more ornate. And the fountain was really lovely, carved out of some sort of white stone with crystal-clear water splashing down from one basin to another. Matt knew almost nothing about art or architecture, but even he could see that there was something about the fountain that wasn't quite English. The same was true of the whole cloister. He cast his eyes from the perfectly mown grass to the brilliant flowers tumbling out of huge, terra-cotta pots. How could a church as shabby and as

85

neglected as St. Meredith's have managed to hold on to a courtyard as perfect as this?

He looked back at the church from which he had just come. And that was another thing. Was he going mad or was the brickwork somehow different on the outside? There was a square tower rising up above him but no sign of a steeple, modern or otherwise. Well, perhaps it was hidden by the angle of the wall. But even so, Matt had to fight to stop himself from thinking an absurd thought.

This was a completely different building from the one he'd just come out of.

No.

It was some sort of illusion. William Morton was deliberately trying to trick him.

The bookseller had told him to bring something back with him. It didn't matter what and he didn't care. All Matt wanted to do was to get out of here, to get back onto familiar ground. He stepped forward and plucked a bright, mauve flower out of one of the pots. He felt stupid, holding a flower, but he couldn't see anything else and he didn't want to spend any more time here searching. He turned round and was about to walk back when someone stepped in front of him. It was a young man, dressed in a brown robe. A monk.

And there was Matt, in his jeans and hooded sweatshirt, caught picking flowers in the middle of the cloister.

"Hi!" Matt didn't know what to say. He held up the flower. "I was told to get this. It's for a friend."

The monk spoke to him. But not in English. Listening to the strange language, Matt thought it might be Spanish or Italian. The monk didn't sound angry. He was trying to be friendly — although he was obviously puzzled.

"Do you speak English?" Matt asked.

The monk held up a finger and a thumb, almost touching. The universal symbol for "a little."

"I have to go," Matt said. He pointed at the door. "I have a friend . . ."

The monk didn't try to stop him. Matt opened the door and went back through.

He was back in St. Meredith's.

But William Morton wasn't there.

Matt looked around him, feeling increasingly foolish with the flower in his hand. It seemed that the bookseller had been playing tricks on him. While Matt had been out in the cloister, Morton had been making his getaway. He had never intended to hand over the diary. It was all for nothing.

And then the woman screamed.

She screamed once, her voice so loud and high-pitched that it must surely have been heard all over Shoreditch. The scream flew up into the church to be joined by a second and then a third, each scream becoming an echo of the other. Matt looked around and saw her, an old woman wrapped up in black, standing a few meters away, pointing down. At the same time, he saw the blood on the cold, stone floor.

He ran forward.

William Morton was lying on his back, his hand clamped to his stomach, trying to hold shut the wound that the knife had made. There was a lot of blood. At first Matt thought he must be dead. The woman was still screaming. None of the other worshippers had come near, although Matt could hear them whispering, murmuring, afraid to show themselves. Then the bookseller opened his eyes and saw Matt, saw what Matt was holding. Despite everything, he smiled to himself. It was as if Matt had brought flowers to the funeral he was about to have.

"You are . . ." he began.

Just two words. Then he died.

At the same time, the doors were flung open and half a dozen men ran in. Matt looked up and saw police uniforms. So the Nexus hadn't been lying to him. There really had been a protective ring around the church. It was just that it hadn't worked. The police had arrived too late.

He was surrounded. More people were screaming. The police were trying to keep them back. More officers came through the door. Matt recognized one of them. It was Tarrant, the assistant commissioner. He looked grim.

Richard Cole arrived a few minutes later, bursting in with Fabian. By now the body had been covered. The congregation had left. More police officers had arrived. Matt was sitting on his own, holding the flower which had already begun to wilt. He was very still. There was blood on one of his sneakers.

"Are you okay?" Richard asked. His face was filled with horror.

"Yeah. Sure." Matt wondered if he was in shock. He didn't feel anything. "I didn't get the diary," he said. "Whoever killed him took it."

"How did they know he was here?" Fabian muttered. "Nobody knew about the meeting. He told only us."

"Somebody knew," Matt said. He waved a hand in the

direction of the dead man. "They took the diary. He had it with him when we met but just now I looked and it wasn't there."

"To hell with the diary," Richard said. "You were with him. You could have been killed, too." He paused and frowned. "What happened?" he asked. "Did you see who it was?"

"No. I was out in the cloister. He made me get him this." Matt held up the flower.

Now it was Fabian's turn to look puzzled. "What cloister?" he asked.

"The church has a cloister," Matt said. "Morton asked me to go there. He said it was some sort of test, but I think he was lying."

"This church has no cloister," Fabian said.

"It's through there." Matt looked in the direction of the door.

"Let's go out," Richard said. "You need some air."

"There is no cloister," Fabian insisted.

Angrily, Matt stood up and walked over to the door. "It's through here," he said.

He opened the door. And stopped dead.

There was no cloister on the other side. There were no flowers, no fountain, no monks. Instead, he found himself looking at an alleyway lined with dustbins and, on the other side, a grimy backyard filled with rubble and broken cement.

He looked down at the flower in his hand and then threw it down as if it were scalding him. The flower lay floating in a puddle of brown rainwater. There was no other color anywhere around.

SEVEN
Danger Area

In the end, it all seemed too easy.

Matt didn't want any part of it. He would have liked to forget the Nexus, the Old Ones, William Morton, the diary, the second gate, and all the other weird things that had somehow closed in on him and taken over his life. Certainly, he had no great desire to visit Peru. And yet, here he was at midday, sitting on a British Airways jumbo jet on the runway at Heathrow Airport, Flight 207 to Lima via Miami. Once again, he got the feeling that he hadn't chosen to be here. It had just happened.

After the death of the bookseller at St. Meredith's church, there had been another meeting of the Nexus — and that was when they had put it to him.

"Matt, we want to send you to Peru." This time, Susan Ashwood had done most of the talking. Maybe they felt she knew him best. "We've lost the diary. It wasn't your fault, but it's a catastrophe. It means that whoever was bidding for it in South America probably has it, or will have it soon. The diary will show them how to find the gate. Worse than that, it may show them how to open it."

"There's nothing Matt can do," Richard said. "You send him all the way across the world . . . what's the point?"

"I can't really answer that, Mr. Cole. How can I explain? Imagine this were a game of chess. Losing Morton was like losing a pawn. Now, sending you to Peru, it's as if we're advancing a knight. In the end, it may be too late. It may not help. But at least it shows we're still on the attack."

"The boy and the gate are linked," Natalie Johnson said. Matt could see that the American woman had already made up her mind. "He's part of it. Something is going to happen in Peru — and whatever it is, he should be there."

"Well, Peru's a big country. Where's he supposed to begin?"

"In the capital. Lima."

"Why there?"

"We may have one lead," Tarrant explained. "William Morton had his cell phone with him when he was murdered. Fortunately for us, his killer left it behind. I've looked at it, and it seems he made a dozen calls in the week before he died. Some of them to us, of course. But three of them were to a number in Lima."

"Salamanda News International," the Frenchman said.

"What's that?" Richard asked.

"It's one of the biggest businesses on the whole damned continent," Natalie Johnson explained. "And the man who fronts it, Diego Salamanda, is one of the richest. I've had dealings with him in the past, but I've never met him. I've heard he's disabled in some way and he keeps himself very much to himself. He runs newspapers, TV and satellite stations, publishing houses, and hotels. He does it out of an office in Lima."

"Was he the one trying to buy the diary?"

91

"Perhaps. We can't know for sure. But not much happens within his organization without him knowing it, so it probably comes down to the same thing. If it's Salamanda we're up against, that's bad news. He's powerful. But on the other hand, maybe it's good that we know who the enemy is. At least it tells us where to start."

"Okay." Richard nodded. "So you send Matt to Lima. Then what does he do?"

"He stays with me as my guest," Fabian replied. "You will both be welcome in my home. I told you already that I have a house in Barranco. It is a quiet part of the city where many artists and writers live. I'm not far from the beach. You will be safe there."

"William Morton thought he was safe," Richard pointed out. "And look what happened to him!"

"We don't know what went wrong," Ashwood admitted. "None of us knew the meeting place until the day before, and of course we didn't tell anyone. We can only assume he must have been followed. However, I agree with you. Your safety is of paramount importance — which is why we've decided to take extra precautions. Nobody must even know you've left England."

"What about passport control?" Richard asked.

"I'm seeing to that." Tarrant took over. "I'm going to arrange false passports for you. This man — Salamanda — may not have any agents at Heathrow Airport, but he's sure to have people on the lookout when you arrive in Lima. So you'll both travel under assumed names. Nobody outside this room will know who you are."

"It still sounds crazy," Richard said. "Your plan is that

you don't have a plan. Go to Peru! Do not pass Go. Do not collect two hundred pounds!"

"No," Matt interrupted. It was almost the first time he had spoken, and the thirteen adults in the room all turned to look at him. "I think Miss Ashwood is right. We can't just walk away. Not after all that's happened. The second gate is in Peru. It's going to open. We have to be there."

Now, hours later on the plane to Peru, Matt wondered why he had been so decisive.

Maybe the twelve members of the Nexus had been right. His life was completely tangled up with the second gate, and there seemed to be no escaping it. Or was there part of him that genuinely wanted to help, to fight back at an ancient enemy? Matt wasn't sure. All he knew was that he was sweating and felt sick. As the engines began to roar in the buildup before takeoff, he was certain they would fall off the wings. And how could this huge machine with its six hundred passengers, suitcases, meal carts, and all the rest of it possibly stay up in the air? Matt had only ever flown twice in his entire life and those had been short hops to Marseilles and Malaga with his parents, when he was very young. This flight was going to last seventeen hours! He wasn't afraid of what he might find in Peru. But he was certainly afraid of flying there.

Twenty minutes later, the 747 was well above cloud level, already leaving the west coast of England behind. A flight attendant came up to them with a menu.

"Would you like a drink, Mr. Carter?" she asked.

It took Matt a moment to realize that she was talking to them. Paul and Robert Carter. Two brothers traveling together. Those were the names on the false passports they had been given.

"I'll have a beer, thanks," Richard said.

"Just some water for me," Matt added.

They were traveling in business class, close to the front of the plane. The tickets had cost thousands of pounds, but the Nexus had been ready to pay millions for the diary. They obviously weren't short of cash. Matt settled back in his seat. He had a personal television set with a choice of about ten films as well as a selection of computer games. Richard had also bought him books and magazines. But he didn't feel like doing anything. Sitting there, suspended in the air somewhere above the Irish Sea, he felt empty, disconnected.

"So do you want to talk about it?" Richard asked.

"What?"

"The door. What you saw on the other side."

Matt shook his head. "I don't know," he said. "I've been thinking about it. William Morton chose the church because of something he'd read in the diary. He used the door as a test, to prove I was who he thought I was."

Richard nodded. "If anyone else went through the door, they'd find themselves standing in a puddle in East London."

"But I went somewhere else. I'm not even sure I was in England." Matt thought for a moment. "Do you remember what it said on that news program? The one we saw on the video? It said something about an Internet working inside the church. . . ."

"It was one of the things in the diary."

"Well, maybe that's what it meant. When you sit at a computer, you can click a mouse and go where you like. You can link up with another computer anywhere in the world. Maybe it's the same sort of thing . . . only for real."

"That's great!" Richard smiled. "So all you have to do is find another church door in Peru and maybe you can go home without having to pay for another flight."

The flight attendant came with the drinks. Sunlight was streaming in through the windows, and the smell of lunch was already spreading through the cabin from the galley just behind them. Only four months ago, Matt had been living with his aunt in Ipswich, failing at school, struggling from Monday to Friday, and wasting time on weekends. And now he was here. It was hard to believe.

Richard seemed to pick up his thoughts. "You didn't have to do this," he said.

"I think I did, Richard." Matt gazed out of the window. There was nothing to look at. Just the clouds and an empty sky. "Miss Ashwood knew it. Even William Morton. I'm part of this and I think I always have been. I tried to pretend otherwise and I nearly got a whole lot of people killed." He sighed. "You don't have to be here. But I think I do."

"Yeah, well, you're not going anywhere without me."

"Then we're stuck in it together."

● ● ●

The flight seemed endless. Matt watched one film, then another. He read part of his book. He tried to sleep, but without success. The noise of the engines was all around him and he couldn't forget the fact that he was hanging in space with the ground far too far away. They landed in Miami and spent two hours in a characterless transit lounge while the plane refueled. By now Matt's inner clock was telling him that it was late in the evening — but it was still light outside. The entire day had been stretched out of shape and he felt exhausted.

They took off again and suddenly the weather turned bad. The sky was dark and a fork of lightning cracked downward, flashing against the silver skin of the 747. They hit a patch of turbulence and Matt felt his stomach heave as the floor momentarily disappeared from beneath his feet. Inside the business section, the lights had been dimmed. A soft, yellow glow illuminated the passengers, sitting in their seats, trying to look relaxed but at the same time gripping the armrests with all their strength. Nobody was talking. But as every buffet of wind made the plane shudder, as the tone of the engines rose and fell in the swirling air pockets, one or two of them swore softly or even muttered a near-silent prayer.

And somehow, in the middle of all this, Matt finally managed to fall asleep. Not that it felt that way. One moment he was next to Richard, half concentrating on yet another film and counting the minutes until they were back on the ground, the next he was somewhere else.

The island. He recognized it at once and knew it so well that he had to remind himself that he had never actually been there. He had only ever visited it in his dreams. There was the shaft of black, broken rock. And there was the sea, as ugly as liquid tar, spread out all around. There was no wind, but the clouds were still racing across a darkening sky. Matt wondered what it all meant. Why was he here? Why did he so frequently return?

He looked down and saw the strange reed boat that had been making its way toward him the last time he came here. It had reached the edge of the island and sat, abandoned, on the gray sand.

"Matt!"

Someone had called his name. He turned round and saw the boy from the boat, standing on a rocky shelf just below him. The two of them were about the same age but the boy was smaller and thinner than he, wearing clothes that were little more than rags. Matt opened his mouth to answer. He knew who the boy was and why he was there. He had come to collect him, to take him to the three others who were still waiting on the mainland, just half a mile away.

But the words never came. There was a scream. Matt looked up just in time to see the swan plunging out of the sky, its neck straining forward. It came at him with all the power of a plane crash. Even as he looked, the swan drew closer, its gaping beak filling his vision as if it were about to swallow him whole.

The other boy cried out. Matt felt himself falling.

There was a bump, and he opened his eyes.

Richard was sitting next to him.

They had arrived in Lima.

• • •

It seemed to Matt that Aeropuerto Jorge Chavez was only half built. After the bright lights and bustle of

97

Heathrow, with crowds milling among the duty-free shops as if every day were Christmas, he had arrived at a blank, empty space where the passengers were invited to queue up at a row of cubicles manned by border guards in black-and-white uniforms. The ceiling of the arrivals lounge was missing tiles and none of the fans were working. A few potted plants sat wilting in the sticky heat. It wasn't so much *Welcome to Peru* as *Welcome to Nowhere in Particular.*

Matt was feeling tired and grimy as he waited in line with Richard — looking just the same — next to him. But there was something else. As he watched the passengers moving ahead of him and heard the clunk of the passport stamps as they were admitted into the country, he realized he was getting nervous. It was only now that he remembered that he and Richard were committing a criminal offense. They were traveling with false passports. He supposed the Nexus knew what it was doing, but even so, it suddenly seemed less of a good idea.

The two of them reached the front of the queue and found themselves facing a tired-looking official with suspicion etched into his face. Presumably that was his job, to be suspicious of everyone. But Matt felt his heartbeat quicken as Richard handed over their documents. He glanced away. Part of the hall was held up by scaffolding and there was a large sign hanging below: NO CRUZAR. ÁREA DE PELIGRO. Richard had followed his eyes.

"Don't cross. Danger area," he translated.

Matt nodded, wondering if the words might be prophetic.

The border guard had run both the passports through

a machine and was studying a television screen. Now he looked up. "What is the purpose of your visit?" He must have asked the same question ten thousand times.

"We're here on holiday," Richard lied.

The stamp came down twice more. That was it. They were through and Matt was annoyed with himself for even being slightly worried in the first place.

It had been agreed that Fabian wouldn't come to the airport himself to collect them. Again, there was always the chance that he might be recognized and followed. Instead, he would send a driver — and sure enough, there was a stocky Peruvian in a white short-sleeve shirt, waiting for them after they had picked up their luggage. He was holding up a sign with their false names: PAUL AND ROBERT CARTER. Two brothers on holiday. Nothing at all to do with Matt Freeman and Richard Cole, who had come here to save the world.

"*Buenos dias,*" the driver said, reaching out to take the cases for them. "I am Alberto. Mr. Fabian sends you his good wishes. I hope you had a good flight."

"It was long," Richard said.

The driver laughed. "Long flight. Yes. You have come very far. But Mr. Fabian is near. I take you to him."

He led them out of the airport, pushing through a crowd of anxious-looking people who immediately surrounded them shouting, "Taxi! Taxi!" and trying to snatch at their hand luggage. Matt was feeling really tired now. It was early evening and a heavy darkness hung in the sky. The air was warm and smelled of diesel. He hoped it wouldn't take them too long to reach the hotel.

Their car was a brand-new shuttle bus. As the door slid shut and the driver turned on the engine, Matt felt the welcome chill of the air-conditioning. He sunk back in the leather seat with Richard beside him.

"Peru . . ." Richard muttered.

"Yeah." Matt didn't know what to say.

"It's not as Peruvian as I'd imagined. Shouldn't there be llamas?"

"We're in the middle of an airport, Richard."

"Well . . . something." Richard closed his eyes tiredly.

Alberto put the car into gear and they moved off.

Matt gazed out the window. After the long journey, the hours spent in the air, it was difficult to believe that he had arrived. He was in South America! Not just a foreign country but a whole new continent. A different world.

They drove past some sort of naval base — the airport had been close to the sea — and joined a six-lane motorway, somehow blending in with about a thousand other vehicles, rushing along on all sides. Brightly colored buses, just big enough for twenty passengers but carrying twice as many, rumbled past. Toyota vans, also crammed with people, swerved in and out of the traffic, horns blaring. On each side of the road there was a wide strip of wasteland, rubble strewn with old tires, oil drums, and garbage. Broken walls covered with graffiti dotted the way, along with ancient watchtowers, some of them sprouting the red-and-white Peruvian flag. To Matt, it seemed as if a war had been fought here, but a very long time ago, and the people were still clearing up the mess.

Somehow the tangle of dust, graffiti, traffic, and concrete

managed to tumble together into something vaguely resembling a city. As they drew closer to the edge of Lima, Matt saw a row of modern office buildings, a garage with its name — REPSOL — flashing in neon, a few shops still open, with people lolling around outside. Signs of everyday life. Green-and-red taxi bikes buzzed past them, their own horns blasting out angry little tunes. Billboards carrying advertisements for computers and mobile phones sprung up, blocking out the view. And then they turned off and came back once again to the sea, gray and uninviting, breaking against sand that seemed to have been mixed with cement, forming a beach that was barely more attractive than a building site.

"How far is it to Fabian's house?" Richard asked.

The driver looked up nervously, meeting Richard's eyes in the mirror. "We don't go to the house," he said.

"Why not?"

"We go to the Hotel Europa in Miraflores. Is not far. Mr. Fabian meets you there."

Richard glanced at Matt. He was puzzled by the change of plan. Nobody had said anything about a hotel.

They stopped at a traffic light, and here the noise was worse than ever. All around them, drivers were leaning on their horns, furious at being kept waiting. There was the crunch of buckled metal, a van colliding with the back of a car. The shrill scream of a whistle as a policeman in a dark green uniform tried to take control. The jangle of a boom box on the back of a motorbike. A figure stepped in front of the car. It was a boy, about his own age, dressed in filthy jeans and a T-shirt, juggling with three balls. He seemed to be enjoying himself, sending the balls spinning in a circle over his head. He performed for a few seconds, then bowed and held out a cupped hand, begging for money. The driver shook his head and at once the boy was transformed, his face contorted with anger. He swore briefly and spat at the window. The lights changed and they moved off again. Matt was relieved. He had never been anywhere like this before. What had he gotten himself into?

Now they were driving down a quieter, more residential street, moving away from the sea. Matt got the feeling they were getting close to the hotel.

"What time is it?" he asked Richard.

"I don't know." Richard turned his wrist to look at his watch. Matt realized he had just nodded off. Both of them were half asleep, half awake, caught somewhere between the two. "My watch is still on English time. But right now it's . . ."

He never finished the sentence.

The car stopped abruptly. Both Matt and Richard were thrown forward. The driver rapped out something guttural in Spanish. Matt saw what had happened. A blue van had driven out of a side street at full speed, blocking the way ahead. At first, he thought it was just an accident, but then he saw the doors of the van open. Four men piled out and began to run toward them — and at that moment he knew there was nothing accidental about it. They had driven into some sort of trap. These people had been waiting for them.

Alberto knew it, too. With a sense of unreality, Matt saw the driver reach into the glove compartment and bring out a gun. Fabian must have been afraid of this from the start. He must have suspected that they might be attacked on the way into the city. Maybe that was why he had changed their destination. And why else would he have ensured that his driver was armed?

He wasn't the only one. Two of the men coming at them from the van were carrying handguns. Everything was happening so quickly that Matt only had time to glimpse their faces — dark, of course, with long black hair. They were wearing jeans and open-neck shirts, the sleeves rolled up. Then somebody fired a shot, and the front windscreen became a frosted maze of cracks with a deadly eye at the center. Alberto cried out. He had been hit in the shoulder. His blood splattered against the back of his seat. But now he brought his own gun round and fired three times. The front window collapsed, the glass cascading down. The men from the van hesitated, then took cover.

And that was when Richard acted. Grabbing hold of Matt with one hand, he threw open the door with the other. He was in the right-hand side, the side farther away from the van.

"Move!" he shouted.

"No, señor!" Alberto twisted round in the front.

Richard ignored him. Dragging Matt, he slid out of the car and into the street. Matt didn't resist. His head was spinning. He didn't know what was happening. But he agreed with Richard. He would feel safer in the open air.

Two more shots. Out of the corner of his eye, Matt saw Alberto heave himself clumsily out of the car and run off into the evening gloom, one hand clutching his wounded shoulder. He was abandoning them! Matt and Richard were in the street now. There were houses on either side, but nobody had come out to see what was happening. Nobody wanted to help.

"Run!" Richard shouted. "Just keep moving! Don't stop for anything!"

Matt didn't need to be told twice. He stumbled away from the car and began to run back up the street, heading in the direction from which they'd come. It was dark now. Streetlamps threw an ugly artificial light over them, turning everything yellow. And it had become even hotter. Matt could feel the sweat trickling underneath his clothes.

And the men were coming after them. Who were they? Who had sent them? Matt didn't dare look round, but he could hear their shoes hitting the pavement, knew they were getting closer.

Richard cried out.

Matt stopped and turned. Two of the men had grabbed hold of the journalist. Matt saw one of them quite clearly. A round, almost feminine face. Unshaven. A small scar next to one eye. He was holding Richard with one arm around his neck. The other two men were coming up fast behind.

Richard was struggling and somehow, for just a brief moment, he managed to break free. "Keep going, Matt!" he shouted. "Move!"

He lashed out with a foot, kicking one of the men in the stomach. The man groaned and collapsed. But the other man, the one with the scar, had grabbed hold of Richard again. As Matt watched, the others reached them, making it three against one. There was no way to save Richard. Matt twisted round and began to run. He heard one of the attackers calling out to him. Although he couldn't be certain, he thought he heard them using his name. His real name. So they knew who he was! The trap must have been set up long before they arrived.

Matt turned a corner and sprinted down an alleyway. At the end, he turned again, came to a main road and crossed it, weaving recklessly between the traffic. Someone yelled at him. A bus shot past, punching at him with a fist of warm air. He came to a patch of wasteland and ran across it. A dog, dirty and half starved, barked at him. A few local women watched him with idle curiosity.

At last he stopped, his breath rasping in his throat. He was covered in sweat. His shirt seemed to have glued itself to him. The jet lag still hadn't left him. He could feel it, sitting on his shoulder, trying to hammer him into the ground. But he was alone. He looked back across the wasteland, with the main road and the traffic in the distance. Nobody was coming after him. He had escaped.

It was only then that the enormity of his situation struck him. He was in a strange country, with no money and no luggage. The driver who had been sent to collect him had run off, saving his own skin, and his only friend had been kidnapped by an unknown enemy. He didn't know where he was. He didn't know how to get to where he was supposed to be. It was night. And he was on his own.

So what did he do now?

EIGHT
Hotel Europa

Matt hadn't even realized he'd fallen asleep until he began to wake up again. He groaned quietly and curled up, not wanting to return to full consciousness. He wasn't ready to face reality quite yet. He was utterly drained. His entire body felt as if it had been hollowed out. Maybe it was the jet lag. More likely it was the shock of what had happened. His arms and shoulders were aching and his mouth was dry. What had woken him up? Oh, yes — a hand in his jacket pocket. Just to add to his troubles, he was being robbed.

Matt opened his eyes and saw a dark-haired boy leaning over him. At the same time, the boy's own eyes widened in alarm. Matt cried out and pushed the boy away. The boy had been crouching on his heels. He lost his balance and fell over backward. Matt sprang to his feet.

"Get off me!" he shouted. "Who are you? Leave me alone!"

The boy said nothing. Of course, it was unlikely that he spoke a word of English. Matt looked down at him and, even after everything that had happened, with all the confusion in his mind, he thought he knew him. It seemed to Matt that they had met long ago, but then he remembered. In the car, on the way from the airport. The boy who had been juggling at the traffic lights and who had sworn at them.

"No hacía cualquier cosa. Era el intentar justo ayudarte," the boy said.

Matt got the general sense of the words, the protestation of innocence, but he didn't believe the boy. It was there in his eyes — deep brown and suspicious — and in the way he held himself like a cornered animal, as if he were going to lash out at any moment. The boy was all bone. If Matt grabbed hold of his arm, he was fairly sure his thumbs and fingers would meet. He was wearing a yellow T-shirt that advertised a drink called Ínca Cola, but the words had faded and the fabric had worn away into holes. His jeans were disgusting, tied with a piece of rope around the waist. He was wearing sandals made out of black rubber. Otherwise, his feet were bare.

The boy got to his feet and brushed himself down, as if the action could remove months of accumulated dirt. Then he looked balefully at Matt.

"No he tomado cualquier cosa." He showed his empty hands to make the point. He hadn't taken anything.

Matt felt in his pockets. He'd had ten pounds when he came from England, and fortunately he had kept it in his trousers. It was still there. His passport was still in his jacket. That was something, anyway. The boy was looking at him with injured pride, as if to say *How can you possibly mistrust me?* But Matt was sure that if he'd slept for another thirty seconds, he would have woken up with nothing.

He looked around him. He had been sitting, slumped against a low, brick wall underneath a tattered poster advertising mobile phones. The wasteland that he had crossed was in front of him with a row of partly built houses on the other side. All the buildings looked as if they had been cut in half with a knife. Wires and metal poles sprouted out where the roofs should have been. It was still dark, the area lit by ugly arc lamps curving high above on concrete posts. But the first gray fingers of the morning light were already creeping through the sky. Matt glanced at his watch. It wasn't there. The boy shuffled uneasily.

"I don't suppose you've got the time?" he asked.

The boy held out his hand. Matt's watch was on his wrist.

It was five o'clock in the morning.

Matt didn't even try to take the watch back. He was a little surprised that the boy hadn't run off and abandoned him. Perhaps he was curious. A foreign tourist in the middle of the city. And one who was about own age. Perhaps he could see a chance to make more money. Well, it was possible that he might be useful — even if he was a thief. After all, he was Peruvian. He knew the city.

It was time to think.

Matt had to get back in contact with the Nexus . . . and in particular with Fabian, who must be searching for him even now. The trouble was, nobody had counted on Richard and Matt being separated. Richard had money and credit cards. He had phone numbers to reach Fabian day or night. But he hadn't shared them with Matt.

Apart from the ten pounds, Matt had nothing. Perhaps if he could work out how to use directory inquiries he might be able to get a number for Susan Ashwood back home in Manchester. But even that seemed complicated and somehow unlikely. How about the police? That was the obvious choice, although Matt doubted that the Peruvian boy would be too keen to show him the way to the nearest station. Perhaps he could find his way to Barranco, the suburb where Fabian lived. It couldn't be too far from here.

Then Matt remembered what the driver, Alberto, had said: Fabian was waiting for them at a hotel. What was its name? It took Matt a few moments to get his brain back into gear. The Hotel Europa. That was it. The Hotel Europa in Miraflores.

The boy was still waiting for him to say something. Matt tapped himself on the chest. "Matt," he said. There was no point in hiding behind a false name just now.

The boy nodded. "Pedro."

So that was what he was called. And the strange thing was, Matt knew it already. He had been expecting it. Could he have heard it when he was asleep?

"Do you know the Hotel Europa in Miraflores?" he asked.

Pedro looked blank.

Matt tried again, more slowly. "Hotel Europa." He pointed to himself. "I go."

"Hotel Europa?" This time Pedro got it. "*Sí . . .*"

"Can you show me the way?" Matt gestured down the street. "Do you understand?"

Pedro understood. But he wasn't agreeing to anything. Matt saw the doubt in his eyes. Why should he help this foreign boy?

Matt took out the ten pounds. "If you take me there, I'll give you this. It's a lot of moncy."

Pedro's eyes lasered in on the banknote. It was what he

had been looking for in the first place. He nodded a second time. "Hotel Europa," he repeated.

"Let's go."

The two of them set off.

• • •

It took them an hour to reach the hotel, a modern building twelve stories high, with a drive sweeping round to the front door, where a uniformed doorman was already standing, waiting to receive early-morning guests. Miraflores was one of the most exclusive parts of Lima, stretching out contentedly in the morning sun. The streets were quiet and ran between well-manicured lawns decorated with palm trees and fountains. There was an expensive-looking arcade boasting the sort of shops and restaurants that wouldn't have been out of place in London. The whole suburb was perched on the end of a miniature cliff. Far below, the sea formed a giant crescent, stretching into the distance with the rest of the city barely visible, a mile away.

Hotel Europa. Matt felt a surge of relief as he saw the name written in large white letters above the entrance lobby. And there was something else. He hadn't noticed them at first, but there were two police cars parked outside. He had no doubt at all that they were there because of him. Fabian would have been waiting for him and Richard to arrive. When they hadn't, he must have raised the alarm.

Matt started forward but Pedro reached out and grabbed hold of him.

"Yeah. All right." Matt took out the ten-pound note and offered it to the other boy. "Here you are. *Gracias.*"

"No!" Pedro was looking scared. He pointed at the two cars and uttered the single word that was almost the same in so many different languages. *"Policía!"*

"It's okay, Pedro. I want to see them. It's not a problem."

But Pedro was worried. He shook his head and seemed unwilling to let Matt go.

Matt broke free. "I'll see you around," he said, knowing that he never actually would.

He walked up the drive and into the hotel. The door-man glanced briefly in his direction and then decided to let him in. He was a child and he was scruffy — but he was a European and that was all that mattered. Somewhere inside him, Matt knew that Pedro wouldn't have been allowed anywhere near the place.

The front doors opened into a large reception area with leather sofas, antique tables, oversize potted plants, and mirrors. Matt had hardly ever been inside a luxury hotel before — and never on his own. He felt uncomfortable walking into this enormous space. The Hotel Europa was a place for rich tourists and business travelers, and he was neither. There were two smartly dressed women standing behind the slab of marble that served as a reception desk. They watched him with faces of frozen politeness as he walked over to them.

"I need your help," he said.

"Yes?" The younger of the two receptionists sounded surprised, as if helping wasn't part of her job description.

"My name is . . ." Matt hesitated. What name should he

111

give? He decided not to bother. "I was meant to meet some-one here."

"Who are you meeting, please?

"His name is Mr. Fabian."

The receptionist tapped at the keyboard of a computer hidden just below the level of the desk. Her nails clacked against the keys. A moment later, she looked up. "I'm sorry. There is nobody of that name staying at the hotel."

"He may not be staying here." Matt tried to keep the impatience out of his voice. "I arrived at the airport yester-day. I was on the way here to meet him. But I got delayed."

"Where are you from?"

"From England." Matt took out his passport and laid it on the desk. He hoped the cover, with its gold lettering, would impress the girl more than he could.

The girl opened it and looked at the name underneath the photograph. "Paul Carter?" She glanced at him strangely, as if she had been expecting him. The other girl picked up a telephone and dialed a number. "Where is your brother?" she asked.

"My brother?" Matt realized that they were talking about Richard. So he was right. They were expected. "I don't know. Where is Mr. Fabian?"

"Mr. Fabian is not here."

Next to her, the second girl had been connected. She spoke briefly in Spanish, then put the telephone down.

A side door opened.

Four men came out, walking purposefully toward him. There was something menacing about the way they moved. They could have been coming out of a bar, half drunk, looking for a fight. If there hadn't been police cars parked outside, Matt would have assumed they were soldiers. They were wearing gray trousers tucked into their boots, dark green jackets that zipped up the front, and caps. Their leader was a huge, potbellied man with a heavy moustache and leathery, pockmarked skin. His hair was dark. Was there a single man in Peru who didn't have dark hair? He had the body of a wrestler. His hands were enormous. Everything about him seemed brutal and oversize. Matt had to remind himself that he was the one who needed the police, that he hadn't himself committed any crime.

Or so he thought.

"You are Paul Carter?" the policeman asked. Even from the four words, Matt could tell that he spoke good English. He had a heavy Peruvian accent, but there was a certain rhythm to the way he spoke. And despite his looks, his voice was soft and intelligent.

"Yes."

"My name is Captain Rodriguez. I have been waiting for you. Where is your friend . . ." He smiled unpleasantly. ". . . Robert Carter?"

"He's not here."

"Where is he?"

Matt was becoming increasingly nervous. The policeman had referred to Richard as his friend, not as his brother — which was what he was supposed to be. And he had spoken the names as if he already knew they were false. Pedro had warned him not to go into the hotel, and Matt was beginning to wish he'd listened. Certainly, he hadn't been expecting this degree of hostility. The senior policeman was standing right in front of him. The other three had moved to surround him. They weren't treating him as if he needed help. It was more as if he were a suspect, a wanted criminal.

"Did Mr. Fabian call you?" Matt asked.

"Fabian? Who is Fabian?"

"Listen . . . I was attacked last night. I need help."

"Your name is Paul Carter?"

"Yes." Even as Matt spoke the word, it died on his lips. The policeman knew who he was. He had only asked the question to test him. Slowly, he reached for the passport and turned it round, handling it as if it were something dirty. Then he picked it up and opened it. For a long moment, he squinted at the photograph at the back.

"Where did you get this?" he asked.

"It's my passport." Matt felt a nameless terror opening up beneath him.

"This passport is a forgery."

"No . . ."

"Tell me your true name."

"I just told you. It's Paul Carter. Didn't you hear what I said? I was attacked last night. There were men with guns. You have to ring Mr. Fabian. . . ."

The girls at the reception desk were watching all this, their eyes filled with fear. One of the policemen rapped something at them and they hurried away, disappearing down a corridor. Another policeman went over to the main door and stood there, making sure nobody was looking in. It was still only six o'clock in the morning. There was nobody to witness what happened next.

The senior policeman — the one who called himself Captain Rodriguez — punched him. Matt barely had time to see the huge fist swing in an arc toward him before it had made contact with his stomach, throwing him off his feet. If he'd eaten anything in the past twelve hours, he would have been sick. As it was, he felt the breath explode out of him as he crashed backward onto the floor. Darkness shimmered in front of his eyes as he hovered at the edge of consciousness and he had to fight with all his strength simply to breathe again. He felt the cold marble against his cheek. He needed it. It helped fight the dark away.

"You are lying to me," Rodriguez said, and Matt knew that he was in more trouble than he could begin to imagine. The policeman knew everything. He had been waiting for Matt at the hotel. Perhaps he had been there all night. "You think, perhaps, that I am an idiot? You think that the police officers of Peru are not worthy of your respect?"

"No . . ." Matt tried to speak, but he still hadn't caught his breath and he was in too much pain. He couldn't believe what had just happened. There was the taste of nausea in his mouth. He forced himself to go on. "I want . . ." he began. He was a British citizen. It didn't matter what he'd done. They couldn't treat him like this.

Captain Rodriguez swung a foot almost lazily; Matt yelled out as it came into contact with his ribs. A second wave of pain exploded through his body. For a few seconds, the hotel went red and he wondered if they were going to kill him, here and now, in this upmarket hotel.

"What do you want?" Rodriguez taunted him, imitating his voice. "You want to confess? I think that would be a

115

good idea, my friend. I think you should tell me who you really are and why you have come here. I think you should tell me now!"

He lashed out again. Matt saw the boot coming and was able to ride with it, rolling over and over across the marble floor. The other policemen laughed.

Rodriguez walked over to him, one slow step at a time.

"You should not have come here, my friend," he crowed.

"I . . . haven't . . . done . . . anything . . . wrong."

"You have no papers. You have no nationality. You have entered this country illegally." Rodriguez reached down and grabbed Matt's hair. He tugged it so hard that Matt cried out. He could feel the tears being squeezed out of his eyes. "Maybe you are a terrorist. Yes. You are young, it is true. But there are others who are younger. Are you prepared to tell me the truth?"

Matt nodded. What else could he do? He would tell this man everything.

"Where is Richard Cole?" Rodriguez asked.

So the charade was over. The policeman knew who they were. He had known them from the start.

"Where is he?" Rodriguez pulled even harder.

"I don't know!" Matt screamed. He was sure the hair was going to be torn out of his skull. There was blood trickling from his nose and down the corner of his mouth. "He said he'd meet me here! I don't know where he went." It was a lie — but it didn't matter. He just had to say anything to stop the pain.

He heard the sound of a bell, and the elevator doors opened. A businessman had appeared, on his way to an

116

early meeting. He stepped out of the elevator and saw the four policemen, the boy lying on the floor between them. Nobody said anything. The businessman blinked and disappeared back into the elevator. Matt could imagine that he wouldn't even draw breath until he was back in his room.

But at least Captain Rodriguez had let go of his hair. Matt lay where he was, sprawled out on the floor like one of those drawings the police make after there's been a murder. He wondered if some of his ribs had been broken. His entire body was in pain.

Rodriguez dropped down next to him and cupped a hand under his cheek. For a moment he could have been a father, consoling an injured son, but every word he spoke dripped with venom and hate. "You are a very foolish child," he muttered. "You have come, uninvited, to my country and nobody can help you. Because, you see, you are 'Paul Carter.' You do not exist. Nobody knows that you are here and nobody will know when you disappear. For that is what will happen to you, my friend. We have places here that nobody knows. Prisons far away where you can go in and never come out. It would be easy to kill you. I could kill you now and go to have my breakfast and not think twice. But that is not what is going to happen to you, Matthew Freeman. You are going to be buried alive in a concrete cell far beneath the ground and you are going to be left to rot and nobody is going to hear from you again."

He raised Matt's head a little farther so that his lips were almost touching his ear. And then the final words came, a whisper of sheer hatred.

"Diego Salamanda sends you his regards."

117

He let Matt's head fall, and Matt felt another spasm of pain as his skull came into contact with the marble floor.

Rodriguez must have given a signal. The other three policemen closed in on Matt and scooped him up. Between them, they dragged him out of the hotel. Matt didn't even try to resist. He could feel his feet, toes downward, sliding along behind him. His vision was blurred. He could just make out the reception desk with Rodriguez standing in front of it, but both of them were out of focus. He was bundled out through the door. There was no sign of the doorman. Like the businessman, he must have gotten out of sight as quickly as he could. Matt remembered the two cars parked out front. They had been waiting for him! And he had just walked in and given himself up.

They dragged him across to the first car, and one of the policemen fumbled in his pockets for his keys. That left just two of them supporting Matt. Did he have the strength left to fight back? No. They were holding him too tightly. What about his powers? Briefly, Matt remembered the chandelier exploding at Forrest Hill. It felt as if it had happened a century ago. He wondered if he could do something similar now. Turn on the power and make the police car blow up. Send these two men spiraling away like puppets in the wind. But it wasn't as easy as that. There was no switch he could throw. Whatever power he had, it still wasn't under control.

But then the policeman holding him on the side nearest to the car cried out and suddenly let go. Looking up, Matt saw blood pouring down his face. Had he done that to him? Matt was so shocked that for a moment he thought he had. But then he saw a fist-size stone come flying through

118

the air and the second policeman staggered back, his hand clutching his face. Matt was free. He fell back against the car and looked away from the hotel, down toward the main street. And there was the answer.

Pedro was there. He was holding a slingshot made out of a strip of some sort of black material — rubber or leather. He had used it twice with deadly accuracy, bringing both the policemen down. But that still left one more, the policeman with the car keys. Matt shouted a warning as the policeman reached down to his holster and pulled out a gun.

But before it had come halfway up, Pedro swung the slingshot a third time. Another rock flashed through the air and slammed into the policeman, catching him just above the eye. The policeman swore and dropped the gun.

"Matt!" Pedro called out his name.

Matt looked back at the hotel. Captain Rodriguez had appeared, alerted by the cries of his men. His own gun was in his hand. Quickly, he took in what had happened. His men were hurt. The English boy was free, leaning against the car that should have been taking him away. And there was another boy, with a slingshot. Rodriguez took aim at this second boy.

Matt dived forward and snatched up the fallen gun. He rolled over on his stomach and fired six shots in the direction of the hotel. He wasn't sure if any of them hit Captain Rodriguez, but he saw the senior policeman dive for cover behind a parked car. The glass doors of the hotel shattered. At the same time, an alarm went off inside the hotel. Matt dropped the gun and got unsteadily to his feet.

The first policeman that Pedro had hit was already

recovering. Matt took one look at him and then, finding some last hidden reserve of strength, lashed out with his foot. His toe cap came into contact with soft flesh. He had kicked the man right between the legs and the man crumpled without a sound.

Another rock sailed past. One of the other policemen was hit a second time and knocked off his feet, stumbling into the side of his car and setting off another alarm. The third policeman had crawled away to hide.

"Matt!" Pedro called again.

Matt didn't need any more encouragement. With his hands gripping his stomach, doubled up in pain, he lurched forward. The Peruvian boy waited for him, a fourth stone ready in his slingshot in case anyone tried to follow. But nobody did.

Pedro reached out and grabbed hold of Matt, and together they ran off as fast as they could. The alarm bells were still jangling, and now they were joined by the scream of sirens as more police cars approached. Seconds later, they pulled up in front of the hotel. Captain Rodriguez had reappeared, his face full of fury. But they were too late. The street was empty.

The two boys had disappeared.

NINE
Poison Town

An hour later, they were still running.

Matt was astonished by how much energy Pedro seemed to have. After all, he looked as if he hadn't eaten for a week. But he had kept up the same pace ever since they had left the hotel, pausing only when a dirty blue van with barred windows and the words POLICÍA NACIONAL painted on the side came speeding past. Then Pedro ducked behind what looked like a broken-down and abandoned truck, dragging Matt with him. He took one look at Matt and signaled to him to rest. The two of them sat on the pavement.

As he regained his breath, Matt remembered what Rodriguez had told him. He had no papers. He had entered Peru illegally. At the time, when the Nexus had suggested it, forged passports had seemed like a good idea. But in fact he and Richard had been delivered, gift wrapped, into enemy hands. Matt couldn't prove who he was. There was no record of his arrival, and even when the Nexus realized he was missing and came looking for him, there would be nothing they could do. He would simply have disappeared.

"*Debemos apresurarnos,*" Pedro said, and stood up again.

They were in a wide, busy road, somewhere on the edge

of Lima, standing in front of a row of shops and a restaurant, all of them missing their front windows and front doors . . . in fact, they had no fronts at all. They were like open boxes with their insides spilling out onto the street, the smell of food mixing with the petrol fumes. Opposite them, a row of men in jeans and baseball caps sat slumped against a low, concrete wall, seemingly with nothing to do. There were also a couple of shoeshine boys with crude, wooden boxes strapped to their backs. The sight gave Matt a jolt. They were both about six years old.

"Where are we going?" Matt asked.

Either Pedro didn't understand or he couldn't be bothered to answer. He was already moving down the pavement. Matt was exhausted, but he forced himself to follow. What else could he do?

They came to a set of traffic lights, and Pedro's face broke into a grin. It was the first time Matt had seen him smile. There was a truck waiting, open-backed and piled with building materials. Pedro had recognized the driver. He ran forward and began to talk, gesturing a couple of times in Matt's direction. The lights changed to green and at once all the cars behind began to blast their horns. But the driver wasn't in any hurry. He waited until Pedro had finished, glanced briefly at Matt, then jerked his thumb. Pedro signaled to him and, with a huge feeling of relief, Matt climbed with him into the back.

They set off again.

Matt was desperately tired. He'd only managed a few hours of troubled sleep the night before. He was also in a bad way following his encounter with Rodriguez. There was a sick pounding in his head and in his stomach and he was sure he'd broken a rib. The police had beaten him up. How could such a thing have happened — and in a public place, in the middle of a hotel? What sort of country was this?

The driver shouted something out the window, and Matt saw his hand appear, holding a small bunch of bananas. Pedro took them and broke some off, offering them to Matt. Matt shook his head. He was starving, but he couldn't bring himself to eat. He was in too much trouble, too much pain. Pedro shrugged, peeled a banana, and took a bite.

Matt wasn't sure what to make of this boy. There was no doubt that Pedro had saved him by waiting with his slingshot, but it was hard to know exactly why. Right now he was ignoring him completely. It was as if Matt were nothing more than an annoyance, like a stray animal following him down the street. Certainly there was nothing very friendly about him. Quite the opposite. Matt had to remind himself that only a few hours before, Pedro had been trying to rob him — and he was still wearing his watch! Maybe he was still interested in Matt's ten-pound note. No. That wasn't fair. Matt had already offered him the money, and Pedro had refused to take it. So where were they going now? Pedro must live somewhere in this great, unwelcoming city. Perhaps he had parents. Hopefully he would know somebody who could help.

About twenty minutes later, the truck stopped and the two of them climbed out, Pedro waving and shouting at the driver. Matt found himself standing at the foot of a mountain with an ugly township, a tangle of bricks and wires, sprawling its way up the slope. He had never seen anything like it. His first impression was that this was a community that had tumbled down the hillside, getting broken and jumbled up along the way. Then he realized that it had been built like this. It was a barrio, a shantytown, home to only the poorest of the poor.

As ever, Pedro was already moving. Matt followed him as he plunged into a maze of narrow streets and passageways, none of them paved, all of them covered in rubbish and other debris. Only now that he was in the middle of it all did Matt see that less than half the houses were made of brick. Most of them had been built out of cardboard, corrugated iron, straw mats, plastic sheeting, or a mixture of all four. They came to a sort of square where a group of old women in bright shawls and bowler hats sat squatting beside a rusty oil drum that had been turned into a makeshift oven. They were cooking some sort of stew, cooking it in cans that they had beaten flat and made into pans. A few scrawny chickens pecked hopelessly at the rubble, and a dog — it was hard to be sure if it was alive or dead — lay stretched out in the sun. There was a terrible smell of sewage. Matt covered his nose and mouth with his hand. He was amazed that anyone could live here — although at the same time, Pedro barely seemed to notice it.

Matt was aware of the women looking at him curiously. He wondered what he must look like. He was grubby and disheveled, but even so, he was white. His clothes were new and expensive . . . certainly compared with what Pedro was wearing. In their eyes, he would be a rich European kid and he doubted that many of those showed up around here. He nodded at them and hurried on after Pedro.

They were climbing farther up the mountain. The effort was hurting Matt's chest — he could feel his ribs aching — and he was beginning to wonder how long he could keep going when Pedro arrived at a small, brick building with two windows covered, from the inside, with some sort of sacking. Pedro cupped a hand, gesturing at him to come in.

Was this where he lived? Suddenly apprehensive, Matt followed him through the doorway. There was no door. He found himself in a square boxlike space, and as his eyes got used to the lack of light, he made out a wooden table, two chairs, a Primus stove — the sort of thing he'd used to go camping — a few tins, and a low, narrow bed. Then he saw that there was a man lying on the bed. Pedro was squatting beside him, talking excitedly. Slowly the man sat up.

He was about sixty years old, wearing a suit that looked about the same age. He had slept in it, and the material was terribly crumpled. Nearly all the buttons were missing and his shirt hung outside his pants. He was unshaven, with gray stubble spreading around a mouth that was thin and rather cruel. The man's eyes were bloodshot and sly. For a long minute he said nothing at all, looking at Matt as if he were weighing him up, trying to work out what he might be worth. He wiped his mouth with the back of his hand and swallowed. Then, at last, he spoke.

"Welcome," he said.

It was the first friendly word of English Matt had heard since he had been separated from Richard, and he felt a flood of relief. But at the same time, examining the man, he began to wonder if his troubles were yet over. Certainly, this wasn't the savior he had been hoping for.

"Pedro tells me that you are American," the man said. His accent was unattractive. Or maybe it was the suspicious tone of his voice, the way he drawled the words.

"No. I'm English," Matt said.

"From England!" The man was amused. "From London?"

"I flew from London. But I live in a place called York."

"York." The man repeated the word but had obviously never heard of it. "Pedro says that you are alone. That you were beaten by the police. That they were going to arrest you."

"Yes. Can you thank him for helping me?"

"He does not need your gratitude. What makes you think he wants anything from you?"

The man reached down beside the bed and produced a bottle, half filled with some transparent liquid. He drank and as he lowered it, Matt caught the scent of alcohol. Next he took out half a cigar from his jacket pocket and lit it. All the time, his eyes never left the new arrival.

"Pedro says you have money," he said.

Matt hesitated — but once again he knew he had no choice. He took out the ten-pound note and gave it to the man.

The man turned the note in his hands, then slid it into his jacket pocket with a twitch of the lips that might have been a smile. A moment later, he snapped something at Pedro. Pedro scowled. The man waited. Pedro slipped Matt's watch off his wrist and handed it over.

"What is your name?" the man asked.

Once again, Matt hesitated. What name should he use? But there was no point trying to pretend he was someone he wasn't. The fake passport had already proved itself to be useless. "I'm Matt," he said.

"And I am Sebastian." The man blew out smoke. It hung in the air, silvery gray. "It seems that you need help, my friend."

"I haven't got any more money to give you," Matt muttered angrily.

"Your money and your watch will buy me food. But right now, I think, they are of no use to you. If you want them, take them and go. You will probably be dead, or in jail, before the sun goes down. But if you want my help, be polite to me. You are in my house. Remember that."

Matt bit his lip. Sebastian was right. The money was irrelevant. "Who are you?" he asked. "What is this place?"

"This community has a name," Sebastian replied. "The local people call it Ciudad del Veneno. In English, you would say . . . Poison Town. They call it that because of the amount of disease that there is here. Cholera. Bronchitis. Pleurisy. Diphtheria. None of us has any right to live in this place. We have stolen this land and built our homes. But the authorities — the police and the landlords — never come here. They are too scared."

Matt looked around him, almost afraid to breathe.

"Don't worry, Matt." Sebastian smiled, showing two gold-capped teeth. "There is no illness in this house or in this street. Nine of us live here. And there are seven more next door. And nobody understands why. We have nothing . . . but we have our health."

"Does Pedro live here?"

127

Pedro glanced up, hearing his name. Until now, he had been examining Matt with a look of complete mistrust. But he had shown no interest in what was being said.

"He sleeps on the floor, right where you are standing now. He works for me. He and the other children. But why are we wasting time, talking about him? There are a million kids like him in Lima. They live. They die. They are of no use at all. But an English boy in Poison Town, that is another matter. How do you come to be here, Matt? Why are the police looking for you? You must tell me everything and then we will see how we can help. *If* we can help. If we want to . . ."

Everything?

Matt didn't know where to start. His story was so huge. It had swallowed up his life. And where did he begin? With the death of his parents six years ago or his involvement with Raven's Gate and the Nexus? It was hopeless. Matt knew that. He could talk all day and this man wouldn't believe a word of it.

"I can't explain it all to you," he said. "I came to Peru because something bad is about to happen and there are people who thought I could stop it. There were two of us. Me and a friend. His name is Richard Cole and he's older than me . . . twenty-six. Neither of us wanted to come here but we were sent . . ."

"To stop this thing from happening."

Matt nodded. "Yes. I have no passport. The passport I was given is a fake. It was meant to protect me. But the moment I arrived, I was attacked. Richard was kid-napped, and the police tried to arrest me. There was a police captain. He said he was working for someone called Diego Salamanda."

Sebastian had been listening to all this with a look of puzzlement and disbelief. The mention of Salamanda was the first thing to provoke any real reaction. His eyes narrowed and he allowed a trickle of cigar smoke to escape from the corner of his mouth. "Salamanda!" he exclaimed. "Do you know who he is?"

"Some sort of businessman."

"One of the richest men in South America. Certainly the richest man in Peru. They say he has more money than the rest of the population put together, with his mobile phones and his newspapers and his satellites in outer space." Sebastian rapped a few words in Spanish at Pedro, who was sitting cross-legged on the floor, leaning against the bed. Pedro shrugged. Then Sebastian turned back to Matt. "If I was going to have an enemy, he is not the man I would choose."

"I think he chose me . . . not the other way round," Matt said. Then: "Where can I find him?"

"Why do you want to?"

"Because I think he must have been the one who kidnapped my friend. He knew we were coming. He got Richard first, and then he tried to get me."

Sebastian raised the bottle to his lips and swallowed some more. The alcohol must have been strong. Matt could smell it from where he was standing. But Sebastian drank it as if it were water.

"Salamanda News International is based here in Lima," he said. "They have offices all over Peru. What do you want to do? Do you want to visit all of them? It doesn't matter, because you won't find him there. He has his main research base near the town of Paracas. That's south of here. But he spends most of his time in a farm — what we call a hacienda — near Ica. He is never seen in public. It is rumored that he is very ugly, that maybe he has three eyes or something wrong with his face. If you want to talk to Señor Salamanda, you go to Ica. I'm sure he will be delighted to see you."

Matt ignored the sarcasm in Sebastian's voice. "Can you help me go there?" he asked.

"No."

"Then maybe I'm wasting my time, talking to you."

"Is that what you believe?" Sebastian stared at Matt, now angry. "Well, let me give you some advice. Don't you worry about your time. Time is cheap here." He stubbed out the cigar. "I must leave you. There are things here I do not understand and there are people I must talk with. Maybe I will help you and maybe I won't. But right now, I would say you need food and you need sleep."

"Can I sleep here?" Matt asked. He was too tired to eat.

"You will be safe in this room. There are blankets. You can sleep on the floor. Not the bed, you understand? The bed is mine! Later today, we will talk again. And we will see what we can do."

Sebastian said something to Pedro. Pedro nodded.

The two of them left the building.

●　　●　　●

It was evening when Matt woke up. Without his watch, he had no idea how long he had been asleep, and the jet lag didn't help. In England it could have been breakfast time, dinnertime, or whenever. It took him a couple of minutes to work some life back into his muscles, which were cramped from lying on the hard floor. At the same time, he tried to make sense of what had been happening. But that wasn't so easy. He was on his own, thousands of miles from home, stuck in a squalid hut in a town that was, even by name, poison. He was the guest of a man he didn't much like and a boy who had recently robbed him. The richest man in Peru wanted him dead, and it seemed that the police were all too happy to help him achieve that aim.

It was all too much. Matt closed his eyes and groaned.

And yet that was another strange thing. He was suddenly aware that the pain in his head had gone. He sat up and ran a hand over his chest. His ribs and his stomach were unhurt. It was as if the beating he had received had never happened. Was this another instance of his powers? Had he in some way managed to cure himself? Matt stood up and stretched. He was starving. He wished now that he'd accepted the food he'd been offered. But apart from that, he had to admit he felt fine.

Weird . . .

There was a movement at the door and Pedro appeared, carrying a steaming tin of food and a spoon. He handed them over. At the same time, his eyes never left Matt. He was examining him, searching for something.

"Thank you," Matt said. He was feeling increasingly ill at ease.

The tin contained some sort of stew. A lot of beans and very little meat. In normal circumstances, Matt might have sniffed it suspiciously — but right now he was too hungry to care. He wolfed the food down, being careful not to look at it too closely. Whatever the meat was, it certainly wasn't lamb or beef. He tried not to think about the dog he had seen lying outside.

When he had finished eating, Pedro produced a battered metal jug of water and handed it to Matt to drink. It tasted warm and brackish and Matt wondered where it had come from. Did Poison Town have wells or water pumps? Did it even have electricity? There were all sorts of questions he wanted to ask but there was no point until Sebastian returned. Pedro understood nothing.

About ten minutes later, Sebastian came in, carrying a bundle of old clothes. From the moment he entered the room, it seemed to Matt that he was more alert, more nervous. He put the clothes down and lit another cigar, almost burning his fingers, and threw the match down.

"I have been speaking to people," he said. "There is a great deal happening in Lima, and none of it is good. You must leave here very soon. You do not have a lot of time."

"They're looking for me," Matt said.

"The police are everywhere. They are asking questions and they are not being very polite. You understand? They have big sticks and they have tear gas. They are searching for an English boy. They say he is a terrorist and they are offering a large reward." He held up a hand before Matt could speak. "Only a few people saw you enter Poison Town, and they won't talk. We have no money. We have no possessions. Maybe that is why we value the things we do have . . . loyalty and friendship. Nobody will talk, but the police will still come here looking for you. They will tear the place apart. Maybe they're already on their way."

"I have to find my friend," Matt said.

"You're wasting your breath. I already told you: If Salamanda does have him, he could be anywhere. He could be in Lima. Or he could be floating facedown in the ocean. If you ask me, that is more likely."

"What about this place you told me about? This farmhouse or whatever you called it."

"The Hacienda Salamanda. I do not believe you will find him there."

"I still want to look."

Sebastian thought for a minute. Then he nodded. "It doesn't matter to me where you go," he said. "The only important thing is that you do not stay here. And Pedro must go with you. I have already explained to him. He attacked three policemen, so now they are looking for him, too. They will kill him if they find him."

"I'm sorry," Matt said. "This is my fault."

"No. It's his fault. If he'd been smarter, he would have stolen your watch and your money without waking you up. I always said he made a lousy thief. But it's too late to worry about that now." Sebastian paused. "There is something else. Your appearance. We must change that."

"What do you mean?"

"A white boy in a white boy's clothes! It doesn't matter where you go in Peru, you'll be seen a mile away." Sebastian gestured at the bundle he had brought in. "Give me everything you're wearing."

"What . . . ?"

"Now!"

Matt was too dazed to argue. He stripped off his jacket, his shirt, and his jeans and gave them to Sebastian. He had no doubt that they'd all turn up in some market the next day.

But that wasn't enough. "Your shoes and socks, too," Sebastian ordered.

He slipped them off and stood in the middle of the room, dressed only in his boxers. Sebastian had produced a bottle and handed it to him. "Rub this in," he commanded. "Your arms, your legs, and especially your face. Pedro will do your shoulders and back."

"What is it?"

"It's a dye made from nuts. It will stain your skin for many weeks. We must also cut your hair." Sebastian took out a pair of scissors. Matt hesitated. "Your hair is nice," Sebastian said. "And it will look good at your funeral. But if you want to live, you must look like one of us. We don't have time to argue."

A short while later, Matt stood wearing his new wardrobe. His hair had been cut in the shape of a pudding bowl, with a straight fringe above his eyes. His entire body was dark brown. There was no mirror in the room, so he had no idea what he fully looked like but he felt disgusting. His new jeans were stained, shapeless, and came to an abrupt halt high above his ankles, revealing his bare legs and feet. He'd been given a green Adidas T-shirt, full of holes, filthy, and faded. Instead of shoes, he had a pair of sandals, made out of black rubber — the same as Pedro's.

"They're made from tires," Sebastian told him.

Matt felt his skin trying to shrink away from the clothes.

He could imagine that several people had worn them before him. He noticed Pedro watching him with a halfsmile. "What's so funny?" he asked.

Sebastian translated the question into Spanish, and Pedro answered. He spoke softly and only uttered a few words.

"He says, now you know how a Peruvian boy feels," Sebastian replied. "But you are still too tall. You must learn to walk in a crouch. Make sure you are never higher than he is. And from now on, you will not be Matt. You will be Matteo. Do you understand?"

"Matteo!" Pedro repeated the word. He seemed amused by Matt's transformation.

But Sebastian was completely serious. "You have to leave Lima," he said. "If you take my advice, you will go south to Ayacucho. I have many friends in the city who will look after you. Perhaps the police won't look for you there."

"I still want to go to Ica," Matt insisted.

"You are stubborn and you are stupid — but you care about your friend and that, I suppose, does you credit," Sebastian spat. "Very well. You can stop in Ica if you think it will do any good. The first bus leaves tomorrow morning at six o'clock. It is almost certain that the police will be watching the bus station, so we will have to think about that."

"I just want to find Richard and go home," Matt said.

"That would be the best thing for all of us. It is a pity that you came in the first place."

Matt nodded. Suddenly he felt awkward. From the moment he had met Sebastian, he had sensed a sort of hostility between them — without knowing why it was there. "Can I ask you something?" he said.

"What?"

135

"You obviously don't like me very much. So why are you helping me?"

"You're wrong. It's not true that I don't like you very much. I don't like you *at all*. The police are crawling through the shantytowns, thanks to you. They are asking questions, making arrests. Everything is going to be difficult until they find you."

"So why don't you just hand me over? It's obviously what you want to do."

"It is exactly what I want to do. But it was Pedro who dissuaded me. He tells me that you are somehow important. He says that we have to help you because you are on our side."

"How does he know that? He doesn't know anything about me."

"I know," Sebastian said. "It's very strange. Normally, he would have taken your watch and your money and anything else that was of any value, and then he would have left you where he found you. He wouldn't have risked getting into trouble with the police. And he wouldn't have brought you here."

"So why did he?"

"Pedro can't understand it. And nor can I. But he tells me . . . he's seen you before." Sebastian shook his head. "He says he's seen you in his dreams."

TEN
Dream Talk

There were eight people sleeping on the floor of Sebastian's house. The youngest of them was only five, the oldest about seventeen. They had arrived one at a time as the light began to fade, some carrying shoeshine boxes, some with buckets and sponges, one with a basket of brightly colored finger puppets. Sebastian must have already told them about Matt, since none of them seemed surprised to find him there. Nobody tried to talk to him. They ate dinner — more beans and stew — then spent the rest of the evening playing a game that involved cups and little wooden dice. The room was lit by fat white candles that Matt suspected had been stolen from a church. He watched them for an hour, listening to the rattle of the dice in the cups as they were shaken and then tipped onto the floor. Pedro was playing with the others. He glanced at Matt once or twice, and for the first time Matt could see a sort of curiosity in his eyes.

"He's seen you before . . . in his dreams."

Sebastian's words echoed in his head. Matt examined the Peruvian boy as he concentrated on his game, furiously rattling his dice, throwing them down and shielding them with both hands, his eyes fixed on the other players. Matt now knew who he was. How many times had the two of them sat together in the reed boat with the wild cat's head for its prow? He was annoyed with himself for not realizing it sooner.

He remembered the moment when he'd woken up to find Pedro stealing his watch. He had recognized him there and then. But in all the confusion of what was happening, he had thought back only as far as the traffic lights, on the way from the airport. He thought that was when he'd seen Pedro for the first time. But of course he'd been aware of him for many years before that.

Pedro was one of the five. Matt could imagine Susan Ashwood saying the words. She would be delighted. Was it a coincidence that Matt had stepped off a plane in a country of twenty million people and Pedro had been almost the first person he'd met? No . . . not at all. There were no coincidences. It was *meant* to happen. That was what the blind medium would have said.

So was Richard meant to be kidnapped? Was Matt meant to be beaten up at the hotel? Did Matt have any control over what was happening or was he simply being pushed around by forces that he couldn't see and which were way outside his own comprehension? And if so, where were they taking him? What did they have in mind?

There were a thousand questions Matt wanted to ask and he didn't have answers to any of them. But he took some comfort in the thought that somehow he and Pedro had found each other. Now there were two of them, and that meant that the other three might not be far behind.

Pedro won the game. Matt saw him laugh delightedly and scoop up his dice. He wished his new companion spoke even a smattering of English. How were they supposed to fight a war together when they couldn't even talk?

The game was over. The smaller children were already asleep and now the others drew up their blankets and joined them. In England, going to bed had always been a routine of getting changed, washing, brushing teeth, and all the rest of it. Here it was very matter-of-fact and happened very quickly. The evening just stopped. Everyone took his place, huddled together around the single, empty bed, and soon the whole floor was a sea of blankets that rose and fell while the candles spluttered, throwing strange shadows across the wall. Matt couldn't sleep, still trapped in the wrong time zone. The room was much too warm with so many people in it, and there was a mosquito droning around his ear. He hadn't gotten used to the smell, either, even though he was now part of it. He hadn't bathed for forty-eight hours and he could feel the grime clinging to him all over. He thought about Richard. Sebastian assumed he was probably dead but Matt wouldn't even consider the possibility. He wondered how the two of them had allowed themselves to walk into all this and whether they would ever see each other again.

About an hour later, Sebastian came in. Matt saw, to his dismay, that the man was quite drunk. He staggered over to his bed and collapsed onto it without removing any of his clothes . . . not even his shoes. Within seconds he was fast asleep and snoring.

It took Matt much longer. Half the night seemed to slip by before his eyelids finally closed — much to his relief. Because this time he knew exactly where he was and he wasn't afraid to be there. He was with Pedro on the beach. The boat was moored just behind them, waiting to take them away.

"Matteo," Pedro said.

"I'm glad to see you, Pedro."

"Yeah. Me, too. I suppose . . ."

And here was the strange thing: Matt was speaking in English; Pedro was speaking in Spanish. And yet somehow the words were changing in midair so that both boys understood each other perfectly. Did this island exist only in a dream? Matt had always thought so. But now that there were two of them, sharing the sand, the sea, the boat, and all the rest of it, and he wasn't so sure. Part of him was aware that even as he stood here facing Pedro, the two of them were also lying just a meter apart in Poison Town. Perhaps this was why they were now finally able to talk to each other — they knew each other now.

"I don't get any of this," Pedro began.

"You're one of the five," Matt said.

"Yes. I know. I've been hearing that all my life, but I don't know what it means. Do you?"

"Some of it. There are five of us. . . ."

"I've seen the others. Over there." Pedro pointed, but there was no sign of the two boys and the girl on the mainland.

"We're gatekeepers."

"What gate?"

"It's a long story, Pedro."

"We've got all night."

Matt nodded. For the moment, they seemed to be out

of any danger. In Poison Town, everything would be quiet. On the island, they were alone with no sign of the swan that had twice come thundering out of the darkness. And what was the significance of that? Matt wondered. There was still so much he didn't understand.

He told Pedro as much as he knew, starting with the death of his parents, his growing awareness that he was never going to have a normal life, his life with Gwenda Davis in Ipswich, his involvement with Raven's Gate, and everything that had happened since then.

"I came to Peru to find the second gate," Matt concluded. "That was two days ago although it feels a lot longer. Everything went wrong the minute we arrived. If I can find the Nexus, maybe they can help. They're probably looking for me. I don't know."

Matt took a deep breath. The reed boat rocked gently on the water. He wondered if they should get into it — and if they did, where it would take them.

"I knew you'd come," Pedro said. "I've always been expecting you. But there's something I want you to know. When you were asleep . . . when I took your watch . . . I thought you were just some rich tourist kid who'd gotten lost. I didn't know it was you. I'm sorry."

"When did you realize?"

"When you woke up. I recognized you then. And the truth is, I wasn't too happy to see you. I wish you hadn't come."

"Why?"

"Because you're going to bring trouble with you. Everything's going to change now." Pedro paused. "You may not think I've got much of a life, but it's the only life I've got, and I was happy with it. I'm sure that's not what you want to hear. But this isn't what I want."

"No, I understand."

Matt knew exactly what Pedro meant. He felt the same.

"I don't know anything about you," he said. "Only your name . . . Pedro. Do you have another name? What do you do in Lima when you aren't juggling in front of cars or stealing from tourists? And who is Sebastian? Why do you live with him?"

"I don't like talking about myself," Pedro said. He paused. "But I will because I suppose you ought to know. But I'm telling you now, there's not a lot to say . . . and anyway, you probably won't remember any of it when you wake up."

That possibility hadn't occurred to Matt. He sat down on the sand, wondering what time of the day it was in this strange dreamland. Was it even day? The sky was dark but he could see quite clearly. The sand was warm although there wasn't any sun. It wasn't day or night but something in between.

Pedro sat down opposite him with his legs crossed.

"First of all, Pedro isn't my real name. Everyone just calls me that. It's what Sebastian called me when I first came to Poison Town. He used to say he named me after his favorite dog. I know I had a family before I met him although I don't remember very much about them. I think I had a sister. She was a few years younger than me.

"I used to live in a village in the province of Canta, which you've probably never heard of. It's about sixty miles from Lima. A three-day walk. It was a very ordinary place. The men went out to work in the fields — they grew potatoes and corn — and the women stayed at home and looked after the kids. There was no school in the village but I went to one that was two miles away. I didn't learn very much, though. I mean, I learned some of the letters in the alphabet but I've never been able to read."

He reached out and drew a capital *P* in the sand with his finger.

"That's *P* for *Pedro*. It's also *P* for *parrot, papagayo*. I remember the letter because it always looked like a parrot to me.

"My mother used to say that I was born under an evil star, but I don't know what she meant. There were four of us in our family, and we had a nice house even if it was mainly made of wood and cardboard. And we had a big bed. All four of us used to sleep in it. I can't tell you much about my mother. I don't want to think about her. Sometimes I remember the feel of her, next to me in the bed, and that makes me sad. That was always the best part of the day for me . . . falling asleep.

"The worst thing about Canta was the weather. The wind used to come down from the mountains and it went right through you. I never had enough clothes to wear. Sometimes I only had a T-shirt and my underpants and I'd think I was going to turn into a block of ice.

"It used to rain at the start of the year. You never saw rain like it, Matteo. Sometimes it would rain so hard that all I could see was water, and I used to wonder how I could live, since I wasn't a fish! It would be raining when I woke

143

up and it would never stop. You couldn't walk from one end of the village to the other because of the great sheets of rain, and if you fell into a puddle you might drown.

"And then there was a day — I must have been about six years old — when it rained so much that the river burst its banks. The River Chillon . . . that was what it was called. There was too much water and it got out of control and this great flood came pouring down. It was like a monster, brown and freezing. It ripped into our house and just threw it away. I remember someone shouted a warning but I didn't know what they meant and then the whole world exploded. Not with fire but with water and mud. It all happened so quickly. All the houses were smashed up together. People and animals . . . they were just killed. I should have died. But someone grabbed me and put me high up in a tree and I was lucky. The tree must have had strong roots, because it wasn't ripped out like the others. I stayed in the branches of that tree all day and all night, and when the morning came, my village wasn't there anymore. It was just a sort of swamp with dead people floating on the surface. I guess my parents and my sister were among those who were killed. I never saw them again and nobody told me. So they must have all drowned."

Pedro stopped. Matt was amazed that he could tell all this in such a matter-of-fact way. He tried to imagine the horror of what it must have been like. A whole community had been destroyed and he realized that this sort of thing must happen often in some parts of the world. But in Britain, it wouldn't have been given more than half an inch in a newspaper.

"After that, things became very difficult," Pedro went on. "I think I wanted to die. Inside me, I thought it was wrong that my parents were dead and I was still alive. But the strange thing is, I knew I was going to be all right. I had nowhere to live. There was no food. People were falling sick all around me. But I knew that whatever happened, I would make it. It was like my life was beginning all over again.

"Anyway, some of the survivors came together — there were quite a lot of them — and they decided to go to Lima. They'd heard there was work there. They thought they'd be able to build themselves a new life. I went with them. I was the youngest and they didn't want to take me. But in the end I followed, and there was nothing they could do.

"And so we came to the city, but it wasn't like we thought. Nobody wanted to see us. Nobody wanted to help us. We were the *desplazados*. That's the word we use for people with no place. There were already enough poor people starving and dying in Lima. They didn't want any more.

"There was a woman looking after me and she had a brother in one of the barrios, and for a while I lived with them. They made me work, searching for food in the garbage. I hated it. I'd leave at five o'clock in the morning, before the dust carts came, and I'd take anything I could find. Vegetables that weren't too rotten. Bits of fat and gristle cut off meat. All the scrapings from rich people's meals. That was what we lived on, and if I didn't find enough or if it was too rotten, they'd give me nothing to eat and they'd beat me. In the end, I ran away. If I stayed, I was afraid they would kill me.

"And that's my story. Did you enjoy it? I'll tell you the rest of it. You asked me about Sebastian. Nobody knows who he is exactly, Matteo, and we don't ask too many questions. I've heard people say he was a university professor until his wife left him and he took to drink. But there are others who say he was a waiter in an expensive hotel, and that's where he learned to speak different languages. Anyway, I went to Poison Town to get away from the sister and her brother. I found Sebastian and he took me in.

"He's not a bad man. He's only ever hurt me when he's very drunk, and he's always apologized the next day. All the kids in his house work for him. He was the one who taught me how to juggle in front of tourists' cars. Sometimes I can get five American dollars — although I have to give four of them to him. We wash car windows. We sell finger puppets. Sometimes we get work collecting tickets on the buses. Sebastian knows all the drivers, and that's how he'll get us out tomorrow."

Pedro fell silent.

"There's one thing you haven't told me," Matt said. "Did you know the river was going to flood?"

"How would I know that?"

"You didn't get any warning . . . perhaps the day before?"

"No."

"When my parents were killed, I knew it was going to happen. I saw it in a dream."

"I never had dreams like that. Forget it, Matteo. I'm not like you. I don't have any special powers, if that's what you're thinking. I'm not special . . . except maybe I have these stupid dreams where I'm with you. And they don't help much, either."

"You're coming with me to Ica," Matt said.

Pedro frowned. "I don't want to. But Sebastian says I can't stay with him anymore. It's too dangerous. And anyway . . ." He relaxed a little and the frown left his face. "Now that we've found each other, I don't see how I can walk away . . . even if I want to. So — yes. I'm coming along."

"Thank you," Matt said.

It was all the help he needed. He was no longer alone.

He stood up, and at that very instant it was as if the entire dreamworld had been cut in half by a vast, white guillotine. He felt no pain. There wasn't even any sense of shock. But suddenly the sea and the island had gone and he was sitting on the floor in the house in Poison Town.

He looked across at Pedro, still fast asleep underneath the blanket. The Peruvian boy hadn't changed, but now Matt saw him differently. He knew everything about him. They could have been friends throughout their entire lives. In a way, Matt reflected, they had been exactly that.

Outside, dawn was breaking, the first ribbons of pink light bleeding through the sky, signaling the start of another day.

• • •

Midnight in London.

Susan Ashwood was sitting in the spacious living room of a penthouse flat, high above Park Lane. Floor-to-ceiling windows provided a panoramic view over Hyde Park, an area of dense black, with the lights of Knightsbridge twinkling far behind. She had her back to it. Sometimes she was able to sense the appearance of a city from the way its sounds traveled, from the feel of the breeze against her face, from the smell of the night air. She knew beauty. But tonight all her attention was focused on the woman who owned the penthouse and who was sitting opposite her now.

"Thank you for seeing me," Ashwood said.

"There's no need to thank me," Natalie Johnson replied.

The American woman was sitting on a sofa with her legs tucked up under her, holding a glass of white wine. Her reddish brown hair was tied back and she was wearing a simple black dress. She had been about to go to bed when the blind medium had called. This was her home when she was in London. She had a similar apartment looking out over the Hudson River in New York.

"I didn't know who else to come to."

"You don't need to worry, Susan. My door's always open to you."

Natalie Johnson had been a member of the Nexus for eleven years. In that time, she had built up a huge business empire selling low-cost computer hardware, mainly to schools and youth clubs. The newspapers called her the female Bill Gates. She found the description sexist and irrelevant.

"Matthew Freeman is still lost," Susan Ashwood continued. "But it's now been confirmed that there was a gunfight near Jorge Chavez airport. Richard Cole was kidnapped but Matt managed to get away. As far as we know, he hasn't been seen since."

"We sent him to Peru because we wanted something to happen," the American woman said. "It seems that we got more than you bargained for."

"None of us could have expected this."

"What shall we do?"

"That's one of the reasons I'm here. I was hoping you might be able to help. You have business interests in South America. . . ."

"I could talk to Diego Salamanda if you like."

"You said you'd had dealings with him."

"I've never met him but we've spoken often on the telephone." Natalie Johnson paused. "I think we should be careful. Salamanda is our number-one suspect. It seems more than likely that he's the one who's trying to open the gate."

"Fabian is trying to find Matthew," Ashwood continued. "He's worried sick and blames himself for not driving personally to the airport. He's already spoken to the police but he's not sure he can trust them. He's suggested an advertising campaign in the national press."

"'Have you seen this boy?'" The idea seemed to amuse the American.

"Someone must know where he is. An English teenager on his own in Peru . . ."

"Assuming, of course, he's still alive." Johnson put down her wineglass. "I'll pay for advertisements if that's what you want," she said. "My New York office can organize it."

"There's something else. . . ." The blind woman paused,

trying to collect her thoughts. Her face was grim. "I've been thinking about what happened. First there was the business with William Morton. We were the only ones who knew where he was going to be, and he only told us twenty-four hours before Matthew met him. But someone still managed to follow him to St. Meredith's. They killed him and took the diary.

"And then there's Matthew and Richard Cole. They traveled to Peru under false names, but it seems that somebody knew they were coming. There was an ambush. Fabian's driver was almost killed. Richard Cole was taken."

"What are you suggesting?"

"That our enemy knows what we're doing. Someone is telling him our every move."

Natalie Johnson stiffened. "That's ridiculous."

"I've come to you because I've known you for a long time, and my instinct tells me I can trust you. I haven't said this to anyone else. But I think we need to be careful. If there's a traitor inside the Nexus, we could all be in danger."

"We should warn the others."

"Not yet. First of all we have to find Matthew Freeman. He's our main priority. The second gate is going to open very soon and he's the only one who can prevent it. It doesn't matter what happens to us, Natalie. If we don't find the boy, we've lost."

• • •

The bus station was like a crazy outdoor circus, a jumble of color and noise with people and packages everywhere, street vendors shouting, old women in shawls sitting behind

150

little piles of papayas and plantain, children and dogs chasing each other around the rubble, and the ancient buses themselves. Nobody was going anywhere yet but everyone seemed to be in a hurry. Great sacks and cardboard packages were being passed from hand to hand before being thrown up to be tied in towering piles on the buses' roofs. There were old tickets strewn all over the ground like confetti and fresh ones being sold from cubicles hardly bigger than a small closet. There was an Indian woman cooking *cau cau* — tripe and potato stew — in a large metal can at the edge of the bus yard, and some of the travelers were squatting on their haunches, eating from plastic bowls, the smell of the food fighting with the exhaust fumes.

Matt took this all in as he approached the bus station with Sebastian and Pedro. They had walked here from Poison Town, leaving just after five o'clock. Sebastian already had the tickets and had announced that he would be coming with them as far as Ica. Although he had been drunk when he went to bed, he seemed clearheaded enough when he woke up. In his own way, he was even cheerful.

"There is almost no chance that you will find your friend in Ica," he had said. "But after you have given your compliments to Señor Salamanda, you can continue down to Ayacucho. I will be waiting for you there."

They walked past a row of shops. Looking through an open door, Matt noticed a dark-skinned boy his own age, dressed in a bright green T-shirt with jeans that stopped a few inches below his knees. He had bare feet, black rubber sandals, and black hair cut in a straight line across his forehead. He was completely disheveled and dirty.

Matt moved . . . and so did the boy. It was only then

151

that Matt realized that he was actually looking at a full-length mirror. The boy was a reflection of himself.

Sebastian had seen what had happened. "You didn't recognize yourself," he chuckled. "Let's hope you can do the same with them."

He glanced in the other direction, and Matt felt his mouth go dry as two policemen appeared, both carrying semiautomatic machine guns. They could have been here for any number of reasons, but instinctively Matt knew that they were looking for him. Pedro asked something in Spanish, and Sebastian reassured him. From the moment the other boy had woken up, Matt had known that he, too, had remembered the conversation of the night before. He might not be happy to be here but he wasn't going to leave.

"Remember, keep yourself hunched," Sebastian whispered. "Your height will give you away. And here, take this. . . ." He had brought with him a large bundle, tied in white sacking. Matt didn't know what was inside. He wasn't even sure if it was luggage or merely a prop to make them look more like real travelers. He understood Sebastian's strategy. Matt looked like a servant, carrying the luggage for his master. He was doubled over, with the bundle balanced on his shoulders and the back of his neck making it impossible to see how tall he was. His face was also hidden, his eyes fixed on the floor.

They made their way forward. The policemen moved slowly through the crowd, which parted to let them pass. People were careful to avoid their eyes.

"This way," Sebastian said quietly.

He was steering Matt toward a half-filled bus. The two

policemen hadn't noticed them. Matt reached the door and his heart missed a beat. A third policeman had appeared, stepping out of the bus. Matt had almost knocked right into him. Bent underneath the bundle, he couldn't see the man's face — just his leather boots and the barrel of his gun. But then the policeman said something and with a hollow feeling in his stomach, Matt knew that he had just been asked a question. He said nothing. The policeman repeated what he had just said.

And then a hand grabbed hold of the bundle and tore it off his back. For a terrible moment, he thought it was the policeman. But it was Sebastian. He was shouting at Matt in Spanish, then slapping him hard on the side of the face. Before he could react, Sebastian hit him a second time, then threw him into the bus. Matt was sent flying onto the floor. Behind him, he heard Sebastian talking to the policeman and laughing. There were about twenty people in the bus, all staring at him. With the skin on his face burning — with pain and embarrassment — he stumbled forward and found himself a free seat.

Pedro got onto the bus and Sebastian followed. The man sat next to Matt but didn't say anything. More people got on, some with tethered goats, others with baskets packed with live chickens. Soon every seat was taken and the aisle was filled with people squatting on the floor. Finally the driver arrived. He swung himself into his seat and turned on the engine. The entire bus began to rattle and shake.

The driver slammed the gear stick forward and the bus lurched and began to cross the yard. Looking out of the window, Matt saw the policeman walking away.

"That was close," Sebastian growled. He went on in a low voice, "I had to hurt you because the policeman was becoming suspicious. I told him you were my nephew and that you were an idiot. I said you had brain damage, which is why you hadn't shown him more respect."

"Was he looking for me?"

"Yes. He told me just now. They're offering a huge reward — many hundreds of dollars — for your discovery. They're still saying that you're involved with terrorists."

"But why? They're the police! Why are they doing this?"

"Because someone has paid them. Why do you think? Maybe Ayacucho won't be so welcoming for you. You'll never be safe so long as you're in Peru. Without a passport, there's no way you're going to get out."

The bus rattled along a track and joined the main road. As it turned the corner, the passengers swayed in their seats and the various animals cried out. Then the driver hit the accelerator, and the engine roared. They had begun the long journey south.

ELEVEN
Salamanda

Ica was a small, busy town, full of dust and traffic. Matt's first impression as he climbed down from the bus was that every building had been painted a uniform white and yellow, giving the place an artificial look. It reminded him of a film set, perhaps for an old western. But real life was all around him. It was there in the rubbish piles, the clothes flapping on lines high above the rooftops, the graffiti that seemed to have spread across every wall. Advertisements for Nike and Coca-Cola. Names of politicians and their parties. NO A LAS DROGAS . . . public warnings applied with a spray can. The old men and women, blinking on benches out in the sun, the *chollo* — "people" — taxis buzzing in and out of the main square, the money changers in their bright green jackets, chasing the tourists who were taking pictures of all this with cameras that must have cost more than most of the local people would earn in a year.

Sebastian had walked with them to the main square. He bought them some food — shish kebabs and rice — and sat on the curb with them as they ate.

"I don't like these provincial towns," he said. "Lima may be a stink hole . . . but at least you know where you are. I never know what country people are thinking. Maybe they're not thinking anything. They're just *indios*." He used the abusive term for native Indians. "They've got nothing in their heads."

"What do we do now?" Matt asked.

"What do we do now? I'll tell you what *I* do now, Matteo." Sebastian had lit another cigar. It occurred to Matt that he had hardly ever seen him without one in his mouth. "I go on to Ayacucho. If you make it there alive, come to the main square. I'll have people looking out for you. They'll bring you to me."

"Aren't you going to help us get into the hacienda?"

Sebastian laughed unpleasantly. "I've helped you enough already. And besides, I enjoy living too much. I'll show you where it is. After that, you're on your own."

After they had finished, he walked with them over a river and on to the edge of the town. He talked to Pedro as they went. He seemed to be giving him advice. Gradually the houses fell away behind them until they came to a dirt track, leading off from the main road.

"The hacienda is five miles down this way," he said. "I hope you'll find your friend there, Matteo — but I've already told you, I doubt it. Maybe you and I will meet again in Ayacucho. I also doubt that. But I hope so."

"I thought you didn't like me," Matt said.

"Pedro tells me that maybe I'm wrong about you, that you're not the same as other rich kids in the west who have everything and never think about people like Pedro and me." He shrugged. "Anyway, you are an enemy of the police, and that is enough to make you my friend."

He reached into his pocket and took out a cloth bag.

"I have some money for you. It's a hundred *soles*. That's a lot . . . almost twenty pounds in your currency. And before you thank me, it's Pedro's. He was the one who stole it — not me. Maybe it'll help keep the two of you alive."

Pedro said something in Spanish. Sebastian went over to him and spoke at length. When he had finished talking, he reached out and tousled the boy's hair. Suddenly he was looking sad.

"I had a son once," he said. He shook his head. "You know how to find me."

He turned and walked away.

Matt glanced at Pedro, who nodded. They still couldn't talk to each other, but they seemed to understand each other more and more. Together they set off.

The track that Sebastian had showed them ran through agricultural land. Some of the fields were planted with maize, beetroot, and asparagus while others held cattle, chewing at the rough, spiky grass. Following Sebastian's advice, the two boys kept to the very edge of the track, ready to drop out of sight if any cars appeared. Once, an open-backed truck came rattling past and they threw themselves under a low shrub and waited until it had disappeared, kicking up clouds of dust. The afternoon was swelteringly hot. Pedro had fished two plastic bottles out of a bin and filled them with water from a tap, but Matt doubted it would be enough. He could feel his bottle leaking in his pants pocket. He was tempted to drink it all now.

As soon as the truck was out of sight, they stood up and trudged on in silence. Matt would have liked to talk — there was still so much he didn't understand — and it seemed crazy to him that they would be able to communicate only when they were asleep. They were two of the five. He wondered what languages the others spoke. The two boys and the girl that he had seen on the beach had been white and fair-haired but they could be Russian, Scandinavian — or even Martian, for all he knew. And what happened when they did finally meet? Was that the end of the adventure or the beginning of something worse?

So many questions, but Matt could only walk on in silence, feeling the sun as it beat down on his shoulders. He still hadn't gotten used to his own smell, to the unfamiliar shape of his hair, and the dye, dark and sticky all over his skin. His clothes no longer disgusted him but they felt strange, like some sort of unpleasant fancy dress. And he kept on stumbling over his rubber sandals. Worst of all, he was worried about Richard. He had to admit that Sebastian was right — the chances of the journalist turning up at this hacienda were probably one in a million. But he had nowhere else to go, no other clues to follow. He had to start somewhere, and it might as well be here.

Pedro stopped and took a quick drink. Matt did the same, wondering if the Peruvian tap water would make him sick. The other boy was doubtless used to it. He had been drinking it all his life. The water was warm and tasted metallic but Matt didn't care. He had to stop himself from drinking it all.

After that, Matt's thoughts wandered. Five miles might not seem much to Pedro, but it was a long way for him, particularly in the heat and in sandals that tried to trip him up every few paces. A car passed, coming the other way, and once again the two of them had to dive for cover. How much security would there be at the hacienda? Sebastian hadn't said anything but it occurred to Matt that anyone as rich and powerful as Salamanda would be sure to have guards.

The sun began to set and a cool breeze crept into the air. Matt's legs were beginning to ache and he only had an inch of water left when they turned a corner and Pedro raised a hand in warning and they ducked back into the undergrowth, crouching low. There was a house directly ahead . . . not just a house but an entire complex complete with barns, storerooms, stables, and even, incredibly, a sixteenth-century church carved out of white stone, with its own soaring bell tower. This was where the lane had brought them — all five miles of it. There was nothing more beyond. Two stone pillars and a twisting metal gate marked the entrance. The gate was open, but somehow Matt didn't feel it was inviting him in.

Carefully he peered round, searching for any sign of life. All the buildings were grouped around a flower-filled courtyard with an elaborate ornamental fountain in the middle. A huge acacia tree grew next to it. The tree had four separate trunks and leaves that spread out to provide a natural shade from the sun. There was a tractor parked outside one of the barns. A man, dressed in white, came out, pushing a wheelbarrow. Apart from the soothing tinkle of water in the fountain, everything was silent.

"Matteo . . ." Pedro tapped Matt's arm and pointed.

Matt looked into the distance and saw a guard tower constructed at the edge of the complex. At the same time, a man appeared with a rifle strapped across his back. He stopped and lit a cigarette, then kept on walking. So Matt had been right. This hacienda might be in the middle of nowhere but Salamanda left nothing to chance. The place was guarded, and Matt was sure that there would be plenty of other security around, too.

"¿Qué hacemos ahora?" Pedro asked.

"We wait." The meaning of Pedro's question was obvious. He wanted to know what they were going to do. Matt looked up. The sun was already setting behind the palm trees that grew tall behind the house. The night might still be an hour away, but the shadows were spreading out. They would help. Two dark-skinned boys in dark clothes in the dark. It wouldn't be too hard to slip inside.

The house itself was completely open. Three wide, wooden stairs ran up to a veranda that ran its full length. There was nobody in the courtyard, no sign of movement in the guard tower. Security cameras? Matt hadn't seen any, and there was always a chance that they wouldn't operate in this low light. He would just have to risk it. The thought that Richard might be here, perhaps only a few meters away, spurred him on. He nudged Pedro and then, keeping low, ran through the gate across one corner of the courtyard, making for the side of the house.

Nobody saw them. Nobody cried out. Matt stopped, breathless, his back against the wall just below the veranda. Pedro was next to him, looking unhappy. He shook his head as if to say *This is a crazy idea and I don't want any part of it.* But at the same time, he was still sticking by him, and right now Matt was grateful that he wasn't alone.

Where would Richard be and how could they possibly find him in a house crawling with guards? There was no obvious prison complex, no windows covered with bars. A basement or cellar, perhaps. That would be the most likely place. But first they had to get in.

At least that wasn't going to be too difficult. Now that he was closer, Matt could see that the veranda continued all the way around the back. On one side, there was a hand-rail, separating the house from the garden and the courtyard. The main body of the house made up the other side with tall, elegant windows standing at intervals about five meters apart. The windows reached down almost to the floor and all of them were open. Matt glanced at Pedro, giving him one last chance to back out. Pedro nodded. *I'm with you.* Matt reached up and used the handrail to pull himself onto the veranda. Now he was as good as inside the house. The roof with its heavy red tiles stretched out over him. Matt waited until Pedro had joined him, then crept round the side.

Almost at once, he heard voices. There was a meeting going on in one of the rooms, but in the stillness of the evening the sounds were carrying out. Matt gestured and the two of them crept along the veranda past more sofas and some terra-cotta pots. They came to an open French window. A man was speaking on the other side. Carefully, an inch at a time, Matt peered round the corner and looked in.

It was a dining room with a vast wooden table that seemed to have been cut from a single tree. The floor was also made of polished wood, and there were wooden panels set into the walls. An iron chandelier — it must have weighed a ton — hung down, illuminating the room not with electric bulbs but with about a hundred candles, each one in its own holder. Matt wondered when they had been lit. A servant or someone must have come in while the meeting was in progress.

There were three men and a woman sitting around the table. Matt recognized one of them instantly and stopped dead, feeling as if the ground was opening up beneath him. It was Rodriguez, the police captain who had beaten him up at the hotel in Miraflores. He was in uniform. The other two men wore suits. The woman had a simple black dress. All of them were listening attentively as they were given their instructions.

The man who was talking to them was sitting in a tall wicker chair with his back to the window. Matt could see nothing of him apart from one arm and a hand, resting on one of the arms. He had long fingers and seemed to be wearing a linen suit. He was speaking quickly, in good English, only occasionally stumbling over some of the words. Matt whistled very softly at Pedro and swung his head over toward the room. Why were they using his own language? If he listened long enough, he might find out.

"I do not care what is a possibility and what is not," the man was saying. "I give you the instructions and you will obey. The swan must be . . . *en la posición* . . . in position, five days from now. At midnight exactly. You understand, Miss Klein?"

The woman nodded. "It will all be done," she said. Her English was worse than his, and heavily accented. "But I am needed soon the . . ." It took her a minute to find the word. "I must have the coordinates," she said.

Now Matt understood. The woman was German and spoke no Spanish. The man was Spanish and spoke no German. They were using English as a common language.

"You will have the coordinates as soon as I have them myself," the man went on. "My agents have been into the Nazca desert but they have still failed to find the platform."

"The diary did not give you the position?"

"It gave me the approximate position, and it is possible that we now know enough to place the swan exactly where it is meant to be. But I prefer to leave nothing to chance. We have to be careful, but the search continues. Just so long as everything is ready at your end."

"Of course, Herr Salamanda. Everything will be as you ask. . . ."

That was the end of it. Matt was listening in with his head pressed against the wall, right next to the window. Pedro was slightly behind him. So he was the one who heard the clunk of boots on wood and realized that at least two guards were making their way toward them, patrolling the full length of the veranda. They were still out of sight, around the front of the house, but in a few seconds they would turn the corner and the two boys would be discovered.

There was only one thing to do. Matt pushed Pedro, and the two of them flitted past the open window, past the dining room. Matt hoped that they wouldn't be seen in the growing darkness — or, if they were, that none of the people in the room would realize they weren't meant to be there. He heard the woman talking as he went past, and wished he could have stayed longer to hear more. But he and Pedro had only just moved in time. A second later, the guards appeared, both of them dressed in loose-fitting khaki overalls and armed with rifles hanging from their shoulders. The veranda they saw was empty.

Matt and Pedro didn't stop moving until they had reached the back of the house, where they came upon an inner courtyard, immaculately laid out with antique benches surrounding a well and a single, dark green *molle* tree in the very center. There were two more wings to the house, one on each side. Matt noticed that here some of the windows on the upper floor *were* barred. Perhaps these were the cells he had been imagining. Could Richard be sitting in one of them even now?

He needed a way up — and saw one, on the opposite side of the yard. An open staircase with a series of arches over a wooden banister, running up to a gallery. But before he could move, a third guard appeared, coming through a doorway on the first floor and making as if to come down. Matt cursed himself. Had he really thought he could just walk in here, find his friend, and walk out with him? Was it likely that one of the richest and most powerful men in Peru wouldn't make sure he had plenty of protection? Sebastian had been right. This was stupid. Worse than that, it was suicide. He and Pedro were going to get caught. They would be handed back to Captain Rodriguez. And neither of them would ever be seen — in Ayacucho or anywhere else — again.

Pedro had obviously had the same thought. He glanced at Matt, who nodded. They would get out of the house and wait. Maybe later, in the middle of the night, it would be safer to take a look around.

Together, they crept round the side of the courtyard, keeping well into the shadows. There were lights on inside the rooms and they could see moths dancing in the doorways, but fortunately no lamps had yet been turned on outside. There was a door leading into the study that they had already seen from the front. They could pass through here and out the other side.

They entered the study.

Matt quickly took in his surroundings. This had to be where Diego Salamanda worked. There was a grandness about the room, the rich tapestries on the walls, the expensive rugs on the floor. A sudden thought occurred to Matt: If this was Salamanda's private office, perhaps the diary of St. Joseph of Cordoba might be here. He hadn't thought about the diary since Richard had disappeared. His entire mind had been focused on finding his friend. But suppose he stumbled across it? If he could get his hands on it, perhaps he could use it as a bargaining chip. The diary for Richard. The Nexus would hate that — but he didn't care. Salamanda and the Old Ones could do what they liked. All he wanted was to get out of Peru.

Pedro was already halfway across the room.

"Wait!" Matt whispered.

Pedro stopped and watched in dismay as Matt began to search the desk. It was an ugly piece of furniture, heavier and bigger than it had any right to be, with a leather square built into the surface and gold rings on the drawers. Matt tried one of them. It wasn't locked but made so much noise as it was opened, wood creaking against wood, that it could surely be heard throughout the house.

"¿Qué estás haciendo?" Pedro hissed.

"The diary . . ." Matt replied, and Pedro understood. The word was almost the same in English and Spanish.

Pedro went over to the side of the room where a number of shelves stretched out over a modern photocopier. Some of the shelves contained books, but before he could examine them, he noticed a sheet of paper in the top of the machine.

"Matteo . . ." he called out.

Matt abandoned the desk — most of the drawers were empty and the rest contained nothing of any interest. He came over to the photocopier and took the paper. It was covered in writing, possibly made with an old-fashioned pen or even a quill. Could it have been taken from the diary? Matt cursed quietly. The words were in Spanish. He couldn't understand them. And Pedro couldn't read. Even if Matt read them out loud, he wouldn't be able to translate them into English. How much more useless could this break-in have been?

He folded the paper and slipped it into his pocket. Maybe he would be able to make sense of it later.

There was a movement at the door.

Pedro had seen it first. He stopped where he was, his eyes widening in disbelief. Matt saw the look on his face, turned round and froze. A shiver, as tangible as an electric shock, ran through him. He felt it travel through his arms and up the back of his neck.

He couldn't see the man who was standing on the other side of the doorway, shrouded in darkness. But he could make out his shape and knew at once that his head was impossibly large, twice as long as it should be, monstrous. The man was holding on to the frame of the door and Matt understood why. He needed help to stand up straight. His neck simply wasn't strong enough to support his head on its own.

"I thought it was you," the man said. He was still speaking English. His voice sounded strained, as if someone were strangling him. "I heard you on the veranda as you went past. But it wasn't just that. I *knew* you were there. I have been feeling your presence all evening, just as I feel it now. One of the five. *Two* of the five! Here, in my hacienda! To what do I owe the pleasure of your company? What do you want?"

There was no point in Matt denying who he was. The man had seen right through his disguise. He seemed to know everything about it.

"Where's Richard?" Matt demanded.

"Your friend the journalist?" Matt could see the lips twist into something that resembled a smile. But this was a face that could never smile properly. There was too much of it. "What made you think *I* had him? Why should he be here?" Salamanda looked genuinely puzzled. "How did you even find your way to me?"

Matt said nothing. There was no point answering.

Salamanda turned to Pedro. "*¿Cuál es tu nombre?*" he demanded.

Pedro spat. Whatever he had been asked, that was his reply.

"What fun I'm going to have with the two of you," Salamanda muttered. "It's almost too good to be true. A gift, if you like — and perfectly timed. A week from now, it will all be over. The gate will have opened and not one but two of the gatekeepers will be mine. I never thought it would be so easy."

Salamanda stepped into the light and Matt saw his colorless eyes, his babyish mouth, his pale, horribly stretched skin. It was enough.

"Go!" Matt shouted.

Pedro didn't need encouraging. The two boys turned and ran, away from the door and out through the window, back into the outer courtyard. They had no plan. Their only desire was to get away — from this house and from the monster who inhabited it. But even as they jumped down from the veranda and made for the main gate, the church bells sounded, metal striking metal and echoing into the night. Searchlights that they hadn't noticed sprang to life, turning black to white and half blinding them in their glare. At the same time, they were aware of guards, half a dozen of them, closing in from all sides. Two of them had Alsatian dogs, straining on thick chains, snapping at the air. Captain Rodriguez had reappeared at the side of the house, watching in anger and disbelief. The strange thing was that nobody seemed to be in a hurry. Two intruders had been discovered. The alarm had been raised. But the guards were almost strolling toward them, deliberately taking their time.

Matt understood why. With a growing sense of hopelessness, he realized that they had nowhere to go. Even if they could escape from the immediate compound, it was a five-mile walk back to the main town with no other building in

168

sight and nowhere to hide. They could run all they wanted. They would simply be hunted down like rats. Matt swallowed, recognizing the bitter taste of defeat. He had been warned not to come here but he hadn't listened, and as a result he had doomed them both.

He began to raise his hands in surrender — but then everything changed. He saw it first on the faces of the guard, heard it a moment later himself. There was the roar of an engine — then, as he turned round, a car burst through the gate and into the courtyard. For a moment, Matt assumed it must belong to Salamanda, another of his men cutting off their last way of escape. But at the same time, he knew that something was wrong. The guards had stopped in their tracks. Rodriguez had taken out his gun and was shouting orders.

The car slid to a halt. The passenger door swung open.

"Get in!" a voice called out, first in English, then in Spanish. *"¡Consiga en el coche!"*

There was a burst of gunfire and suddenly Matt was back in Lima on his way from the airport. He had never been shot at in his life. Now it had happened twice in the space of a week. Two shots had been fired from the watchtower that he had seen earlier. One bullet hit the ground, kicking up a cloud of dust. The other hit the trunk of the car. That told him everything he needed to know. Whoever was in the car was on his side.

Matt ran forward. There were more shots. The guards seemed to be shooting at the car rather than at Pedro and him. Were they obeying instructions from Salamanda? It seemed the boys were wanted alive. Then Matt saw that the

169

dogs had been released. They were bounding forward, their eyes aflame, mouths wide open to reveal white, vicious teeth. He and Pedro might not get shot, but if they didn't reach the car soon, they would be torn apart.

"Faster!" the driver shouted.

Pedro got there first. He opened the back door and threw himself onto the seat. Matt lunged for the front door. And despite the guns still firing all around him, despite the dogs bounding ever closer through the brilliant, electric light, he froze.

He knew the driver of the car.

The slightly feminine face. Long eyelashes. A thin face with sculpted cheekbones, covered by the beginnings of a beard. A half-moon scar next to one eye.

It was one of the men who had kidnapped Richard.

"Get into the car or you will die!" the man shouted.

Two more bullets slammed into the metalwork. A third smashed one of the mirrors. Matt didn't need any more persuading. He dived forward at the same time the man slammed the car into reverse, skidding backward and taking Matt with him. Matt was half in and half out, the door still open. Pedro was sitting, surprisingly calm, in the backseat. The car continued backward. Matt saw a guard raising his gun. There was a terrible thump and the guard disappeared.

"The door —" the driver warned.

There was a hideous snarling, and Matt turned just in time to see one of the Alsatians leap at him. It landed on his leg and he felt its teeth snapping, inches away from his thigh. With a cry, he drew back his other leg and kicked out. His foot slammed into the dog's head. The dog screamed and fell back. Matt drew himself into the car and pulled the door shut. The driver had already changed gears. The car shot forward.

But it wasn't over yet. As if afraid of losing them, the remaining guards all fired at once and Matt yelled out as glass and bullets exploded over his head. Next to him, the driver jerked in his seat and Matt felt something wet splatter across his face. He wiped his cheek with the back of his hand and looked down. His fingers were covered in blood.

He hadn't been shot. It was the driver. It was Lima all over again, except that this time the roles had been reversed. The man with the scar wasn't firing at them, he was helping him. And he was wounded. He had been hit twice: in the shoulder and the side of the neck. There was blood on the seat and on the dashboard. More blood was spreading rapidly down his shirt. But he was still gripping the wheel, his foot pressed on the accelerator. The car swerved round the courtyard and into the darkness. The driver reached out and turned on the headlamps. The car bounced and rattled back down the lane.

"They'll follow us!" Matt said. He expected to see Salamanda's men already following in cars or trucks.

"I don't think so." The man was trying to keep the pain out of his voice, but Matt could tell he had been badly hurt. The blood had spread all the way down to his chest. Soon the whole shirt would be red. He muttered a few words in Spanish. Pedro leaned down. When he sat up again, he was holding a handful of wires and fuses. Matt smiled. Somehow

171

the man had reached the hacienda ahead of them. And he had disabled all the vehicles he could find.

"Who are you?" Matt demanded.

"My name is Micos."

"How did you find us? Where's Richard?" There were a dozen more questions Matt wanted to ask.

"Not now. Later . . ."

Matt fell silent. He understood. Micos didn't have the strength to drive and to talk at the same time.

It seemed to take them forever to reach the end of the lane. It was completely dark and the headlights illuminated only a small area ahead of them. Matt only knew they were back on the main road when the wheels began to turn smoothly on an asphalt surface. A few moments later, Micos pulled over to the side and stopped.

"Listen to me," he said, and with a jolt of alarm Matt saw that he had been even more badly wounded than Matt had feared, that Micos had very little time left. "You must go to Cuzco." Micos coughed and swallowed with difficulty. More blood appeared, on his lower lip. "On Friday . . . the temple of Coricancha. In Cuzco. At sunset."

He seemed to take a deep breath, as if preparing to tell them more.

"Please, tell Atoc . . ." he began. But that was all. He was sitting still, his eyes fixed on something in the distance. Matt realized he had just died.

In the backseat, Pedro whimpered.

"We can't stay here," Matt said. He didn't care if the other boy understood or not. "Salamanda will come after us eventually. We have to go."

The two of them got out. The car was parked right on the edge of the road with a slope leading into brushwood. For a brief moment, Matt wondered if they could get back in and drive away. He couldn't drive, but Pedro . . . ?

He glanced at the other boy. As if reading his mind, Pedro shook his head. Well, if they couldn't use it, they had to get rid of it. Otherwise, Salamanda would know they were nearby and on foot. Matt turned out the headlamps and released the hand brake. He signaled to Pedro, and the two of them began to push the car. It rolled off the road, out of sight.

The moon had come out, showing the way ahead. Ica couldn't be more than half a mile away.

"Are you ready?" Matt asked.

"Yes." Pedro had understood. And he had replied in English.

Together they set off along the road.

173

TWELVE
The Holy City

Once again, Matt and Pedro found themselves in the main square at Ica, and this time they were even more nervous than they had been before. It was half past five in the morning, but there were already plenty of people around. It seemed to Matt that life began early in Peru. Even so, everything was quiet. There were no tourists yet. The money changers hadn't come out. If anyone came looking for them, they wouldn't be too hard to find.

Matt was fairly sure that nobody would be looking for them here. As far as Salamanda knew, they could be a hundred miles down the Pan-American Highway — the single road that ran the full length of the country. But he wasn't taking any chances. He had left Pedro to buy the bus tickets for the next leg of their journey while he squatted in the shadows. He was crouching on the edge of the pavement, his arms wrapped around himself, pretending to be asleep. It wasn't all pretense. He was exhausted. He wasn't sure how much longer he could keep going.

Pedro returned with the tickets and sat down next to him.

"Cuzco," Matt said.

"Cuzco," Pedro agreed, and showed him the two slips of paper.

Matt hadn't been certain that he would really buy them. He knew that Pedro would have preferred to continue south to the city of Ayacucho — where Sebastian and his friends would be waiting. As he took the tickets, Matt glanced at the other boy. Pedro wasn't looking happy about what he had done but he had evidently come to a decision and would stick by it.

Matt and Pedro ate a quick breakfast of rolls and coffee bought from a stall, then crept on board the bus at the last moment. Almost every seat was taken and they had to sit apart. *Not that it matters,* Matt thought to himself. When they were awake, they couldn't speak anyway.

Cuzco.

It meant nothing to him. A name spoken by a dying man. It was a town . . . a city . . . it could be anywhere in Peru. He guessed it must be far away because the tickets had cost almost half their remaining money. As they set off, jolting through the half-empty main square, Matt looked across the aisle at Pedro, who was sitting, cramped, next to the window on the other side of a plump, sweating man. What was he thinking? From the moment he had met Matt, his entire life had been thrown into turmoil. Despite everything, Matt was beginning to worry about him. Pedro had said nothing and had shown little emotion since the death of the man called Micos. Of course, he was used to violence and sudden death. But he surely hadn't been expecting so much more of it.

The Pan-American Highway was long and very straight, running through the landscape as if it had been cut with a knife. For the first couple of hours, there was no real view out the window. The edges of the road were lined with garbage — old tires, pieces of plastic sheeting, tangled coils of wire, and mounds of rubble that seemed determined to follow them every inch of the way. Matt had never been anywhere like this before. He had seen garbage dumps in England. There had been parts of Ipswich that were run-down and depressing. But the poverty in this country was endless. It had spread like a disease.

The sun rose, and suddenly it was hot. Matt looked around him at the other passengers, a mixture of city people, farmers, Indians, and — once again — animals. The woman sitting next to him was dressed in brilliant colors, with a bright red shawl tied around her neck, and a floppy hat. Her skin looked like beaten leather. She could have been a hundred years old. She was examining him curiously, and Matt wondered if she had seen through the skin dye, the clothes, and the haircut and recognized the English boy underneath. He turned away, afraid she might try to speak to him.

Another hour passed. Then several more. It was impossible to tell how long he had been sitting there. Even worse, Matt was thirsty. His mouth seemed to be full of dust and diesel fumes. He closed his eyes. Almost immediately he was asleep.

"We should have gone to Ayacucho," Pedro said.

"I know. I'm sorry. Why did you decide to come along?"

"Because of the man who died. Micos. He died because he wanted to help us. And at the end, when he only had one breath left, he told us to go to Cuzco. It was that important to him. If we didn't do as he said, his ghost would never forgive us."

"Do you know anything about Cuzco?" Matt asked.

"Not much. Sebastian went there once and he didn't like it. It's a long way away . . . high up in the mountains. Sebastian told me that you can't breathe properly because there isn't enough air. A lot of tourists go there." Pedro thought for a moment. "It's not far from a place called Machu Picchu, which is where the Incas used to live."

"What about the temple of Coricancha?"

"I've never heard of it."

The two of them sat in silence for a minute. But in this strange world, a minute could have been an hour or even a day.

"So who do you think he was?" Pedro asked. "He said his name was Micos but he didn't tell us anything else. And what about the man with the big head? That was Salamanda. . . ."

"Yes." Matt shuddered.

"I've never seen anyone like that. I mean, there are people in Lima with no legs and no arms and stuff like that. You see it all the time. But he was a freak. A real freak. And he was evil. It was like it was oozing out of him. He made me want to be sick."

"Yes. I felt the same."

Matt glanced at the boat with the cat's-head prow. He thought that, quite soon, he and Pedro must leave the dream island. There was a whole dream world to explore.

"Listen, Pedro," he said. "I've been thinking about everything that's been happening. It's all happened so fast — the airport, meeting you, all the rest of it — I haven't had a chance to work it out. But now I have. And maybe I've been stupid. I may have got it all wrong."

He paused.

"Let's start with Salamanda. He's our enemy. He's the one who wants to open the gate. He must have paid someone to kill William Morton and take the diary. But it wasn't Salamanda who snatched Richard. He more or less told me that himself. He seemed surprised we thought Richard was with him."

"Then who . . . ?"

"That's what I've been wondering. Richard and I arrive in Lima and we're met by a driver who says that he's working for Fabian. He tells us his name is Alberto but he could have been anyone. He drives us to a hotel where Captain Rodriguez and the police are waiting for us. We're walking into a trap.

"But on the way, another bunch of people run into us. They shoot at the driver and try to grab us. They take Richard, but I get away."

"They were trying to stop you! They didn't want you to go to the hotel because they knew the police were there!"

Matt nodded. "That's right. Micos was one of them. I recognized him at the hacienda. He was there, with them, in Lima. And last night he must have somehow followed us to Salamanda's place. Or maybe he was always waiting for me to show up."

"Maybe he could have told you where your friend is."

"I wish he'd told us more. Who he was. Who he was working for."

"Maybe he didn't know he was going to die." Pedro thought for a moment. "This temple . . ."

"Coricancha. If we can find it, maybe we can find Richard." Matt picked up a pebble and threw it into the

178

sea. It made no sound as it hit the water. "How long will it take us to reach Cuzco?"

"They said twenty hours when I bought the tickets."

"Well, if we can sleep most of the time, at least we can talk."

"Yes." Pedro frowned. "What about this place, Matteo? Where are we now? How come we can understand each other . . . and remember everything when we wake up?"

"I don't know," Matt said. "When I met you here on this island, I hoped you'd be able to tell me."

"No chance. I don't know anything about anything. I'm just me. I do juggling and I steal from tourists. It's all a mystery, and how I got mixed up with you is the biggest mystery of all."

"Then let's get moving." Matt stood up. "I think we should get off this island. You've got a boat. We can take it."

"Where?"

"There are five of us, Pedro. That's what this is all about. We have to find the other three."

The two of them went over to the boat and dragged it off the shingle. Matt climbed in and Pedro pushed off. Suddenly, the mainland looked a long way away. Matt looked up. The sky, still black, was clear. The huge swan hadn't returned.

The swan. Salamanda had been talking about it in his dining room.

"The swan must be in position five days from now. . . ."

That was what Salamanda had said, but what did he mean? Did he have the power to enter this dreamworld? Was the swan in some way controlled by him?

Matt shivered. Pedro leaped in, water dripping from

his ankles and feet. The boat seemed to have a life of its own. Almost at once it turned away from the island and, picking up speed, it carried them out to sea.

•   •   •

Matt jolted awake again.

The bus had stopped at a crossroads with a few ram-shackle buildings and stalls selling food and drink. The old woman who had been sitting next to him got off. Pedro, carrying two bottles of water and some more rolls, was able to join him. As the doors hissed shut and they set off again, Matt remembered the piece of paper that they had found in Salamanda's study and took it out again.

It had been photocopied from the diary. He was sure of it. The entire page was covered in lines, some of them form-ing shapes. There was a sort of rectangle that narrowed at one end. A drawing of what looked like an elaborate spi-der. And there was writing everywhere, going in every direction, some of it so tiny that it would have been unread-able even if it had been in English. There were four lines in the very center of the page. They looked like a verse from a poem. And in the bottom left-hand corner, a blazing sun and two words in capital letters:

INTI RAYMI

Was that Spanish? Somehow it didn't sound like it. What did the page mean and why had Salamanda felt the need to photocopy it? Matt folded the page away. He would solve the mystery later, once he had found Richard.

Matt looked outside and noticed the countryside was changing. It was much more mountainous, covered in dense green vegetation. The road, which had been straight before, now continued in a series of hairpin bends as the bus climbed ever higher. Matt remembered what Pedro had said and sniffed the air cautiously. It was definitely getting thinner. Even the color of the sky was different — a harder, more electric blue. There were farmhouses, thrown onto the upper slopes as if by chance, and strange fortresses, small and circular, made out of solid stone. It would be impossible to grow anything here, or so Matt thought. But then they turned another corner and he saw that someone — the local Indians or some civilization before them — had carved fantastic terraces into the sides of the hills, shoring them up with boulders and then planting them with crops. It must have been the labor of a thousand years.

Then the bus reached the top of a valley and Matt saw the city of Cuzco spread out in front of him. It was like nothing he had ever seen in his life.

It really wasn't like a city at all. There were no skyscrapers, no office buildings, no main roads, no traffic lights or even very much traffic. Cuzco was like something out of a storybook written a long time ago. Matt saw a central square dominated by two Spanish cathedrals and a sprawl of neat, white-fronted houses with terra-cotta roofs that continued for what looked like several miles to the foothills on the other side.

It was only when they had left the bus and began to make their way on foot toward the center that Matt was able to get the measure of the place. Cuzco was a beautiful city of archways and verandas, wrought-iron lamps, cobbled streets, and pavements so highly polished that they could have been indoors . . . in a museum or a palace. Every building seemed to be a restaurant, an Internet café, or a shop piled high with textiles, jewelry, and souvenirs. There was poverty here, too. Matt saw a tiny boy, barefoot and dirty, asleep in a doorway. Old women sat in the street, blinking in the sunlight. Shoeshine boys looked for trade around the churches. But the poverty seemed almost picturesque here — just something else for the tourists to photograph.

And there were tourists and backpackers everywhere. As they entered the main square, Matt heard English voices and his immediate instinct was to throw himself into the arms of the first person he met. He needed help. A rich English tourist was the perfect answer. At the very least, they would help him reach a British embassy and they in turn would arrange his flight home.

But even as he started forward, he knew he couldn't do it. First of all, there was Richard. If Matt left the country, he might well be condemning the journalist to death. After all, he was the one they wanted. Not Richard. He couldn't just abandon his friend.

And then there was Pedro. Whatever happened to Matt and however much he hated being there, he had managed to find one of the five. They were meant to stay together. It was as simple as that. Running away wouldn't help anyone. Despite everything, Matt knew he had to see this through.

He stood back and watched as the group walked past, following a woman waving an umbrella. He fell in with them. At least it gave him a little comfort to hear his own language.

"Cuzco has always been known as the holy city," she was saying. "It was certainly holy to the Incas, who made this the center of their empire. They were ruling here in 1533 when the Spanish conquistadors, led by Francis Pizarro, invaded. The Spanish destroyed much of the city and built their own palaces and cathedrals on what was left, but even today you will see a great deal of Inca influence. In particular, you should look at the amazing walls, fitted together without the use of cement. We'll have plenty of chances to examine Inca building methods this afternoon, when we visit the temple of Coricancha. . . ."

Coricancha. That was where Matt had been told to go. He was tempted to follow this woman now — but there was no point. He had imagined something small and hard to find, but it seemed that the temple was a major tourist attraction. And anyway, he was meant to be there on Friday evening at sunset. What day was it now? Matt had no real idea. He had just spent an entire night in a bus. That would make it Wednesday or Thursday. He hardly knew where he was and he had no idea when he'd arrived. In a way, he was just like Pedro: *desplazado*. Utterly displaced.

The woman with the umbrella moved off. The tourists obediently followed. Matt turned to Pedro, who was standing in the square, looking lost. Of course, he had barely been out of Lima in his life and in many ways the city of Cuzco must have been as strange to him as it was to Matt.

"We need to find somewhere to stay," he said.

Pedro looked blank.

"A hotel . . ." Matt added. He knew they couldn't afford one but it was the only word that Pedro would understand.

Pedro shook his head. He looked doubtful.

Matt rubbed a finger and thumb together. The universal symbol for money. "Somewhere cheap," he said.

They walked together out of the square and along a straight, narrow street with a wall about five meters high on one side. Matt knew nothing about Peruvian history or architecture but he guessed that the wall must have been built by the people that the tour guide had been talking about — the Incas. It could have been made as long ago as a thousand years, when they were in command of the city. The stones were huge — each one must have weighed a ton. But at the same time, they were all irregular in shape, with seven or eight edges. Somehow they had all been locked together without cement.

The first hotel Matt and Pedro came to refused to take them. It was a small, rough-looking place filled with students and backpackers, smoking and sipping beer in the open courtyard. Matt crouched in the street beside the door, once again disguising his height, while Pedro spoke to the receptionist — an elderly woman with suspicious eyes. He had money, but she wasn't having any of it. The money, she said, was certainly stolen. Why would two Peruvian beggar boys want to stay in a tourist hotel unless it was to rob the other guests?

The second hotel was the same. At the third, Matt went in and tried to book a room, speaking in English. The owner stared at him in something close to shock — and he could understand why. The language he was speaking simply didn't fit in with his appearance and was drawing too much attention to himself. He had no need to remind himself that the police were looking for him. The fact that Captain Rodriguez had been at the hacienda proved that he was in the pay of Diego Salamanda — if any more proof were needed. Matt had no papers, no identity. If the police got their hands on him a second time, he would disappear for good. He backed away quickly from the receptionist, knowing he couldn't stay.

By now it was late morning. Matt was thirsty, hungry, and exhausted. He could feel the lack of oxygen in the air. Every time he exerted himself, he had to stop for a moment to catch his breath. How high up were they? On the bus, it felt as if they had been climbing for hours.

He looked at Pedro. "Do you want to eat?"

Pedro nodded. *"Estoy muerto de hambre."*

They chose the shabbiest, quietest restaurant they could find, but even so, the owner refused to serve them until they had paid. Once he had their money and knew they wouldn't run away, he took pity on them and served a huge meal of *chicharrones* — chunks of deep-fried pork ribs — and a jug of *chicha*, which tasted sweet and fruity and was some sort of ancient Inca beer.

Matt and Pedro ate in silence. They had no choice. But even so Matt was beginning to feel closer to the other boy — as if the two of them had known each other all their lives and really had no need to talk. A few other tourists came in, but they paid no attention to them, and Matt was able to relax and collect his thoughts.

One of the travelers at the next table was reading a Spanish newspaper. He turned a page, and at that moment everything changed. Pedro nudged him and pointed. Matt turned and saw a photograph of himself — taken by Richard in the middle of York. Matt jolted upright in his chair when he saw the white skin, the neat hair, the smiling face. The picture belonged to another time, another world. He could hardly believe it was him.

And then came the fear. Had the Peruvian police published the photograph to try to track him down? How had they gotten it? He didn't want to draw attention to himself, but he had to know what the newspaper said. He leaned forward. And there it was: a message from the Nexus.

MATT FREEMAN
CONTACT US FOR HELP. CALL US AT ANY TIME.

There was a telephone number printed below.

So someone had finally realized he was missing and had taken steps to find him! But could he trust it? Salamanda owned newspapers. Could he have placed the message there as a trap? Matt quickly read it again. They had called him Matt, not Matthew. That was something. Salamanda wouldn't have known that was the name he preferred. It wasn't much to go on, but Matt realized he had nothing to lose. He would call the number and see what happened next.

He memorized it quickly before the traveler turned the page. The table had a paper tablecloth and he wrote it down in tomato sauce, using a toothpick. As soon as they had finished eating, he tore out the number and hurried into the street.

"We need to find a telephone," he told Pedro.

"*Sí . . . un teléfono.*" Pedro was the one who had seen the photograph. He knew what was going on.

Just about every hotel and café in Cuzco had telephone and Internet facilities. Matt went into the first one he found, threw down some money and made his demand in English. He wasn't worrying about his safety anymore. He was shown into a creaky wooden cabinet where he took out the scrap of torn paper and dialed the number. There was a pause, a dial tone, then . . .

"Matthew? Is that you?" It was Fabian speaking. He sounded exhausted and excited at the same time, and it occurred to Matt that this was a dedicated telephone line. Fabian must have been sitting beside the receiver, waiting for the call.

"Mr. Fabian . . . ?"

"Where are you? How are you? Are you all right . . . ?"

"Yeah. I'm fine."

"I can't believe it's you. We've all been so worried about you. I nearly went crazy when you and Richard didn't show up in Lima. Then Alberto told me what happened. Is Richard with you?"

"No. He's not." Matt felt a sense of relief just talking to Fabian, hearing his voice once again. "I'm okay. But I need your help."

"Of course. We've been waiting for you to ring. You don't need to worry about anything now, Matt. You just need to tell me where you are and how I can reach you."

"I'm in Cuzco."

"Cuzco!" Fabian sounded astonished. "What are you doing there?"

"It's a long story."

"Tell me. And as soon as I put this phone down, I'm on my way. . . ."

• • •

Half an hour later, Susan Ashwood received a telephone call at her home in Manchester, England. It was Fabian, calling from Lima.

"I've spoken to Matthew," he told her. "You won't believe the things that have been happening to him but he's alive and he's all right. He's in Cuzco. Don't ask me how he got there. It's too long a story. But I've already booked a flight and I'll be there this evening. I'm going to bring him in. And there's wonderful news — another one of the five . . ."

The two of them spoke for some time as Fabian filled her in on what Matt had told him. Then he rang off, and Susan Ashwood telephoned Natalie Johnson to pass on the news.

"Matthew is in Cuzco," she said. "He saw the advertisements and telephoned Fabian. . . ."

The two women spoke for about ten minutes.

Shortly after that, Diego Salamanda received a call at his hacienda near Ica. He barely spoke at all, holding the receiver against his ear. The mouthpiece, of course, came nowhere near his mouth. When he did want to talk, he had to slide the receiver down his face.

Eventually, he smiled and hung up. The caller had told him exactly what he wanted to hear.

Now he knew where Matt was, too.

THIRTEEN
Into Thin Air

The next available flight from Lima didn't get in until nine o'clock. Fabian had arranged to meet Matt and Pedro one hour after that, in front of the cathedral in the main square. That gave them the rest of the day to kill until he arrived.

They spent the time walking around Cuzco, trying to keep out of everyone's way. It was a weird experience for Matt. Normally, someone like him would only come here as a tourist — and if he had been dressed differently, that was what people would think he was. He could imagine himself stopping to photograph the long galleries with their stone archways and the bustling shops behind.

But his disguise had put him right at the heart of the city. He had become part of it. At one point, as he and Pedro sat on a step outside a museum, he even found himself being photographed by two Americans. For reasons he couldn't quite understand, he was annoyed to see the expensive zoom lens being focused on him. Before the camera had clicked, he sprang to his feet.

"Why don't you take a picture of someone else?" he snapped at the astonished couple. He knew he wasn't being fair, but he still felt a brief sense of victory as the man and his wife backed away, confused.

Later that afternoon, he and Pedro came upon the temple of Coricancha. In fact, they could hardly have missed it. It was a major tourist attraction, located in the southern part of the city and surrounded by coach buses with a nonstop flow of visitors around the main entrance. Once again there were Inca walls — with a terrace high above, giving panoramic views over the city. There was also a Spanish church on the site. In fact, it had been constructed over it — one building on top of another — as if it had been dropped there from outer space. Why had Micos sent them here? There didn't seem to be any reason, and Matt wasn't prepared to waste any of their money paying to get in.

Even so, he lingered around the entrance and listened as the tour organizers delivered the same lecture to each group of tourists. Coricancha was the ancient word for "golden courtyard." There had once been a great temple with four thousand priests living here. Every wall had been lined with solid plates of gold, and the rooms had been filled with statues and altars . . . also gold. It had been used by the Incas as a religious center and a celestial observatory. Then the conquistadors had come and taken everything. They had melted down the gold, ripped out the altars, and built their own church on the ruins that remained.

Would Fabian bring them here on Friday night? Matt wondered. Was there a chance that Richard might turn up? A guard walked out of the entrance and gestured at Matt and Pedro to move away. Pedro muttered something ugly and guttural in Spanish and tugged at Matt's sleeve. Matt understood. The guard thought they were trying to beg from the tourists. They had no place here. Poor people in Cuzco really had no place anywhere.

As the evening drew in, they walked back to the square and sat on the long step between the cathedral and the fountain. Matt wondered what Pedro was thinking about. He had tried to explain that Fabian was coming, but he wasn't sure how much the other boy had understood. Pedro didn't look happy to him — but then, he hardly ever did. Matt knew how he felt. He had never asked for any of this. He was completely out of his depth. Pedro probably wished he was back in Lima and that the two of them had never met.

At last, the darkness came, and with it Cuzco was transformed into something almost magical. Matt had noticed how strange the light was by day. At night, the sky became a luminous blue with the mountains stretching out, deep black, below. Thousands of orange lights sparkled in the outlying suburbs, and streetlamps glowed all around in the square. After the heat of the day, the evening was cool. The restaurants were filling up, the pavements packed with people in no hurry to go anywhere, like extras on some huge open-air stage.

The police car entered the square just after nine o'clock. Matt noticed it first — a low, white vehicle with a yellow-and-blue stripe and a strip light mounted on the roof. There were two men inside. He watched the car as it cruised slowly along the far side and parked in front of one of the money change shops. The two men didn't get out.

He thought nothing of it. There were police everywhere in Cuzco, just as there had been in Lima. It seemed that their main job was to keep the tourists happy. Tourists were worth millions to the Peruvian economy. They had to feel safe.

But then a second police car joined the first, and Matt began to grow uneasy. They couldn't be looking for him! Apart from Fabian, nobody knew he and Pedro were there. Pedro nudged him, glancing in the direction of the second car. The expression on his face was clear: The police in this country were bad news. The two of them had been moved on plenty of times throughout the day and Matt had no doubt that he and Pedro could be arrested just for sitting here. What was the time? Surely it must be getting close to ten o'clock? He wished Pedro hadn't stolen his watch.

The two police cars and more policemen on foot were entering the square from all sides, moving slowly, seemingly with no particular purpose. What was going on? Pedro was becoming more and more agitated. There was something animal about him now. His eyes were wide and alert. Every muscle in his body seemed to be locked. He was sensing danger, even if he hadn't seen it yet.

"I think we should move," Matt said. *"Vamos!"*

He didn't want to go. Fabian would arrive any minute now. If he could wait just a few minutes longer, the whole ordeal might be over. Getting up, walking, might draw attention to himself. Every fiber of his being screamed at him to stay where he was. While he was sitting down, unnoticed, he was safe. But at the same time, there were more than a dozen policemen in the square now, fanning out, all of them armed. Had the police come by coincidence or did they know Matt was here? Was this just another raid, or were they looking for him?

The question was answered in an instant as the passenger door of one of the police cars opened and a man got out.

It was Captain Rodriguez. He was standing directly under a streetlamp, which cast a glow across his face with its rough, pitted skin and heavy moustache. He looked like a boxer stepping into the ring, and as his eyes swung across the square, Matt knew without any doubt at all that his telephone call to Fabian had been intercepted and that he had walked straight into another trap.

He stood up, forcing himself not to panic. Rodriguez hadn't seen him since the Hotel Europa and didn't know what he looked like now that he was in disguise. There were still plenty of people around. The two of them could just walk away, mingling with the crowd.

Pedro dug his hand into his trouser pocket. When he brought it out, he was holding his rubber slingshot. Matt shook his head.

"Not now, Pedro," he said. "There are too many of them."

Pedro frowned, then seemed to understand. He put the slingshot away again.

The scream of a whistle cut through the air.

It was as if someone had thrown a switch. Suddenly, all the policemen were running toward them as if they had known where they were all along and had simply been playing a game. Another car cut in from behind. Rodriguez was pointing directly at them and shouting. Tourists and travelers stood gaping, afraid, finding themselves caught up in the middle of something they didn't want to see. The friendly face of the country they had come to visit had slipped to reveal the brutality beneath. There were armed police everywhere.

Matt saw at once that all four corners of the square were cut off. The trap had closed in from every side. There were two police cars speeding toward him . . . they would reach him in seconds. That left just one direction — up. The cars couldn't follow him up the steps. He looked round and saw that Pedro had worked this out for himself. He was already halfway up, heading for a group of Europeans, standing together at the top. They'd been about to have their photograph taken in front of the cathedral when the police raid began, but now they were just staring out, slack-jawed. Matt saw Pedro barge through them. Why? He glanced back and understood. Some of the policemen had taken out their guns. Pedro had seen the danger — but at the same time he had guessed that they weren't going to fire anywhere near tourists. He was using the Europeans as a human shield.

Matt joined him, clambering up the last five steps and then across the top, next to the cathedral. The tourists scattered. Someone cried out. Pedro was moving like the wind, and Matt wondered if he would be able to keep up. Already he had discovered something he had guessed all along: It was almost impossible to run in Cuzco. The air was too thin. He couldn't have been going for more than half a minute and his head was pounding, his throat was sore, and he felt as though he was about to faint. He forced himself on, not wanting to be left behind. Pedro was one of the five. Matt couldn't lose him now.

Luckily, Pedro was looking out for Matt. As a police-man swung round the corner, Pedro shouted out a warning. Matt ducked low. There was an explosion and one of the stone steps spat dust. They were shooting at him! Matt felt a tremor of disbelief. Rodriguez had given orders to take them dead or alive.

The gunshot had been a mistake. Now everyone in the square was panicking, running in all directions, desperate to get away. For a moment, the police found themselves powerless. The boys were out of sight. Then something strange happened. The policeman who had fired the shot threw himself backward and lay sprawling. Matt twisted round and saw that the slingshot was in Pedro's hand. He certainly knew how to use it. The policeman had been standing in front of a road that was otherwise unguarded. Matt forced some air into his lungs and set off.

Out of sight. That was the key. Matt knew they had to get under cover. They had to find somewhere to hide. Give them a bit of time and maybe they could work out what to do next. Pedro ran through an open gateway, leading off the street, signaling Matt to follow. Matt did just that and found himself in a rough courtyard with patches of grass growing through the rubble and the dust. There was another market here. Stalls, lit by oil lamps, stood haphazardly against the walls. They were open even at this time of the night, and a few backpackers were wandering idly between them, examining the hats and the ponchos, the rugs, beads, and bags on sale. The great mass of the cathedral rose up behind them.

The two boys didn't stop. They came to a second archway and burst out to find themselves in another street. But this time they were not alone.

A very old Indian woman sat facing them, squatting on

the pavement with a little pile of handmade jewelry. Her hair hung down in two long pigtails, and there was a baby, wrapped in a striped blanket, nestling against her chest. She was looking straight at them, and as they stood there, panting, wondering which way to go, she suddenly smiled, showing yellow teeth that were little more than stumps. At the same time, she pointed toward an alleyway that led off behind her.

Matt wasn't sure what to do. The old woman was behaving as if she knew them. It was almost as if she had been sitting there all evening, waiting for them to come so she could point out the best way. Matt fought to get more air into his system and to keep the dizziness at bay.

"Which way?" he shouted at Pedro.

The old woman raised a finger to her lips. This was no time for a discussion. Once again, she pointed the way. Behind them, they heard shouting. The police had entered the marketplace.

"*Gracias, señora,*" Pedro muttered. He had decided to believe her.

The two of them ran up the alleyway, disappearing into the shadows that pushed in from both sides. Tattered posters hung on the walls, and wooden balconies jutted out over their heads. The street was cobbled, and Matt's rubber sandals were almost torn off his feet as he tried to run.

But was it worth going on? Matt could hear sirens and whistles echoing all over the city. With a heavy heart he knew that he and Pedro were never going to get out of this, no matter how fast they ran. They were two rats in a maze. They could scurry round the streets and passageways of Cuzco until they were exhausted or they could find a building to hide in . . . but it would make no difference. It might take the police all night to find them, but they would do it in the end. Cuzco was surrounded by mountains. There was no way out.

Somewhere, just out of sight, another car pulled up. Boots stamped down on concrete. A whistle blew. Even Pedro was beginning to slow down. Sweat was dripping down his face. It would all be over very soon.

The alleyway led to another narrow street with a T-junction at one end. Pedro started toward it, but almost at once a blue van came skidding to a halt and three policemen piled out. One of them shouted excitedly into a radio while the other two took out their guns and began heading toward them. Matt didn't have the strength to move. His heart was about to burst. He could only watch as the two men approached.

And then it happened again.

Another Indian appeared, stepping out of a doorway, pushing a heavy cart laden with food and drink. He was wearing white trousers and a dark jacket but no shirt. Nor did he have any shoes. Long hair hung down, obscuring most of his face. He stopped in the road, completely blocking it, and it seemed to Matt that he had acted quite deliberately. He had known they were coming and wanted to give them more time. The policeman began shouting. One of them was trying to push past. The Indian nodded and smiled at the two boys. With renewed strength, they set off the other way.

Something was happening in Cuzco. Someone was

trying to help them. First it had been the old woman, now it was the food seller. But who were they? How had they even known that he and Pedro were there? Matt wondered if he was imagining things. And no matter how many people tried to help them, he still couldn't see how they were going to get away.

They turned another corner and suddenly Matt knew where they were. This was one of the most famous streets in the city. Just a few hours earlier, it had been filled with tourist groups and guides. Now it was completely empty, lit only by the glow reflecting from the sky. One side of the street was lined by old Inca walls, ten meters high. Matt recognized the huge stones, slotted so ingeniously together. Pedro was leaning against one of them, straining for breath.

"Which way?" Matt asked.

Pedro shrugged. Either he was too exhausted to talk or he had come to the same conclusion as Matt: There was no way out, so it didn't matter where they went.

They started forward, slowly, making their way down the deserted street. They could hear shouting all around them, disembodied voices flitting like night creatures, everywhere and nowhere. Only one thing was certain. Their pursuers were getting closer all the time.

The street led nowhere. It was blocked by a tall, metal gate that had been swung across the end and locked.

There was no way back. Matt could hear footsteps rushing up behind them and knew that the police were only seconds away. He no longer had the heart to run or to hide. He reached out and rattled the gate. It was too high to climb. Pedro had given up, too. He was looking angry and exhausted — with the bitterness of defeat obvious in his eyes.

"Amigos!"

The voice came from just behind them. Matt turned. Incredibly, there was a young man standing in the street, just a couple of meters away. He was wearing a red-and-mauve poncho, jeans, and a woven hat that had flaps hanging down over his ears. He seemed to have appeared out of nowhere.

And Matt was sure he knew him. For a strange, unnerving moment, he was sure it was Micos. But Micos was dead. So who . . . ?

"Amigos," the man repeated. "Come quickly!"

Amigos. It was one word of Spanish that Matt knew. Friends.

The man gestured. Matt looked past him and saw an incredible sight. Part of the wall had swung open, revealing a secret door with at least seven sides. It was impossible to imagine the hinge mechanism that had made it work, but when the door was closed, it was completely invisible. Matt and Pedro had just walked past it without realizing it was there. Millions of tourists must have done the same. Matt took a step forward. There was a passage inside the wall. He could just make out a narrow corridor, but it ended almost at once in total blackness.

"No." Pedro shook his head. He was afraid.

The man spoke to him quietly and quickly in Spanish, then turned back to Matt. "The police will be here very soon," he said. "If you want to live, you must trust me. Come now. . . ."

"Who are you?" Matt asked.

The man made no reply and Matt understood. He wasn't prepared to talk about this, not now. An amazing secret, this hidden door, had been revealed to them. It had to be closed before the police, or anyone else, saw it.

Pedro was looking at him, waiting for him to make a decision. Matt nodded. The two of them stepped into the wall. The man followed. The door swung shut behind them.

●　　●　　●

Darkness.

Matt couldn't hear anything apart from the sound of his own breathing. He stood in pitch-black, and it occurred to him that he could have died — that death might not be so different from this. He had been cut off from the city of Cuzco the moment the wall closed. There was a slight dampness to the air that clung to his skin, but apart from that he felt nothing. He had to force himself not to panic, to avoid the thought that he might be buried alive.

The man in the poncho turned on a flashlight, and the light sprang out to reveal a narrow corridor with a staircase leading down. They were *inside* the wall. The great stones were on both sides. Where did the steps lead? Matt couldn't even begin to guess.

The light also showed the face of the man who had come to their rescue. Matt had only glimpsed him in the street, and the earflaps of his hat had concealed much of his face. Looking at him more closely, he saw that he did have a very close resemblance to Micos — though without the scar. He was also slightly thinner, with a narrow chin and the beginnings of a beard. He couldn't have been more than twenty-two or twenty-three years old.

"Who are you?" Matt asked. He wondered if his voice would carry out into the street. But that was impossible. The walls were at least a meter thick.

"My name is Atoc," the man replied. His accent was strange. There was a hint of Spanish in it but also something else.

Atoc was the name that Micos had spoken just before he died. He had wanted to get a message to this man. His brother? That would explain why they looked so alike.

"What is this place?" he asked.

"It is an old Inca passage. Very secret. Very few people know."

"Where does it lead?"

"I take you somewhere safe where Salamanda cannot find you. There are friends waiting, but it is far and there is still much danger. Police are looking everywhere. We cannot talk now."

Atoc turned to Pedro and spoke briefly in Spanish. Once again, to Matt's ears, his accent sounded strange. Presumably, he was repeating what he had just said. Pedro nodded. A decision had been made.

"This way," Atoc said. He swung the light at the stairs. "We go down. It will be easier soon."

They began to climb down. Matt tried to count the steps, but after twenty-five he gave up. The walls were very narrow, pressing in on them from both sides, and he could feel the weight of the earth pushing down from above. There was a heaviness in his ears, and the air was getting cold. He could see only a few steps at a time. The flashlight wasn't powerful enough to light much more. But as they reached the bottom, with a second passageway bending round ahead of them, he became aware of a strange, yellow glow coming from somewhere just out of sight. They began to walk forward and after a few steps, Atoc turned off the flashlight. The way ahead was lit, but not by an electric light. Matt turned the corner and gasped.

The passage ran on for as far as he could see, with flames burning in small silver cups, set into the walls about twenty meters apart. They must have been fed by a hidden oil supply. But it was the walls themselves that caught the light, magnified it, and reflected it back. The walls, miles of them, were lined with sheets of what looked like brass but — Matt somehow knew — were actually solid gold.

How much gold was there in the world? Matt had always thought it was precious because it was rare. He remembered what he had heard outside the temple of Coricancha: The Spanish conquistadors had looted the city. They had been mad with greed. They had taken all the gold they could lay their hands on. Or that was what they had thought. But now he could see that they had found only a fraction of what was there. Tons and tons of it had been used to make this incredible roadway far below the city. It was stretching ever farther into the distance, picking up the light from the lamps, turning night into day.

They were not intended to make the journey on foot. Another Indian, dressed like Atoc, was waiting for them with four mules. Matt wondered how the animals could bear to stand here, so far underground, but he supposed they must be used to it. The Indian bowed low as he approached. Matt smiled, feeling increasingly uneasy.

"Please. We must hurry," Atoc said.

Matt and Pedro climbed onto the first two mules. Atoc and the Indian took the next two. There were no saddles, just brightly colored blankets tied underneath. Matt had never ridden an animal in his life and wondered how he was meant to make this one go. But the mule knew what it was doing. The moment all four of them had mounted, it set off at a fast pace, its hooves thudding rhythmically on the soft, earth-covered floor.

One after another, the flickering oil lamps lit their progress. Nobody spoke. Matt noticed that some of the gold panels had designs beaten into them: faces and warrior figures bristling with weapons. After a while, the passage widened and they passed countless treasures lined up against the walls: jars and pitchers, cups and trays, idols and funeral masks — many of them made out of silver and gold. He wondered how long it would take them to reach wherever they were going. The fact that he had no idea where that was only made the journey feel longer. And it was almost impossible to measure the passing of time. All he knew was that they were climbing. The path had been sloping upward almost from the start, although the ceiling felt as heavy as ever and he was sure they were getting no closer to the surface. So they were heading out of Cuzco, into the mountains. That was the only possible explanation.

After at least an hour and possibly as much as two, they suddenly stopped. Despite everything, Matt had been drifting into sleep and he was nearly thrown right over the animal's head. His legs were sore from constantly rubbing against the coarse hair. He added the smell of mule to the many other odors he had picked up since Lima.

"We walk from here," Atoc said.

203

They all dismounted, leaving the animals with the other Indian, who had never spoken, not even to tell them his name. Matt assumed that there must be another exit from the tunnel, some other way to bring the mules into the open air. Ahead of them was another narrow staircase and a lever set in the wall. Atoc raised a finger to his lips and pulled the lever. Matt heard a slight creaking, the turning of a wheel, and guessed that a mechanism like the one that had opened the first wall was being used.

Atoc waited a moment, listening. Somebody whistled, two single notes that sounded like a bird. At once, he relaxed. "We can go up," he said, then repeated it in Spanish for Pedro.

They began to climb. Matt could see a circle ahead of him, lit by a white light that seemed to hang in the far distance. Some sort of tattered curtain hung down. It was only as he passed through that he realized this was the mouth of a cave, surrounded by foliage. The light was a full moon. Matt walked back out into the open, on a hillside high above Cuzco, with two more Indians in ponchos bowing at him.

Pedro joined him and they saluted him, too. Then Atoc appeared. Matt looked back. There was a round hole in the ground, the entrance to the cave. But it was only a couple of meters deep, with a solid back wall. The steps had disappeared. Matt realized that the lever must have been pulled a second time and some sort of huge boulder had rolled into place. The exit from the tunnel was as impossible to find as the entrance.

The two Indians gestured and he followed them away from the edge of the hill and into what looked like the ruin of an ancient stadium, a theater, a fortress . . . or perhaps a mix of all three. There was a flat area, roughly circular, covered by grass and surrounded by gigantic boulders that had been arranged in a zigzagging line. There were three levels to the stadium, so whatever activity had once taken place in the circle could have been witnessed by thousands of people, standing or sitting above. The place was lit by floodlights and there were still twenty or thirty tourists wandering through the ruins. Nobody took any notice of Matt, Pedro, and Atoc. They had come out of nowhere, but Atoc had made sure nobody had seen them arrive.

"This . . . Sacsayhuaman," he told Matt. "Sacsayhuaman means 'Royal Eagle' and this place was a great fortress until the Spanish came. You see the throne of the Inca!" He pointed to the rough shape of a seat that had actually been cut into the rock on the opposite side. There was a girl in a fleece jacket sitting there, having her photograph taken. Atoc frowned in distaste. "Now we leave," he said.

There were a few taxis and a single bus parked in a car park on the other side of the ruin. Matt could see a road twisting back down the hill and into Cuzco. But that wasn't where they were heading. For the second or third time that night, Matt stopped in total amazement. Right in front of them, parked out of sight behind the Inca throne, a helicopter stood waiting for them with two more Indians on guard, looking out anxiously for any sign of the police. Matt could see now how much organization had gone into finding him. From the moment that he had run out of the main square in Cuzco, an invisible net had been drawing in on him, waiting to scoop him out.

"You're not serious," Matt muttered.

"We must go long way," Atoc said.

"Where's the pilot?"

"I'm the pilot."

There were just four seats in the helicopter, two in the front, two behind. The cabin was little more than a glass bubble in a metal frame with the rotors hanging limp above. One of the Indians opened the door. Matt hesitated. But wherever they were going, it had to be better than Cuzco. Captain Rodriguez was there, looking for him. The helicopter would take him out of the city. Maybe it would even take him out of Peru.

But before he could move, he heard the sound he had most dreaded: sirens. The police were on their way, coming to investigate. Someone must have seen the helicopter land. And suddenly, there they were, two cars no bigger than toys, bouncing up the road still far below but getting nearer all the time. Atoc pushed Matt forward. It was definitely time to go.

But Pedro wasn't budging. Matt could see how tense he was, his fists clenched, refusing to move. Pedro turned to Atoc and let loose a torrent of Spanish. Atoc tried to reason with him. Matt remembered how he had felt as they took off from Heathrow. He had been sweating all the way. Pedro would never have flown in his life, so this helicopter had to look to him like some sort of oversize nightmare insect.

The police cars were getting closer. Their headlights seemed to be reaching out in front of them, eager to arrive first. Pedro stayed where he was. He pointed at the helicopter and snapped out a few ugly words. Atoc held up his hands — a gesture of surrender — but at the same time, he spoke again. His voice was soft despite the urgency. The first police car was perhaps a quarter of a mile away.

At last Pedro turned to Matt. *"¿Qué piensas tú?"* he asked.

Matt hoped he'd understood. "It's okay," he said. "I think we should go."

Pedro let out a deep breath. He unclenched his fists, ran forward, and climbed in. Matt could see how much effort it took him. He followed. Atoc climbed into the front seat and punched at the controls. The rotors began to turn.

Matt wondered if they had left it too late. It would be several minutes before the helicopter was ready for takeoff. The rotors were still turning so slowly he could see them. The police cars were close enough now for him to make out the men inside. Pedro wasn't even watching. As the engines began to scream, he went completely white and sat frozen, staring out at the sky. The first police car reached the car park and leaped over the gravel, heading toward them. But then its windscreen shattered and Matt saw that the Indian who had opened the door for them was holding a slingshot, the same weapon that Pedro had used. He had hurled a stone at the car and scored a direct hit. The police car wheeled round and came to a sudden halt. The second police car smashed straight into it, spinning it round. Both police cars stalled and sat still.

The doors opened, and uniformed men tumbled out, pulling guns out of their holsters. The two Indians next to the helicopter turned and ran. Matt wondered what would happen next. They were sitting targets. The rotors still weren't turning fast enough. He glanced round and saw the tourists diving for cover. One of the policemen took aim.

But the rotors had picked up speed. Suddenly the dust rose in a cloud. The policemen disappeared from sight — Matt guessed they must have been blinded. Pedro cried out. The entire cabin rocked as Atoc played with the controls. Then he pushed forward and the helicopter lurched into the air, hovered for a moment, then spun round and flew into the moonlight. Behind them, the great stones of Sacsayhuaman quickly dwindled away.

The policemen cursed and rubbed grit out of their eyes. But by the time they were able to look up, the helicopter had gone.

FOURTEEN
Through the Cloud Forest

There was no view. As the helicopter droned on through the night, Matt was as disoriented as he had been when he'd first entered the wall. The lights of Cuzco had long since faded away behind them, and for a time the moon had been their only guide. But even that had disappeared, swallowed up by clouds so thick it was hard to believe they could actually float. Atoc remained clamped over the controls, his face lit by a soft, green light. The helicopter blades thudded at the air, but sometimes Matt got the impression that they weren't moving at all but had somehow got stuck in the gluey stillness of the night.

Pedro hadn't spoken a word since the takeoff. Nor had he tried to look out the window. His whole body was rigid, his eyes fixed on the pilot as if he couldn't believe he knew how to fly this machine — or might forget at any time. Eventually, he fell asleep and Matt must have followed him, because suddenly he was back at sea, making an altogether different journey, drifting with the tide.

"Do you still think I'm one of the five?" Pedro asked.

"Of course." Matt was surprised by the question. "Why do you ask?"

"I'm a stupid coward. I was too scared to get into the

helicopter. I almost got us caught by the police. I'm still scared now, even though I'm asleep."

Matt shook his head. "You're not a coward," he said. "If you want the truth, I'm afraid of flying, too."

"I saw planes flying out of Lima. When I was doing my juggling, near the airport. I could never understand how anything so heavy could fly. I still don't." Pedro scowled. "You really think I'm one of the five?"

"I know you are. And I'm glad you're with me, Pedro. When I think about it, I've never had a real friend. Not for as long as I can remember."

"I stole your watch!"

"I'll get another. . . ."

They both woke at the same moment. The helicopter had landed.

Matt looked out the window while Pedro stretched and yawned. They had come to a halt in a field in the middle of nowhere. Three oil lamps had been laid out on the grass — Atoc would have been able to see them from the air and had used them to know where to land. But there were no other lights anywhere. Instead, the flames illuminated a line of trees, the edge of what must have been thick jungle. A hand slapped against the helicopter window and Matt started. Atoc, however, had been expecting it.

"Is all right . . . friends," he said.

There were two more Indians waiting for them outside. One of them opened the door and helped the boys to climb down. They were both wearing ponchos and woven hats and kept their heads down as if unwilling to meet the boys' eyes. It was cold outside the helicopter, much colder than it had been in Cuzco. Matt wondered if they had climbed to an even greater altitude. He breathed in. Very little oxygen made its way to his lungs. He was obviously high up. But where? The second Indian hurried forward, holding out ponchos for Pedro and himself. They were beautifully woven, with gold thread forming intricate patterns against a dark green background. Matt slipped his head through the hole in the middle and let the rich material hang around him. He was surprised how effectively the poncho protected him from the chill.

"We stay here tonight," Atoc said. "Travel tomorrow in the light."

"Where are we?" Matt asked.

"This place . . . Vilcabamba." The answer left him none the wiser. "We are in cloud forest," Atoc went on. "Tomorrow we must walk for many hours. Not possible to go in helicopter."

"So where do we sleep?"

"We make ready. . . ."

The Indians led them to the edge of the clearing, where three tents had been prepared. Atoc indicated that the two boys were to share. "You need sleep," he said. "Tomorrow is very hard."

He left them together. The tent was brand-new and there were two sleeping bags rolled out on foam mattresses inside. A battery-operated light hung from the main support. Matt didn't bother undressing. He slipped out of the poncho and rolled it up, using it as a pillow. Then he slid into the sleeping bag. Pedro did the same.

For a brief moment, he thought about Richard. He

wondered if he was being carried even farther away from his friend. And what of Fabian? Was he somewhere in Cuzco, searching for them even now?

There was so much he didn't understand, but he was too tired to think about it now. He was asleep before he knew it.

This time there were no dreams.

• • •

He was woken up by the light trying to break through the fabric of the tent. Pedro was still asleep, his body curled up and his head facing the other way. Matt stretched himself with difficulty inside his sleeping bag. The foam had done little to protect him from the hard ground, and his back and shoulders were stiff. He thought of staying where he was and trying to get back to sleep, but there was no chance of that. He was too uncomfortable — and, anyway, Pedro was snoring. Making as little noise as possible, Matt crawled out of the tent, dragging the poncho with him. Once he was outside, he stood up and put it on.

It was still cold. Dawn had broken, but there was still no sign of the sun. Matt shivered in the morning air as he took stock of his surroundings. The night before, he had got the impression of jungle — thick undergrowth and mountains. But nothing could have prepared him for the sights that were all around him now.

He seemed to be on the edge of the world. The helicopter landing pad had been carved into the side of a fantastically steep hillside. Looking up or looking down, all he could see was green — a spidery tangle of trees and bushes with vines and creepers knotted among them and continuing, it seemed, forever. Atoc had said they had a long walk ahead of them, but Matt couldn't even see where they'd begin. There was no way up. The foliage seemed impenetrable. And yet if they climbed down, they would surely fall into a brilliant green vortex. The area where they were sitting was flat. Everything else was vertical. It was as if the whole world had been tipped onto its side.

Atoc and the two Indians were already awake, putting together a breakfast of bread and cheese. They had lit a small bonfire with a kettle hanging over it, but the water had not yet boiled.

Atoc walked over to him. "Did you sleep all right, Matteo?" he asked. Like Pedro, he was using the Spanish version of his name. "We take food soon. . . ."

"Thank you."

In the daylight, Atoc looked younger and less threatening than he had in the shadows of Cuzco. He also looked even more like the man he had known so briefly as Micos. He had to know.

"There's something I want to ask you," Matt began nervously.

"I will tell you what I can."

"When I was in Lima, I met someone who was very much like you. And he was there again in Ica."

"Micos."

"Yes." Matt wasn't sure how to continue. "Your brother?"

"Yes. Do you know where he is?"

"I'm sorry, Atoc. I'm afraid he's dead."

Atoc nodded slowly as if this was what he had expected to hear. But his dark, brown eyes filled with grief and he stood, completely silent, as Matt told him what had happened at the hacienda.

"I'm so sorry that he died because of us," Matt said.

"But I am glad that if he had to die, it was for you," Atoc replied. He took a deep breath. "Micos was my younger brother. There were two years between us. *Micos* in our language is *monkey*. He was the funny one, always in trouble. *Atoc* is *fox*. I was the one who was meant to be clever. And yet when we were playing once, when I was eight years old, I threw a stone at him and I almost took out his eye. He had a scar . . . just here." Atoc raised a finger and drew a crescent moon next to his eye. "My father took his belt to me for that. But Micos forgave me.

"He wanted to help you, Matteo, because he believed in you. You are one of the five. He will not be sad that he died if he knew that you were safe. So it would be wrong for me to be sad, too. There will be more deaths. Many more. We must grow used to it."

He turned his head and looked into the distance, his eyes focused on something far away.

"Now I shall walk alone for a few minutes," he said. "But when I return, we shall forget what has been said and we will not speak of it again."

He walked away into the undergrowth.

"Matteo . . . !" Pedro had woken up and was calling to him from the tent.

Behind them, a trickle of white smoke from the bonfire rose uncertainly up into the morning sky.

· · ·

After breakfast, the two Indians put out the bonfire and packed up the tents. They had already tied down the helicopter and covered it with a green tarpaulin, camouflaging it in case anyone happened to fly overhead. Matt could see that these people thought of everything . . . although he still wasn't sure who they actually were.

Atoc had eaten with them. Whatever grief he might be feeling, he didn't show it. "We leave now," he said and signaled to one of the Indians who came forward, carrying two new pairs of sneakers. "You cannot walk in those shoes."

Matt gratefully removed the rubber tire sandals he had been wearing since Lima. Somehow he wasn't surprised that the new sneakers fit him perfectly. All of this had been planned. As he pulled them on, he noticed Pedro holding his own pair with a look of complete awe. It occurred to him that the Peruvian boy had probably never owned a new piece of clothing in his life.

When they were both ready, Atoc reached into his poncho and produced a handful of dark green leaves and what looked like two small pebbles. "You put this in mouth," he explained, first in English and then, for Pedro, in Spanish. He wrapped the pebble in the leaves, forming a small bundle. "The leaves are *coca*," he went on. "The stone we call *llibta*. The two mix with saliva in mouth and give you strength."

Matt did as he was told. The coca leaves tasted disgusting and he couldn't imagine how they would work, but there didn't seem any point arguing.

215

They set off. The two Indians went first. Matt followed, with Pedro just behind him, tripping several times as he got used to the new footwear. Atoc went last. Matt had rather hoped that they would be heading downhill, but it seemed that their path was going to be up all the way. The jungle wasn't as impenetrable as it had seemed. Someone, a long time ago, had cut a staircase. The steps were almost invisible, uneven and covered in lichen, but they wove between the trees, twisting up the face of the hill.

"If you need rest, you say," Atoc said.

Matt gritted his teeth. He had walked only a few steps and already he needed to rest. It wasn't the steepness of the slope. The air was even thinner than it had been in Cuzco. If he walked too fast, his head would begin to thump and he would feel the burning in his lungs. The secret was to measure out a careful pace, one step at a time, and not to look up. That would only remind him how far he had to go. He turned the *llibta* over in his mouth. Now he understood why he needed it. He just hoped it would actually work.

The sun climbed higher and so did the heat. Matt could feel the sweat trickling down his back. Everything was wet. Once, he reached out to steady himself against a tree, and his hand sank into it like a sponge. Beads of moisture hung in the air. Water dripped through his hair and ran down the sides of his face. Pedro stopped and took off his poncho. Matt did the same. One of the Indians took them, his face making it clear that he would accept no argument. Matt didn't mind. He was using all his strength just to keep going. He must have already climbed five hundred steps. And the staircase showed no sign of ending.

Something bit him. Matt cried out and slapped his arm. A second later, he was bitten again, this time on the side of his neck. He almost wanted to cry ... or swear ... or scream. How much worse could this journey get? Atoc caught up with him and handed him a cloth filled with some evil-smelling ointment.

"Midges," he explained. "We call them *puma waqachis.* It means ... 'insects who make the puma cry.'"

"I know how the puma feels," Matt groaned. He scooped up some of the ointment and rubbed it into his skin. It mixed instantly with his sweat. Matt felt it trickle down his stomach and around his hips. His clothes were sticking to him like a second skin. Another midge bit him on the ankle. Matt closed his eyes for a moment, then set off again.

They stopped twice for water. The Indian guides had plastic bottles in their backpacks. Matt forced himself to drink only a little, aware that all five of them had to share the same supply. The sun was high above them now and he began to wonder if there was something wrong with his vision. The forest seemed hazy and out of focus. Then he realized that in the heat, all the moisture was turning to steam. Soon he was completely wrapped in a dense white fog, barely able to see the man in front of him.

"Stay close!" Atoc called out. His voice came from nowhere. He could have been on another planet. "Not far now ..."

They emerged from the cloud forest suddenly and unexpectedly. One moment, Matt was fighting his way through the undergrowth, the next he had emerged on the edge of a huge canyon. The sky was clear. A vast mountain range stretched out in front of him, many of the peaks covered in snow. Matt was close to exhaustion. He was soaking wet and had a vicious headache. But even so, he felt a sense of elation. He had never thought mountains could be so huge. Some of them seemed to be touching the edge of space. Looking down, he saw that it was raining in the canyon. But the rain was below him. He had climbed above cloud level.

"You see . . . ?" Atoc pointed to one of the mountains. From where they were standing, it looked a little like a human head. "Mandango," he explained. "The Sleeping God."

Pedro had caught up with Matt. He stood panting on the edge of the abyss. He rasped out a few words in Spanish. Atoc smiled for the first time since he and Matt had spoken. "He says he feels terrible," he translated for Matt. "But you look worse."

"Where now?" Matt gasped. He couldn't believe they had climbed all this way up just to go down again.

"It is not so far," Atoc said. "But take care. It is very far if you fall. . . ."

Atoc wasn't exaggerating. A single, well-defined path led down the side of the canyon. Somehow Matt knew that it must have been cut into the rock face by hand. There was something completely unnatural about it. The path was flat and the surface was almost as polished as the streets of Cuzco. The one thing it wasn't, though, was wide. In places there was barely a meter between the wall and the hideous drop over the side. If Matt had taken one false step, he would have fallen . . . and fallen. He felt as far up as he had been in the helicopter. Perhaps he was that high. He saw a herd of sheep or llamas grazing in the pampas at the very bottom of the canyon. To him, they were no more than pinpricks. There were no trees here to protect them from the sun, and Matt could feel it burning his face and arms. He was nothing in this immense landscape. He could be soaked by the rain or fried by the sun. In his entire life, he had never felt so insignificant.

They walked for more than an hour, descending all the time. Matt could feel the pressure changing in his ears. How long had it been since breakfast? He had no idea, but he knew he couldn't go on much longer. His legs were aching and his feet — despite the new sneakers — were getting blisters. They turned a corner and Matt saw that the path had brought them to a platform of solid rock with steps leading down on the other side. He took a deep breath. It seemed that their journey was over.

They had arrived.

There was a miniature city built, incredibly, on the edge of the canyon. It wasn't a modern city. Parts of it reminded Matt of Cuzco, and he knew at once that it had been built by the same people, surely around the same time.

First, terraces had been cut into the rock. These were the foundation of the city, and there must have been fifty or sixty of them, jutting out of the mountainside like giant shelves. Some of the terraces had been planted with crops, some were dotted with grazing sheep and llamas. The city itself consisted of temples, palaces, houses, and storerooms, all built out of blocks of stone that must have been carried at some time through the cloud forest and over the mountains. A great rectangle of grass ran through the center: a meeting place, a sports ground, the focus of everyday life. Matt knew instantly that there would be no electricity here, no cars, nothing from the modern age. And yet he wasn't looking at a ruin. The city was alive. There were people everywhere. They lived here. This was their home.

"What is this place?" he whispered.

"Vilcabamba!" Pedro replied.

Atoc nodded slowly. "The lost city of the Incas. Many great men search for it. For hundreds of years, they search. But none have found it. Vilcabamba cannot be found. It cannot be reached."

"Why not?" It seemed easy enough to Matt. After all, they had reached it without too much difficulty. The path that had brought them down the side of the canyon must be clearly visible. Anyone could follow it here. "The path . . ." he began.

Atoc shook his head. "There is no path," he said.

"No. What I'm trying to say is . . ." Matt took a couple of steps back and looked round the corner again.

Impossible . . .

The path wasn't there anymore. He couldn't go back the way he had come. The canyon wall was a sheer, vertical drop with no way up or down. The path that they had just taken, which they had walked down for more than an hour, had vanished.

"Do not ask questions," Atoc said. "You have friends who wait for you."

"Yes. But . . ."

The Indian rested a hand on his shoulder and together

the two of them walked round the corner. Pedro and the other men had already gone ahead. Matt saw them walk through a stone archway and into the crowd. At the same time, a man appeared, climbing up the steps toward them. He was in a hurry. And he was white.

The man drew closer and Matt felt a huge surge of pleasure and relief. He shouted out and ran forward.

It was Richard Cole.

FIFTEEN
Last of the Incas

"I can't tell you how glad I am to see you," Richard said. "Everyone's been very kind to me. These people are . . . well, you'll find out for yourself. But ever since that mess in Lima, I've been worrying about you and telling myself we should never have come here. I blamed myself for that and I was afraid I'd never see you again."

"So where are we?" Matt asked.

"This city is called Vilcabamba." Richard shook his head in wonder. "It's one of the great legends of Peru, which is to say it's not even meant to exist! It's a bit like El Dorado. A whole lot of explorers have looked for it. Some of them thought they'd found it. And here we are, right in the middle of it! Amazing!"

Richard had taken Matt to the small, stone-built house on one of the upper terraces of the city, where he had been living. They were sitting in the main room, a single living space with two beds, a sofa, and a multicolored rug spread out over the stone floor. Two of the walls were lined with windows. These were strangely shaped, narrower at the top than at the bottom, like cut-off triangles. Matt had seen the same design all over Cuzco. There was no glass, no electricity, no running water. At night, it would be lit by candles.

There was a fast-flowing stream, a tributary of the River Chamba, on the other side of the city. The toilets and bath houses were all located here.

The two of them had been given lunch: a large bowl of something called *locro*, a mixture of meat and vegetables somewhere between a soup and a stew. They were on their own. Pedro had gone off with Atoc — presumably to rest in one of the other houses. Matt was glad to have a bit of time with Richard. Just being with him reminded him of the normal life he'd once had.

Matt told his story first, beginning with his meeting with Pedro, his time at Poison Town, the escape from Salamanda's hacienda. Then there was the journey to Cuzco, the chase through the streets at night, and finally his arrival here. The two of them had been given a jug of beer — the same stuff that Matt had tried in Cuzco. Richard had drunk it all by the time he had finished.

"So this boy, Pedro, is one of the five," Richard said.

"Yes."

"And you talk to him in your dreams."

"That's right."

Richard sighed. "You know what really worries me? I believe you! Six months ago, if anyone had told me all this, I'd have laughed in their face." He thought for a moment. "Does Pedro have . . . you know . . . any special powers? Can he see into the future or anything like that?"

"No. He's very ordinary. And he doesn't want to be involved."

Richard's story was more straightforward. After being seized on the way from the airport, he had been taken to a room in Lima where he had come face-to-face with his kidnappers. Matt knew who they were by now. One was Atoc. The other had been Micos.

"I was feeling pretty pleased with myself because you'd got away," Richard said. "I figured they wouldn't be interested in me and they'd just let me go. But then they explained to me that they were on our side. They'd tried to intercept us before we walked into a trap. The police were at the hotel."

"I know." Matt shivered. "I met them."

"Atoc and the others always knew we'd come to Peru. They were waiting for us from the very start. The trouble was, so were Salamanda and his people. The Incas had to try the kidnap thing because that was the only way they could get hold of us. Of course, they weren't too pleased that you'd got away. In fact, they've been looking for you ever since. They've had people out all over the country. As for me, they took me by car to a private airport, then by plane to Cuzco, and finally by helicopter to the middle of nowhere. Just like you. I got bitten to death in the cloud forest and I nearly threw up coming down into the canyon. Did I ever tell you that I don't have a head for heights?"

"No."

"Well, I've been here ever since. They've looked after me, and the food's good. But like I said, I've been worrying about you. I couldn't believe it when they told me they'd found you in Cuzco. I'd love to have seen that secret passage. One day maybe you can show me. Perhaps on the way out . . ."

"Who are they, Richard?" It was the one thing Matt still

224

didn't understand. "They say this is the lost city of the Incas. But there aren't any Incas anymore, are there?"

"There aren't meant to be. Most of them died out." Richard lifted the jug of beer, realized it was empty, and put it down again. "These people are the only survivors, the descendants of the tens of thousands killed all those years ago. And this city is like their secret headquarters. Did you notice the path along the edge of the canyon? They have a way of making it disappear after you've walked down it. No planes can fly over here because of the surrounding mountains and the weird air currents. Nobody knows about this place apart from the people who live here — and you and me, now that we're their guests."

"And they want to help us."

"That's right. You've got Diego Salamanda on the one hand. At least this time we know who the bad guy is. And you've got the Incas on the other."

"Why can't they stop him?" This was something Matt didn't understand. "They know who he is. They know where to find him. . . ."

"What do you want them to do, Matt? Murder him?"

Matt shrugged. "It doesn't seem like a bad idea."

"They'd have to get to him first, and he's well protected."

"They could go to the police."

"He owns the police. Diego Salamanda is one of the most powerful men in Peru. What does he call his company? Salamanda News International. He should call it Salamanda International News because that would spell SIN, which sounds right to me. Salamanda's worth billions, and if he went out of business, half the country would go with him. News, telecommunications, software . . . only last week he sent an enormously expensive satellite into space, paid for out of his own pocket. He plays chess with the president. They do it over the telephone, and Salamanda is the one who put in the direct line."

"If Salamanda is so rich and so successful, why does he want to open the gate? What's in it for him?"

"I don't know, Matt. Maybe the Old Ones can shrink his head back to normal for him. Maybe they can give him eternal life. Why did the last lot want to open Raven's Gate? If you ask me, they're all mad."

Richard fell silent. Someone had begun to play panpipes outside the house. The notes hovered eerily in the air. Matt looked out the window, across the canyon. He had forgotten how high up they were. The ground fell away forever.

"You said the Incas were waiting for us," he said. "How did they know we were coming?"

"Yes. I asked Atoc about that. I wish I could tell you they read about it in the newspapers, but it's a bit more complicated. The Incas know more or less everything that's happening in Peru. They've got people everywhere. But there's something else. They use magic."

"Magic?"

"They have these people — they call them *amautas*. They're like sorcerers . . . a bit like dear old Miss Ashwood. They know about the Old Ones. And they know about you. You may meet one of them later. He's an old chap. I've spent a bit of time with him. I think he's about a hundred and twelve."

It took Matt a moment to absorb all this. "They knew I was coming," he said. "But so did Salamanda. Who do you think told him?"

"I've been thinking about that. I'm afraid it looks as if it was someone in the Nexus."

"That's what I thought. I rang Mr. Fabian, but the police arrived before he did."

"Well, I don't have any real idea, but if it was anyone, Tarrant's the one I'd most suspect. Do you remember him? He was the policeman who gave us the false passports. That's what caused half the trouble. Having fake passports turned us into criminals . . . and they were his idea."

"So what happens now?"

Richard thought for a moment. "We can't get in touch with the Nexus again, that's for sure. We can't trust them. So it looks like we're on our own."

"Again . . ." Matt yawned, suddenly tired.

"You'd better get some sleep," Richard said. "You must be exhausted. Then you'd better wash and change those clothes. I have to say, I hardly recognized you when I saw you just now. You look ridiculous!"

"Thanks."

"And then you can introduce me to your friend, Pedro. We've all got to be in the main square at sunset." Richard smiled. "The Incas are having a party and we're invited!"

•   •   •

Matt slept until the middle of the afternoon. When he woke up, Richard took him to the bath house — a series of wooden cubicles in a stone building with a jet of water pouring through a hole in the wall in a nonstop stream. The water was ice cold but sparkling clean. It couldn't wash off the dye, so Matt felt he came out looking much as he had when he went in. But he was certainly refreshed.

He had been given new clothes to wear. The Indians who lived in Vilcabamba wore clothes that were a strange mix of the ancient and the modern, with brightly colored hats and ponchos above and jeans and sneakers below. When he came out of the shower, he was given his own poncho — a deep red with a green diamond pattern around the border. The strange thing was, he didn't feel self-conscious wearing it. Perhaps he had changed so much in the last few days that he no longer had any idea who he really was.

Then he and Richard were taken to a grand building, twice the size of any of the others, at the very heart of the city. All around them, there were Indians preparing the feast to come, setting up wooden tables, building fires, and carrying out trays of food and drink. The sun had turned red and was already below them, sinking fast behind the mountains. It was a new experience for Matt to see the sun this way. Normally he would look up at it. Now he seemed to be above it and he could actually see it slipping over the edge of the world.

The building they were entering was a palace. Matt knew it without being told. There were two guards, bare-legged, ceremoniously dressed in tunics and carrying golden spears — one on each side of the door. More guards lined the passageway inside. And there, in front of them, was a throne, mounted on a platform, and on it a man wearing a long robe with a headdress and golden discs attached to his ears. He wasn't much older than Richard, but there was a sense of confidence and seriousness about him that made him look somehow ageless. Matt stopped and bowed. The Incas, it seemed, had a prince. And this was surely him.

"You are welcome, Matteo," the man said, speaking in perfect English. He had the same accent as Atoc: foreign, but not Spanish. In fact, his first language was Quechua. It was what his people had spoken before the Spanish arrived. "My name is Huascar and I am very glad to meet you at last. I have been waiting for you a long time. My people have been waiting even longer. Please, sit down."

There were four low stools set out in front of the throne. Richard and Matt sat down. A moment later, Pedro and Atoc entered through a side door. Pedro had also been given fresh clothes. His poncho was a soft blue. He bowed to the Inca prince and took his place beside Matt. Atoc sat on the fourth stool.

"You are also welcome, Pedro," Huascar continued. He was still speaking in English for the benefit of Richard and Matt, but Atoc whispered quietly in Pedro's ear, translating. "We have very little time remaining to us and there is a great deal to discuss."

He raised a hand, and servants stepped forward carrying four golden goblets of red wine that they set down on the floor in front of the guests. The Inca drank nothing himself.

"Five hundred years ago," the prince resumed, "one of the mightiest empires ever built fell and died. With the

229

coming of Francisco Pizarro and the conquistadors from Spain, everything my people had created was destroyed. Our cities were burned down, our gold looted, our temples desecrated, my ancestors ruthlessly killed. So began for us the time of the great darkness.

"Today the glory of the Inca world is almost forgotten. Our cities are ruins, the broken pieces laid bare for tourists. Our art is locked away in museums. Only this place, Vilcabamba, remains undiscovered. Only here can we live as we once did. We are the last of the Incas."

He fell silent. Atoc whispered for a few seconds more, then stopped. Pedro nodded.

"But we haven't lost our strength." The Inca looked Matt in the eyes. "You have seen only a small part of our secret world, a fraction of the gold we hid from the Spaniards. We do not live here all the time. We cannot hide from modern life. But we have come here from all over Peru and South America to show ourselves to you. Because, when the final struggle comes, you must know that you can call on us.

"This is more than a new millennium. We are on the threshold of a new world and we believe that one day we will be able to regain our rightful place. The Incas will live again with our own laws, our own justice, our own peace. But we will have to fight for it — and our enemies today are more deadly than the conquistadors ever were. We know about the Old Ones. We've *always* known about them. They mean to destroy the new world before it is even born. And they are here in Peru."

Again, the Inca raised his hand. At once, another man entered the throne room, walking with the help of a stick.

He was wearing a poncho that was as gray as he was. His entire body was hunched over. His arms and legs were all bone. Richard nudged Matt. This was the *amauta* he'd been talking about.

"Tell them," Huascar commanded.

"Before the sun has risen and set three times, the Old Ones will break through the gate that was created in Peru before the world began," the *amauta* said in English. His voice was surprisingly strong. "I have read the signs in the sky and on the land. The birds fly where they should not fly. There are too many stars in the heavens at night. A terrible disaster is a heartbeat away, and perhaps all our hopes will come to nothing. One boy will stand against the Old Ones and alone he will fall. Maybe he will die. This I do not know.

"But not all will be lost. Five defeated them at the dawn of time, and five will defeat them again. That is the prophecy. This boy is one of the five. This boy also." He pointed first at Matt, then at Pedro. "The others will follow and when the five come together, they will have the strength to defeat the Old Ones. Then the last great war will take place and the new world will begin."

He fell silent.

"You say the gate will open three days from now," Richard muttered. "Do you know where it is?"

The Inca shook his head. "We have searched for it. We have never found it."

"Then where do you suggest we go next?" Richard hadn't meant to sound rude, but he was aware that he had been. He flinched, wondering if he was about to find out what it felt like to have two meters of golden spear in his back.

231

But the Inca didn't seem offended. His face hadn't changed. He gestured at Atoc, who took out a sheet of paper and laid it in front of them. Matt recognized it at once. It was the page that Pedro had taken from the photocopier. It had been in the back pocket of his jeans. He wondered when Atoc had taken it.

"This the only clue," Atoc said.

"What does it say?" Matt asked. He had been wondering about the strange verse ever since Pedro had found it.

Atoc translated the words out loud and Matt felt his heart sink.

> *On the night when the white bird flies*
> *Before the place of Qolqa,*
> *There will the light be seen,*
> *The light that is the end of all light.*

And below that, the two words — *INTI RAYMI* — and the blazing sun.

The sheet of paper had obviously been important enough for Salamanda to want to copy it. But why did its message have to be so complicated? Matt had thought the lines would tell him what he needed to know about the gate. They told him nothing at all.

The old *amauta* shook his head. *"Inti Raymi . . ."* he said.

"Inti Raymi is the most important day in the Inca calendar," the prince explained. "It is the time of the summer solstice when the sun is at its farthest point south of the Equator. June twenty-fourth. Today is June twenty-first."

"What about the place of Qolqa?" Richard asked. "Do you know where that is?"

232

The *amauta* glanced at the Inca ruler but he knew the answer already. "Qolqa is a Nazca word," he said.

"They were talking about Nazca," Matt said, excitedly. "Salamanda and the others. They said they were looking for a platform in the Nazca desert."

"The pictures on this paper would very much indicate the desert," the Inca agreed. "But that is on the other side of Peru, back where you've come from. We must give serious thought to what we do next. This page may have told Salamanda what he needs to know, but if so, it can tell us, too. There is a professor who lives in Nazca and who has made many studies of the area. If there is anyone in the country who can make sense of this, she can. I will speak with her tonight."

"Are you on the phone here?" Richard asked.

Huascar smiled for the first time. "This is an ancient city," he said. "We are very remote. But this is still the twenty-first century. We have mobile phones and we even have a satellite connection to the Internet. Please, try not to think of us as primitives."

He stood up.

"My people wish to see you," he said. "The fact that two of the five are with us is a cause for celebration, no matter what the future may bring." He raised his hands. "Let the feast begin."

• • •

Night had fallen once again and the stars had come out in their millions. The entire city of Vilcabamba was filled with lights and music, the thin wail of the panpipes

233

echoing above the deeper beating of the drums. Several bonfires had been lit and there were pigs turning on spits, chickens and lambs baking in clay pots, great chunks of pork on skewers, and bubbling cauldrons of stew. The air carried the smell of burning fat and the sparks leaped up and crackled.

There were at least five hundred people — men, women, and children — in the sacred plaza. This was the rectangle of grass around which everything else had been built. More people looked down from the platforms and terraces above. Many of the Incas had put on their ceremonial clothes. There were headdresses made of feathers and gold, brilliantly colored robes, gold collars and bracelets, golden shields and swords, and gold jewelry, fabulously carved in the shape of pumas, crouching warriors, and gods. Some of the people were dancing. Many were eating and drinking. All of them wanted to see Matt and Pedro, to greet them, and to shake their hands.

Matt was sitting with Richard and Pedro. He had introduced them to each other before the feast had begun.

"I'm really glad to meet you, Pedro," Richard had said. "Thank you for looking after Matt."

Pedro nodded, although Matt wondered if he had really understood.

The night drew on. The music became louder and the wine and beer flowed faster. Matt noticed Richard emptying yet another goblet — but he himself had drunk more beer than was probably good for him. And why not, he thought? For just one night he was safe, among friends. He remembered what the *amauta* had said. The gate would open in three days. One boy would stand against the Old Ones and one boy would fall. Would it be him or Pedro? Or had the *amauta* been talking about someone else? Whatever the answer, Matt knew that this might be his only chance to relax and enjoy himself before he was plunged back into the dangers that lay outside. Richard had already told him they were going to leave the next day.

Then the music stopped and the crowd grew silent and the prince of the Incas stepped out onto a terrace in front of his palace. He spoke once again in English, and although he didn't raise his voice, the words rang out for all to hear.

"This is how the Inca world began," he exclaimed. "This is the story that has been passed down through the generations. . . ."

He paused. Somewhere a baby cried until its mother shushed it.

"According to our ancestors, a long time ago there was only darkness. The land was bare and the people lived like animals. Then the father of all things — we call him Viracocha, the Sun — decided to send his son down to teach the people how to live properly, how to cultivate the fields and build houses for themselves.

"And that is how Manco Capac came into the world. He rose out of the waters of Lake Titicaca, son of the Sun, the first of the Incas. Manco traveled across South America until at last he came to a valley near Cuzco. Here he plunged a gold rod into the earth, for this was the place where he had decided to found the Inca Empire.

"For many years, he ruled wisely and strongly before returning to the heavens. In that time, one image — and

235

only one — was made of him. It was engraved on a great circle of gold. This treasure, more precious to us than any other was called the Sun of Viracocha. When the conquistadors came, it was hidden away and nobody has seen it since, though many have tried to find it."

He raised a hand. On the far side of the plaza, two lines of soldiers moved forward, holding flaming beacons. Then eight more Incas appeared, bowing under the weight of a great litter. Something flat and circular rested on the top, covered by a cloth. All around the city, heads turned silently to follow it. The bearers set it down on the grass, just in front of the table where Matt and Pedro were sitting.

"Why do we celebrate today?" the Inca called out. "Look on the face of Manco Capac and you will understand."

The cloth was removed.

For a moment the golden disc dazzled Matt and he was unable to see. It seemed to shine with a light of its own. Resting on its side, the disc was almost as tall as he was. It had been fashioned like a sun, with golden flames twisting round its rim. Matt blinked. Gradually, he was able to make out a face engraved on the surface. It was a face that he recognized, but of course that was impossible. The image had been made more than a thousand years ago. He heard Richard let out a gasp. Next to him, Pedro stood up, backing away, his face filled with terror and disbelief.

The two faces were the same.

There could be no mistake.

The disc showed a picture of Manco Capac, founder of the Inca Empire. But Pedro was also looking at a portrait of himself.

SIXTEEN
Professor Chambers

They met the Inca prince the next morning — the four of them sitting cross-legged once again in front of his throne. Richard, Matt, and Pedro were to leave before midday.

"I have spoken to Professor Chambers," Huascar said, "and she has agreed to see you. I'm afraid it means another long journey for you, all the way back to the western coast. The professor lives in Nazca. Atoc has asked me if he can go with you there."

"I must finish what my brother began,"Atoc said.

The Inca gazed at them for a moment, and Matt wondered if there wasn't a tinge of sadness in his eyes. "We will meet again one day at Vilcabamba," the prince went on. "But what is important now is that you are safe. Salamanda may have the police and much of the government on his side, but my people are everywhere, and now that we have found you, we will watch over you. Is there anything you wish to ask?"

Richard and Matt exchanged a glance. They had so many questions in their heads. How could a thousand-year-old image so resemble Pedro? One of them was going to be hurt, perhaps killed, at the gate. But which one? And — for Matt, the most burning question of all — if the Old Ones were going to break through the gate as the Inca had prophesied, was there any point even trying to stop them?

But neither of them spoke. Somehow Matt knew that there were no easy answers. He felt as if he had fallen into a fast-flowing river. If he struggled or tried to get out, he would waste his strength and drown. All he could do was swim with the current and see where it took him.

The Inca stood up and raised his hands, palms forward. "I wish you a safe journey and success," he said. "May the spirit of Viracocha go with you."

The audience was over. Richard, Atoc, Matt, and Pedro stood up, bowed, and began to leave. But it wasn't quite over yet.

"Señor Cole," the Inca called out. "I would like, if I may, to have one last word with you? But in private . . ."

Richard stopped. "Don't worry," he whispered to Matt. "If he wants me to stay behind in Vilcabamba, the answer's no."

He waited while Matt and Pedro left. The Inca walked down to him. The *amauta* was also there. Richard hadn't seen him enter the palace.

"What are you thinking?" the Inca asked.

"I'm thinking that one day I'll write about all this," Richard said. "Maybe you'll try to stop me, but I will, anyway. What difference will it make? Nobody will believe me. When I look back, I may not believe it myself."

"Let me ask you this question. Why do you believe the boy was chosen?"

"Matt?" Richard shrugged. "He's one of the five. . . ."

"And Pedro, too. But why you?"

"Was I chosen?" Richard couldn't help smiling. "The way I see it, Matt just happened to stumble into my office in

Greater Malling. If I hadn't been there that day, I wouldn't even have met him and it would be someone else standing here now. Kate or Julia. They both worked at the newspaper. Maybe it would have been one of them."

"No, Mr. Cole. You are wrong. You also have a part to play in this adventure, and that part was written for you long before you were born."

"Are you saying I have no choice?"

"We all have choices. But our decisions are already known."

The Inca held out a hand, and the old Indian, the *amauta*, produced a small leather bag with two drawstrings so that it could be worn across the shoulder or around the neck. "I have a gift for you, Mr. Cole," the Inca said. "Do not thank me, because one day, I assure you, you will curse me for giving it to you. But nonetheless it is yours. It was made for you."

The *amauta* opened the bag and handed Richard a golden object, about fifteen centimeters high. Richard found himself holding a statue of a god. At least, that was what it looked like at first. It was an Inca figure with staring eyes and a grim-looking face, its arms folded across its chest. It was standing on top of a triangle that tapered down to a sharp point. The whole thing was made of solid gold, studded with semiprecious stones; jade and lapis lazuli. Richard had no idea how old it was but guessed it must be worth thousands of pounds.

Then he realized how he was holding it. Quite instinctively, he had let it rest in the palm of his hand with the point jutting out. It wasn't just a statue. It was some sort of knife.

239

"We call this a *tumi*," the Inca explained. "It is a sacrificial knife. The edges of the blade are not sharp, but the point is. You must look after it and keep it safe."

"It's beautiful," Richard said. He remembered the Inca's warning. "Why wouldn't I want to have something like this? And what do you mean when you say it was made for me?"

"This *tumi* has another name," the Inca said. He wasn't answering Richard's questions — but then, it occurred to Richard, he never did. "It has always been known as the invisible blade. You can see it, but it cannot be found. When you carry it with you, nobody will notice it is there."

"How about in airports?" Richard was thinking of the metal detectors. They'd go crazy if he tried to walk through with this.

"You can take it wherever you wish. No policeman or security person will ever find it on you. It is part of you now. And one day you will find it has a use."

"Well . . . thanks." Richard reached out and took the leather bag. He dropped the knife in and closed it. He was surprised how light it all was. "Thank you for helping us. And thank you for finding Matt."

"Good luck, Mr. Cole. Look after Pedro and Matteo. They have need of you."

Richard turned and walked out of the palace. The prince of the Incas and his *amauta* watched him until he had gone.

• • •

The helicopter took them to Cuzco, where a five-seater Cessna plane was waiting to carry them on the longer leg of

240

the journey to Nazca. Matt was amazed how smoothly every-thing had been organized. There were no passports needed, no travel documents. They simply landed at Cuzco's airport, walked across the tarmac, and took off again. Not one offi-cial so much as glanced in their direction. It seemed that the Incas still had plenty of influence in Peru — and that while Matt was with them, he would be safe.

The flight took three hours. Pedro seemed more com-fortable in the plane than he had in the helicopter. He had barely spoken since the golden disc had been shown to them in Vilcabamba, and Matt wondered what was going on in his head. In the seat next to him, Richard was also unusually quiet. He hadn't told Matt what the Inca prince had said to him. Matt had decided not to ask, but obviously it hadn't been good news.

Atoc had flown the helicopter, but on the plane he was just a passenger, sitting on his own at the back, deep in thought. The pilot of the Cessna was behind the controls, almost completely invisible in a leather jacket, flying hel-met, and goggles. He had said nothing as they came on board and nothing during the flight, but suddenly he called out, shouting to make himself heard above the noise of the engine. Atoc leaned across the aisle.

"Look out of windows," he said. "We pass over the Nazca Lines."

The plane dipped, dropping ever lower, as if about to land. Matt felt his stomach rise. They were well below the level of the clouds, flying over a flat, empty desert and he wondered what he was meant to see. The Nazca Lines? There didn't seem to be anything here.

And then he caught his breath.

There was a line, drawn in the sand, running dead straight for as far as his eye could see. It must have been carved in the earth and it couldn't have been done by chance. It was too precise. Next to it, he saw a shape, a huge rectangle, narrower at one end than the other, at least a mile long. A runway? No. Like the line, it had simply been drawn in the ground.

"Over there . . ." Richard said, leaning across him.

There were more lines, running in every direction, crossing over one another, all as straight as arrows. Matt had never seen anything like it. The whole desert was nothing less than a fantastic doodling pad on a gigantic scale. He couldn't imagine how it had been done or when. Nor did he understand how the lines had survived when surely the first puff of wind should have blown them away.

The pilot called out to them again and the plane tilted and curved. Now Matt saw pictures, even more incredible than the lines. The first showed a hummingbird. It wasn't drawn naturalistically, but even so, it was unmistakable, with a long, pointed beak, wings, and a tail. Matt tried to work out its size. It was hard to say, but if he could see it so clearly this high up, it had to be at least a hundred meters long.

One by one, a fantastic menagerie of creatures appeared on the surface of the desert as the plane passed directly overhead. There was a monkey with a spiraling tail, a whale, a condor, and a huge spider with a bloated body and eight legs reaching out. Matt recognized the spider. It was identical to the one he had seen on the page copied from Salamanda's diary.

The drawings were simple, almost childlike. But no

child could possibly have produced them on this scale. Each creature must surely have been the work of dozens of men. And there was something very precise about the way each one had been executed. The legs of the spider, for example, were mirror images of each other, as were the wings of the bird. Every line was straight. Every circle was perfectly formed. It was obvious even at first glance that the entire tapestry had been produced with mathematical precision.

A single road — the Pan-American Highway — ran through the center of the desert, actually dissecting some of the lines. It was completely straight, too, but next to the drawings it appeared cold and lifeless. A piece of modern vandalism, cutting through a work of ancient art.

The pilot turned in his seat, pulling off his helmet and goggles. And that was when Matt saw that he wasn't a man but a woman, about fifty years old, with a square, rather plain face and long, almost colorless hair. She wore no makeup and it would have done little good if she had. Long exposure to sun and desert winds had wrinkled her skin beyond hope. But she had lively, bright blue eyes. She was smiling.

"So what do you think?" she called out.

Nobody spoke. They were all too surprised.

"I'm Joanna Chambers," the woman said. "I heard you wanted to see me so I thought I'd come and collect you myself." The plane shuddered, caught in an air pocket, and briefly she returned to the controls. Then she turned round again. "They told me you've come to Peru looking for a gate," she went on. "Well, if there really is such a thing — if it exists and it's about to be opened — you'd better take a good look. Five hundred square kilometers of some of the emptiest, driest desert in the world. That's where your gate is to be found."

• • •

Professor Chambers lived about a mile from the small, pretty airport that mainly served tourists wanting to visit the Nazca Lines. She had one of the most beautiful houses Matt had ever seen; a low, white building with a green-tiled roof and a broad veranda shaded by a colonnade. It had been built in a garden the size of a park, with llamas wandering freely across the lawn and dozens of birds filling the air with color and song. A low, white wall surrounded it but there was no gate, no guards. Everything about the place suggested that visitors were always welcome.

Richard, Matt, Pedro, and Atoc were sitting in the dining room, eating a late lunch of cold meat and fried yucca chips — which were like potato, only sweeter. The room had a bare tiled floor and a fan turning slowly above. It led directly onto the veranda. The professor was at the head of the table. Now that Matt could examine her more closely, he saw that she was a large, rather masculine woman, though not as unattractive as he had first thought. She looked like the sort of woman who should have been teaching gym at an expensive girls' school. She had changed into white trousers and a baggy white shirt tucked in at the waist. She had a bottle of iced beer in one hand, a thin cigar in the other. The smell of its smoke hung around them.

"I'm very pleased to meet you," Chambers said. "You're welcome to my house."

"Nice place," Richard muttered.

"I was fortunate to be able to buy it. I've made a certain amount of money out of writing books. About Peru — and in particular the Nazca Lines."

"What are the Nazca Lines?" Matt asked.

Chambers sucked on her cigar and the tip glowed an angry red. "I find it astonishing that you haven't heard of them," she remarked. "They just happen to be one of the great wonders of the ancient world. I'm afraid it's all part of this dumbing-down. English schoolchildren! They don't seem to teach you anything these days."

"I haven't heard of them, either," Richard said.

"Bizarre!" Chambers swallowed smoke the wrong way and burst into a fit of coughing. She took another swig of beer and sat back in her chair. "Well, I'm not going to give you a history lesson. Not yet, anyway. First I want to know about you. I got a telephone call from a very special friend. Apparently, you've been to Vilcabamba?"

Nobody said anything. They hadn't realized how much she knew.

"I'm green with envy!" Chambers exploded. "I know that the Incas survived. They consider me their friend and I've spoken with them frequently. But I've never been to their lost city. As far as I know, nobody has — unless they've had pure Inca blood . . . apart from you." She nodded at Matt and Pedro. "They must think very highly of you. I can assure you, it's a great honor."

"They are gatekeepers," Atoc muttered. He seemed offended by the way Chambers had spoken.

"Gatekeepers! Yes, of course! Two of the five! The Old Ones . . ."

"You know about that, too?" Richard asked.

"I know a great deal about a great many things, Mr. Cole." She reached forward and took a grape from a bowl, then flicked it out of the window. A large tropical bird swooped down and caught it. "And yes, I had heard stories about the Mad Monk of Cordoba and this alternative history of his. I was never sure whether to believe it or not. But now that these children have turned up, I suppose I'd better! Now what about this page of yours? The one from the diary?"

Matt still had it in his pocket. He took it out and gave it to her. She read it briefly, once, then again. "Well, some of this is fairly straightforward," she said. "The place of Qolqa. *Inti Raymi* . . . that's only two days from now. Doesn't leave us a lot of time. I'm not sure about this white bird, though. It could be a condor, I suppose. . . ."

"What about a swan?" Matt said.

"A swan? What makes you think of that?"

"I heard Salamanda talking about a swan," he explained. He could have mentioned his dream but decided not to. "He said to be in position. At midnight."

"Are you *sure*?"

"Yes."

Professor Chambers had irritated Matt and she saw it. "I'm sorry," she said. "It's just that it seems so unlikely. There's a condor and a hummingbird in the Nazca desert. You saw them today. But there's no swan. As far as I know, there are no swans in Peru."

"That's what he said," Matt insisted.

"What about the rest of the poem?" Richard asked.

"Well, the whole page refers to the Nazca Lines. There's no doubt about that. The place of Qolqa, for example." She stopped herself. "There's no point talking about the Nazca Lines until you know what they are, so I'm going to have to give you a history lesson after all. It would actually take me a week to describe them to you and even then I would only scratch the surface. But we don't have a week. And anyway, young people these days have no concentration. So let me try and put it as simply as I can."

Professor Chambers got up and helped herself to another beer, flicking the cap off with a penknife. Matt was almost surprised that she hadn't used her teeth.

"There are all sorts of mysteries in the world," she began. "Even now, in the twenty-first century. Stonehenge. The Pyramids. Ulure in Australia. There are all sorts of places and things — some of them man-made, some of them natural — that science can't explain. But if you ask me, the Nazca Lines are the biggest mystery of the lot.

"Let's start with the Nazca desert. It's huge. It's hot. And it's empty. And about two thousand years ago, the ancient Indians of Nazca decided to trudge out here and draw a series of extraordinary pictures in the ground. They did this by removing the darker stones from the surface of the desert and exposing the lighter soil underneath. There's almost no rain in Nazca and very little wind. That's how the lines have survived.

"Are you with me so far?"

She glanced at Atoc, who was rapidly translating for Pedro. He nodded.

"Good. Well, some of these pictures are very beautiful.

247

You saw them from the plane. There are animals — a whale, a condor, a monkey, a hummingbird, and a huge spider. And there are all sorts of triangles, spirals, and star shapes as well as hundreds of perfectly straight lines, some of them stretching for up to twenty-five miles."

She took a quick swig of beer.

"Now, this is where the mystery begins. The Nazca Lines can only be seen from the air. In fact, they were only discovered in 1927 when one of the first airplanes in Peru flew over them. I wish I'd been on board — that's all I can say! Anyway, obviously the Nazca people didn't have airplanes. So the question is: Why go to all the trouble of making the lines and the pictures if they'd never be able to see them?

"There have been all sorts of theories," Professor Chambers went on. "One writer believed that the lines were some sort of airport for spaceships from another planet. It's true that one of the pictures does show a man with a round head, and some people believe it to be an astronaut. A lot of people think they were drawn for the benefit of the ancient gods. They'd be up in the sky, so they'd be able to see them. My own feeling has always been that they are in some way connected to the stars . . . perhaps they were used to forecast stars. Or perhaps . . ." She paused. "I've often wondered if they weren't put there to warn us about something."

Her cigar glowed red. Smoke crept up the side of her face. She seemed to be deep in thought. But then, abruptly, she sat down again.

"Many theories. But the point is — nobody knows for sure."

"Is the place of Qolqa in the desert?" Matt asked.

248

"Yes, it is." Chambers nodded. "Once again, you should have seen it from the plane. Qolqa is a word in Quechua, the ancient language of Peru. It means 'granary.' And it's the name given to the great rectangle we flew over this morning."

"'Before the place of Qolqa . . .'" Matt read out the second line of the poem. "That means the gate must be in front of the rectangle!"

"It may not mean anything of the sort!" the professor snapped. "There is no gate in the desert. That is to say, there are no standing stones, no markers, no buildings. There's just the sand and the lines."

"But there's a platform," Matt returned. "Salamanda said he needed to find the platform."

"Well, good luck to him. I've been into the desert a thousand times and I've never seen a platform." Chambers tapped ash into a saucer on the table. "Mind you, it could be buried," she muttered. "I suppose that's always a possibility."

"Are you sure there's no swan?" Richard asked.

Professor Chambers slammed her cigar down, extinguishing it. "Mr. Cole!" she exclaimed. "The day I started studying the lines, you were still in diapers. How dare you suggest . . . ?"

Matt thought she was going to throw something at the journalist, but she forced herself to calm down.

"I'm sorry," she said. "But you have to understand. The Nazca Lines are my life. I've devoted my whole life to them. I visited them for the first time when I was twenty-three years old, and since then they've never let me go. Can you understand that? There are so few things left in the world

that we don't know. Science has explained almost everything away. And yet here we have one last, great mystery. A
whole desert filled with drawings that nobody understands.
It's been my life's journey to solve the mystery before I die.

"And the fact that you should walk into my life right
now — just three days before Inti Raymi — is mysterious as
well. You come with your extraordinary story and maybe
what you've told me will finally unlock everything. I've been
waiting for this for more than thirty years. So I mustn't
quarrel with you. You have to let me think about what
you've had to say."

"Inti Raymi . . ." Richard muttered.

He was remembering what the Inca had said.

Before the sun had risen and set three times . . .

"That's right, Mr. Cole. That's the one thing we do
know. We have less than forty-eight hours. At midnight,
two days from now, the gate is going to open."

SEVENTEEN
Night in the Desert

They drove out of Nazca as the sun began to set. Professor Chambers was behind the wheel. Richard was next to her, while Matt, Pedro, and Atoc were in the back. The car was a soft-top Jeep. They were planning to go off road. But it was an uncomfortable journey for the two boys. The vehicle had little suspension and they felt every bump and crack in the road. Although the windows were closed, dust came in underneath the flaps and it was often hard to breathe. The engine was deafening and made the seats vibrate. It was like traveling in an oversize washing machine.

"I'd much rather do this by day," the professor shouted. "But all things considered, it looks as if we may be a little short of time. And anyway, we may find it easier to sniff around without planeloads of tourists buzzing over our heads every ten minutes."

"Won't there be guards?" Richard asked.

"There are supposed to be. But there's never enough of them, and the ones who are out here will probably be asleep. Anyway, I have a special permit to go into the desert... which is more than I can say for Mr. Salamanda! If I'd found him or his people tramping over the lines, I'd have had his guts for garters — and I don't care how important he thinks he is."

Matt glanced at Pedro, who was looking out the window, even though there was very little to see. "You okay?" he asked.

Pedro nodded.

"You should get some sleep," the professor said. "This could be a long night."

Two hours later, she stopped and checked her map. The sun had virtually disappeared below the horizon but there was still a red glow in the sky, as if it were unwilling to let go of the heat of the day. The professor pushed the gear stick into four-wheel drive and spun the wheel. Almost at once the Jeep began to bounce up and down as it swapped the bitumen surface of the highway for the rough sand and rock of the desert floor.

They drove for another hour. The professor glanced a couple more times at the map but she had a good idea where they were going. After all, she had been visiting this place for more than thirty years and knew just about every inch of it. At last she stopped.

"We can walk this final part," she said. "There are three spades in the back. Also water bottles, sandwiches, and — most important of all — chocolate. Peruvian chocolate is absolutely first-rate, by the way. Nothing like those sickly little bars you get in England."

Matt stepped out of the Jeep.

He guessed that the great rectangle — the place of Qolqa — must be somewhere in front of him but he could see nothing of it. The rapidly fading light didn't help. He understood now why the Nazca Lines had remained undiscovered for so long. There was nothing to see at ground level apart from a flat, empty plateau. He was like an ant, crawling across a tabletop. The landscape was simply too big to make any sense. Only from above would the pictures become visible. He had seen them clearly from the plane. Now he was among them and they were gone.

"Look here!" Professor Chambers called out.

She turned on the flashlight and pointed it down. The beam of light picked out tire tracks — freshly made, Matt guessed. It seemed that the desert was a bit like the surface of the moon in that any mark stayed there permanently. The professor followed the tire tracks a short way, then swung the flashlight around. Two cars had come. This was where they had stopped. There were dozens of footprints. Several people must have gotten out.

"This is going to be easier than I thought," Professor Chambers muttered.

"What do you mean?" Richard asked.

"Your poem tells us to stand in front of the place of Qolqa. That's where we are now. And somewhere here there must be . . . something. As I've already made perfectly clear, it must be below the surface, because if it wasn't, I'd have seen it. In which case, I thought we'd have to spend half the night digging. But that's not the case. All we have to do is follow the footsteps. Mr. Salamanda may think he's clever but he's left us a path."

They followed the footsteps away from the Jeep and ever farther into the desert. After about two hundred meters, they came to an area where some sort of digging had obviously taken place. The earth was loose. And in the light of the flashlight, the color was quite different.

"This is it!" Richard said.

"Yes." Professor Chambers handed him the flashlight. "The four of you can start digging. I'm going back to the Jeep."

"What for?"

"Isn't it obvious? I'm going to make the tea!"

There was one spade for each of them, and together they began to dig. There was barely enough light left to see by. To Matt, it seemed that the other three were little more than shadows. It was still hot. After just a few minutes of digging, the dust had clogged in Matt's throat. It stung his eyes and settled in his hair. He could feel the sweat making muddy tracks as it trickled down his face. Pedro had stopped digging. He was now holding a flashlight for the others.

Luckily the earth, already disturbed once, came away easily. In just a few minutes, they had dug a trench half a meter deep. Meanwhile, the professor had returned with the food hamper and a Primus stove. Matt heard the hiss of gas and then the pop of the flame as she lit it and began to boil some water for tea. She clearly had no fear of being seen — but then, the stove let out only a tiny pinprick of light in the great emptiness of the desert, and it was highly unlikely there was a guard anywhere near.

Atoc's spade hit something with a loud clang. "Here . . ." he said.

Richard and Matt stopped and went over to where he was working. He had struck some sort of brickwork.

"Be careful!" Professor Chambers called out. Was she afraid of what they might find? Or was it that she didn't want them to do any damage to something that might be of archaeological interest?

254

Quickly, the three of them began to scoop away the earth, using the side edges of their spades. Professor Chambers came back over, adding her flashlight beam to Pedro's. Something flat and square had been revealed. She swung the light over it and saw a brick platform, decorated with a design in the center. As they scraped off the last of the earth, more of the design was revealed. At last they could see it.

Professor Chambers looked down and frowned. "I take it that this is the sign that you described to me," she said. "The sign of the Old Ones."

"Yes," Matt whispered. He shivered. The heat seemed to have evaporated. "This is the sign."

"But what is this thing that it's on?" Richard asked.

"It's a platform." The professor peered more closely at it. "About five meters square, I would say. The bricks are made of andesite. Nothing unusual about that. But the design! Arrows and squiggly lines. That's quite wrong!"

Pedro asked a question. Atoc translated. "What is it doing here?"

"Do you know?" Matt asked.

"As a matter of fact, I do have a pretty good idea." Professor Chambers ran the flashlight over the surface one last time. "Let's have some tea before we cover this back up," she suggested. "And while we're sitting down, we can have a talk."

They went back to the stove, and Professor Chambers filled five mugs with hot, sweet tea made with mint leaves she had picked from her garden. Apart from the hiss of the gas, all was silent in the great emptiness of the desert.

"I'll try to keep this simple," she began. "Although it

isn't. It's actually bloody complicated. But I've told you about the mystery of the Nazca Lines. Now I've got to explain to you my solution to the mystery. I actually wrote a book about it a while ago, although not many people believed me." She fell silent for a moment. "Maybe Salamanda read it. Maybe I'm partly responsible for everything that's happened. I'll try to explain.

"As I told you, I've studied the lines for most of my life. I was fascinated by them, the moment I first saw them. At the time I thought it was because they were so beautiful . . . so very perfect. But as the years went on, I realized that I was wrong. I can't explain how it happened but I began to believe that they . . . that there was something evil about them. The pictures of the animals are wonderful. I don't deny it. But it crossed my mind that to the ancient Nazca people two thousand years ago, they must have been terrifying, too. Huge spiders. Monstrous whales. Even the monkey is grotesque, reaching out with its spindly arms. It has only four fingers on one hand. Why do you think the people who drew the lines gave it one finger too few?"

"Maybe they couldn't count," Richard said.

"No, no. They could count perfectly well. But, you see, in primitive societies, deformity is something to be feared, a bad omen. Maybe that's the point. All the animals could have been drawn simply to scare people."

She took out another cigar and lit it. The smoke shone silver against the black night sky.

"Most people now agree that the Nazca Lines have something to do with the stars," she went on. "I actually studied astronomy at university a long time ago, and from the very start it was my opinion that the lines were nothing more or less than a huge star map.

"This is how it would work. A line would point to a star at certain times of the year. That is to say, you'd stand on the line and look down it and if you saw a star rising up over the horizon right in front of you, you'd know it was April fifth and time to start planting the grain or whatever. Easy enough! But later on, I started to think. What would happen if there was a moment, perhaps no more than a few minutes in a thousand years, when *all* the lines pointed to *all* the visible stars — at exactly the same time? Now that would be . . ." She stopped. "Am I boring you, Matthew?"

Matt's head was craned upward. His eyes were searching the night sky. He had been listening to begin with, but something had distracted him. What was it? There were no sounds in the desert. Could he have imagined it? No. There it was again, a soft beating in the air like a flag caught in the wind. He waited, his ears pricked. But it had gone.

"Are you listening?" Professor Chambers asked.

Matt turned to her. "Yes. Of course."

"Good. Because this is where things get a bit more complicated.

"As I was saying, I wondered if all the stars could align with the all the Nazca Lines. But how would this happen? Well, imagine that you could lie on your back on the desert floor and take a photograph of the night sky. You'd end up with a big sheet of paper with lots of little dots on it. Then you could go up in the air and take a photograph of the lines, making a second picture. What I was looking for was a time when the stars in the first picture would fall exactly on the lines in the second picture. . . ."

"A sort of connect-the-dots on a cosmic scale," Richard said.

"Exactly. Of course, this wouldn't happen very often. It might never happen at all. You see, the stars always seem to be moving when you look at them from the Earth. The reason for this is that it's the Earth that's actually moving — spinning on its own axis. That's why the stars never seem to be in the same position.

"And the Earth isn't only spinning. It's also orbiting around the sun. And as it orbits, it wobbles. Astronomers call this wobble *precession*. And what it means is that the Earth is in exactly the same position only once every twenty-six thousand years.

"So to go right back to where I started, what I wondered and what I wrote about in my book was, suppose that the Nazca Lines were drawn as a sort of terrible warning. Suppose that what they were doing was recording one moment in twenty-six thousand years when they would finally line up with the stars, and the world would come to an end. That would explain why the pictures were so frightening. It would explain why they had to be drawn in the first place."

"And you think the lines will align with the stars two nights from now?" Richard asked.

"I was never able to test my theory before now because I never had an observation platform. Don't forget that this desert covers five hundred square kilometers! I had to know exactly where to stand to see the stars in their right position."

"And now you do."

"Yes. . . ."

Suddenly, Pedro sprang to his feet.

"Pedro?" The professor examined him. *"¿Cuál es él?"*

"Está . . . " Pedro began.

Matt stood up, too. "I heard it just a moment ago," he said.

The stove was still burning, the little gas jet throwing a blue glow across the ground. The Jeep stood where it had been parked. The night had grown cool and now there was a faint touch of breeze in the air. Matt looked up at the sky, at the millions of glistening stars. For a moment, he thought he saw two tiny green lights. He shook his head. There was no such thing as a green star.

"You're imagining things," Richard said. "There's nothing out here."

Unwillingly, Pedro and Matt sat down again. They couldn't leave until they had covered their tracks, and they weren't ready to begin work again yet.

"The platform marks the exact position where you have to stand to see the alignment of the stars," the professor continued. "That's what it said in the verse you showed me. 'Before the place of Qolqa, there will the light be seen . . .'"

"'The light that is the end of all light.'" Matt finished the poem.

Professor Chambers nodded gravely. "There you have it again. This is the place. And we also know the time. Two days from now. Inti Raymi."

"That's when the gate opens."

"Except we don't know where the gate is," Richard cut in. "There are no stone circles in the desert."

259

"What makes you think it has to be a stone circle?"

Atoc was the first to see them. Suddenly he cried out and pointed. And there they were — two green lights, burning in the air, high above them but already moving downward. Matt stared into the darkness. There was something large and bulky behind the lights. He could make out wings.

There was a ghastly shriek. Matt dived onto his stomach as an enormous bird plummeted toward him, steel-like claws reaching out for his eyes. He felt a searing pain in his shoulder, heard the cloth of his shirt tear as the claws ripped through. Then it had wheeled away, and the desert was silent once again but for the beating of its wings in the night air.

Matt rolled over and got dizzily to his feet.

"*¿Cuál era él?*" Pedro demanded.

"It was a condor," Chambers said. "But it's impossible. There are no condors in this part of Peru."

Once again, Matt remembered what the *amauta* had said in the lost city.

"*The birds fly where they should not fly.*"

Condors. In the Nazca desert. At night.

"It's coming back!" Richard shouted.

There was a second scream and a thudding in the air. All of them fell back as the monstrous bird rushed into them, its green eyes blazing. The bird was black and gray with a thick white collar of feathers around its neck. It was huge, the rest of its plumage hanging off its body like a ragged cloak. Its beak curved out of its head like a dagger. Its claws were stretched out and the points were knife-sharp. For a moment it was between them and they felt the air beat against their faces. There was a smell of rotting meat. Then it swooped up, disappearing into the darkness.

Richard snatched up the stove as if it were a weapon, although he knew that the tiny flame would do no good. "Get into the Jeep!" he shouted. "We have to move —"

"Watch out!" Matt warned.

A second bird had dived down, aiming for Richard. The journalist dropped to one knee and its claws missed his head by centimeters. Its huge wings beat at the air, making the flame dance. Like the other bird, it stank of death and decay.

"The Jeep!" Richard shouted a second time.

A third condor swooped out of the sky. Then a fourth and a fifth. Suddenly the entire sky seemed to be filled with shrieking, savage creatures. Atoc shouted. One of the condors had landed on his shoulder. As Matt stared in horror, it twisted round and began to attack Atoc's neck, ripping out skin and flesh with its beak. Atoc tried to beat it off but it refused to let go. Blood was pouring from his neck and down his shirt. Then Matt ran forward. He picked up a spade and with all his strength he swung it, slamming the metal end into the bird, barely centimeters away from Atoc's head. He felt the jolt as the spade came into contact with flesh and bone. The bird was smashed to the ground, its own neck broken. But still it wouldn't die. It thrashed around, its wings beating uselessly. Its beak was sticky with Atoc's blood.

"Matteo!"

It was Pedro who had cried out. Another bird had landed on his back, its claws acting like grappling irons. It was pecking at his skull, over and over again, its beak disappearing into his hair. To Matt it seemed as if the boy and the bird had become one. All he could see was Pedro flailing with his hands, with two gigantic wings spreading out of his back.

Richard saved him. With one hand, he ripped the bird off Pedro's shoulders, then shoved the stove into the condor with his other. The blue flame touched the feathers, and the bird seemed to explode as the fire took it instantly. It screamed again and again. Then it collapsed to the sand, kicked its legs feebly, and lay still.

The stove had gone out.

"Are you all right?" Richard shouted.

"Yes!" Pedro touched the back of his head. When his hand came away, there was blood on his fingers.

"We have to get to the Jeep. . . ."

Professor Chambers was already there. So far she hadn't been touched. She fumbled the keys out of her pocket and threw herself into the driver's seat. Even as she reached out to close the door, another condor swooped down, aiming for her hand. She slammed the door in its face, pushed the keys into the ignition, and turned the engine on.

Richard, Pedro, and Matt all had spades now. Together they made for the Jeep, swinging at the air, keeping close as a group. Matt was supporting Atoc, who seemed dazed, his hand clamped to the wound on his neck. Blood was trickling between his fingers. There was a roar from the engine and the Jeep charged toward them and stopped. Matt helped Atoc into the front seat. He saw Richard lash out with his spade. There was a screech, and a body thumped onto the ground.

Somehow, the three of them managed to get into the back.

"This is impossible!" Chambers cried.

"Just get us out of here!" Richard yelled back. "We can talk about it later."

Chambers slammed her foot onto the accelerator and the Jeep's wheels spun. For a horrible moment, Matt thought they were stuck. But then the tires found a grip and they were propelled forward, heading toward the highway.

But it wasn't over yet.

Even as Matt slumped gratefully back, something hammered into the roof of the Jeep. The next thing he knew, there was a ripping sound, and the head of a condor burst down into the car. At the same time, two more condors swung into the sides, holding on with their claws and tearing through the soft material with their beaks. The Jeep zigzagged. Matt and Pedro were thrown left and right. It seemed that Chambers had lost control. But she had seen what was happening. She was deliberately wrenching the wheel, trying to throw the birds off.

Richard punched upward. His fist caught one of the condors in the stomach and at once it was gone, whipped away into the night. Matt felt a sharp pain and cried out. Another condor had managed to get halfway in. It was pecking at his face and had drawn blood on his cheek. An inch higher and to the left and it would have taken out his eye.

"They're breaking in!" he shouted.

"Can you go any faster?" Richard demanded.

"Not on this surface! I'm going as fast as I can!"

"We're not going to make it!" Richard looked up. The roof had been torn through in several places. There were still condors attached to the Jeep. He could see them through the gaps. He heard another hideous, unearthly screech, and what was left of the roof disintegrated as yet another condor burst through. It was inside the Jeep, a stinking, flapping ball of bone, feather, and claw. It lunged at Matt.

There was an explosion, so loud it was deafening. On the backseat, Pedro jerked back in shock. Matt felt his ears ringing.

It was Atoc. He had one hand clasped over the wound on his neck but in the other he was holding a gun. He had never even mentioned that he had it. Now, when it was almost too late, he had used it, firing at point-blank range into the bird's body. The bullet tore through it. The condor's beak snapped open, impossibly wide. The light in its eyes went out. Atoc fired five more times, aiming at different points of the roof. The other condors fell away.

And then the Jeep hit the highway. Matt felt the tires bump onto the asphalt, and a moment later they had picked up speed. He looked back. A few condors were still circling but they were already far behind.

"I . . . sorry," Atoc said. "I leave gun in Jeep."

"Are you okay?" Richard asked.

Atoc nodded. "Not hurt too bad."

"I have bandages at the house," Chambers said.

The Jeep tore down the Pan-American Highway, leaving a cloud of dust in its wake. The last condors watched it disappear, then wheeled back into the darkness from which they'd come.

EIGHTEEN
Evil Star

"I'm wrong," Professor Chambers said. "I don't understand it. But I've checked and double-checked."

"What do you mean?" Richard asked.

"The stars! That's what I mean. I was sure I was right. But I've looked at them and they simply don't add up."

It was eleven o'clock the following morning. Matt, Pedro, and Richard had eaten a late breakfast, which the professor had brought to them in the garden. All three of them felt a little guilty, knowing that she had worked all night — but she didn't seem even slightly tired. Atoc was in his room, resting. A local doctor had stitched up the wound in his neck and given him tetanus and penicillin shots. He was still in pain but he was going to be all right. Pedro had been luckier. The skull is the toughest part of the human body and it had protected him from the condor's attack. He was missing a few bits of hair and he, too, had been given an anti-tetanus jab, but he was otherwise fine.

Matt had spoken to him the night before, while they slept.

"Where did they come from?" Pedro asked. "The condors . . ."

"From the Old Ones," Matt replied. "They must have been guardians. They were protecting the place of Qolqa.

I knew there was something wrong, something evil the moment we arrived."

"It was cold."

"Yes. When something bad's about to happen, I always feel cold."

"Me, too."

The mainland was getting nearer. Very soon they would arrive.

"The old man in Vilcabamba . . . he said that one of us was going to get killed," Pedro muttered.

"He said one of us *might*."

"Which one?"

"I don't know."

"He also said that whichever one of us it was, he'd be on his own. But I'm not going to let that happen. I'm going to stick with you."

Matt sighed. "I wish it was as easy as that. But it feels like everything's already been decided."

"No, Matteo. Nobody makes decisions for me. You and me . . . we're the ones in charge."

Now Matt was dragged back to reality as Professor Chambers produced a sheaf of computer printouts and laid them on the breakfast table. It seemed strange to be in a beautiful garden on this warm summer's day. The birds were singing. A gardener was mowing the lawn. And here they were talking about the end of the world.

"I've made my calculations based on the position of the platform and the position of the stars on Inti Raymi," Professor Chambers went on. "Remember what I told you? My idea . . . ?"

"You told us they'd line up," Richard said.

"I told you it would happen once every twenty-six thousand years. And the extraordinary thing is that it does happen, very, very nearly . . . tomorrow night. It's quite incredible. It's what I've been saying for thirty years. But there's one star missing. I've gone over it a dozen times, but there's no mistake. One star won't be there."

"Which star?" Matt asked.

"Cygnus. It's actually made up of seven stars and it's also known as the Northern Cross. It's seventy thousand times brighter than the sun, and it's so far away that when you look at it, you're actually seeing it as it was in the time of Christ.

"If you were standing on the platform at the place of Qolqa tomorrow, you'd look for it between the two mountain ranges. All the other stars would be in the right place. But Cygnus wouldn't be anywhere to be seen. It would be about thirty degrees off course, hidden behind the moon."

"So that's the end of it," Richard exclaimed. "Salamanda stole the diary and tried to kill Matt for nothing. It doesn't matter how rich or powerful he is. There's nothing he can do. He can't move a star."

"'There are too many stars,'" Matt said.

"What?"

"It's what the old man said. 'The birds fly in the wrong places and there are too many stars in the night sky.' That was how he knew the gate was going to open."

"Well, he wasn't wrong with the first part," Richard agreed.

"But why did he say there were too many? Professor Chambers says there's one star too few!"

Nobody spoke. The gardener, a cheerful man in a straw hat, had finished mowing the lawn. Now he had disappeared behind the bushes but they could hear the snapping of his shears as he trimmed the leaves.

"St. Joseph of Cordoba predicted that the second gate would open on Inti Raymi," Richard said. Professor Chambers leaned over and began to translate quietly for Pedro. "He was here with the conquistadors. He somehow discovered the secret of the lines and it drove him mad. Salamanda stole the diary because he wanted to know the secret. And he hasn't given up! He's chased Matt all over Peru because he's afraid of him. There must be something he knows that we don't."

"*¿Qué sobre el pájaro en su sueño?*" Pedro asked.

"He's asking — what about the bird in your dream?" Professor Chambers translated.

Matt wondered how much of the conversation Pedro had been able to follow, even without Atoc being there. It seemed that the more time they spent together, the more he was able to understand.

"What does he mean?" Chambers asked.

"I was going to tell you," Matt said. "But I didn't because I wasn't sure if it was part of it. But it's true. I've been having bad dreams about a swan."

"God! I'm an idiot. . . ." Professor Chambers closed her eyes for a moment. "Cygnus," she said. "That's Latin . . ."

Everyone looked at her.

". . . for swan." Richard completed the sentence.

Chambers held up a hand for silence. Matt could see the thought processes going through her head. At last, she looked up. Her blue eyes had never been more alive.

"Listen," she began, "I thought the lines were a warning, but suppose I was only half right. Let's imagine they were something more than that. You came to Peru looking for a gate. We still don't know where it is. But if it's closed, there must be something that keeps it closed."

"You mean . . . a sort of lock," Matt said.

"That's right. And if so, why can't it be a combination lock?"

"I don't understand."

"It's simple. Think of the Nazca Lines as a fantastic time lock. They sit there, keeping the gate closed. That's why they were built. Only when the stars form the right patterns, only then will the gate open and the Old Ones will be free. That's how it works."

"But the whole purpose of the gate was that it should *never* open," Richard said.

"That's right," Chambers continued. "Which is why the gatekeepers made sure that the stars would never align. But two nights from now, they'll come close. In fact, it's as close as they'll ever get. Just one star is going to be missing. . . ."

"And Salamanda is going to replace it!" Matt interrupted. "When I was in his house, I heard him talking." It was all coming back to him. "He said something about a silver swan. There were coordinates. He had to move it exactly into position."

He stopped. Suddenly the answer was obvious.

"A satellite," he said.

"Exactly," Professor Chambers agreed. "Salamanda launched a new satellite just a week ago. It's been in the newspapers. Everyone knows. And what he's going to do is, he's going to position it exactly where Cygnus ought to be.

An artificial star instead of the real one. The satellite will complete the pattern of light. The time lock will be activated. And . . ."

"And the gate will open," Matt said, fear in his voice.

"We can stop him!" Richard said.

Chambers shook her head. "I don't see how. The satellite's already in space. Salamanda will be controlling it by radio. If we knew the frequency, perhaps we might be able to jam the signal, but we'd have to get our hands on the right equipment and I wouldn't even know where to begin. Anyway, the transmitter will be at the SNI compound at Paracas and we could never get in."

"Where is Paracas?" Matt asked.

"Not too far from here. That makes it perfect for Salamanda. It's on the coast, about three hundred miles north. Not too far from the Nazca Lines . . ."

"Can we see it?"

"We can drive there. But I've gone past it a couple of times, Matt — and I'm telling you, you'd need a small army to break in."

• • •

Salamanda's Research and Telecommunications Center at Paracas was a few miles inland, a hi-tech compound surrounded by desert. Not one but two fences surrounded it. The first was ten meters high, with razor wire stretched endlessly around the top. The second carried bright yellow signs that warned would-be trespassers in three languages. The outer fence was electrified. The space in between was patrolled, day and night, by guards with dogs. Two watchtowers looked over the desert, one at each corner. The only way in was through a gate that slid open electronically to allow vehicles to pass. But there was a control room and a barrier that only rose once every driver had been checked.

The compound itself consisted of a cluster of low, ugly buildings made of red bricks, with panels of mirrored glass. The scientists and staff might be able to look out, but nobody could look in. A radio mast loomed over them, standing on metal legs with satellite dishes turned up toward the sky. The building closest to it was also the most modern, a glass dome at the center of the roof but no windows at all. This had to be the control center.

Three lines of identical, whitewashed houses stood at the perimeter. They were also made of brick but looked more primitive. Matt suspected this was where the staff had to live. They had been constructed around a rough, concrete square which seemed to double as an eating area and a soccer field. There was even a television on a metal stand, surrounded by wooden benches. At night, the workers could watch TV in the open air.

There seemed to be at least two hundred people working there. Matt had seen some of them, dressed in gray overalls with the letters *SNI* in red print on their sleeves. He had also seen laboratory technicians and scientists. Salamanda had a fleet of electric cars, little more than golf carts, to ferry them between buildings. There was also a launchpad with a small black helicopter parked in the middle. Armed guards in military dress patrolled the entire compound on foot, and security cameras, mounted on corners, swiveled to take in anyone who passed.

Matt, Pedro, Richard, and Atoc were lying on a sand

271

dune, some distance away, examining the compound through binoculars that Professor Chambers had found for them. She herself was waiting in Paracas. Atoc had a bandage around his neck and moved slowly — but he had insisted on making the journey with them.

"What do you think?" Richard said.

"Professor Chambers was right," Matt said. "We'd need a small army to break in here."

"Yes." Atoc nodded. "And we have one."

•　　•　　•

They came the next day with the setting sun. It had taken them twenty-four hours to cross Peru, coming by car and by train, but Atoc had called for them and now they were here, assembling on the beach at Paracas.

The Inca army was about fifty strong, dressed in dark jeans and black shirts, ready for the attack that would take place that evening. But if their clothes were modern, their weapons were not. They had brought with them the arms and armor that their ancestors had used. As deadly as they looked, Matt couldn't help but think that it looked like a bizarre mix.

Some of the Incas wore padded cotton jackets. Some had helmets made out of some sort of wood that was pitch-black and as hard as iron. Some carried wooden shields covered with deerskin and many of them had a club with a strange, star-shaped head made out of stone. This was the *macana*, a favorite weapon of the ancient Incas. One blow could crack open a skull or fracture a leg.

There were other weapons, too. Matt saw spears, slingshots, and halberds — which were a combination of spear, hook, and ax at the end of a long pole. A few of the Incas carried bolas, three copper balls tied together on leather cords. Thrown properly at a man's neck, they would swing round and strangle him, perhaps knocking him senseless at the same time.

Professor Chambers had watched the arrival in silent astonishment. If she hadn't known about the Incas before, she certainly knew now. The soldiers were all physically similar — more Indian than Peruvian. And their weapons were instantly recognizable. She sat down heavily on a rock and began to fan herself. A crab scuttled in front of her and she nudged it away.

Fifty men. They stood silently on the sand, with the silver waves beating down behind them. A few pelicans eyed them warily, sitting on a broken jetty. A flamingo took fright and hurried along on its way. There was nobody else in sight. Perhaps they knew what was happening here. Perhaps they had been warned to stay out of the way.

Atoc had told the men what they had to do, speaking in their own language. Now he turned to Matt.

"We are ready," he said. "You stay here with Pedro, the professor, and your friend. We return when job is done."

"No." Matt didn't know what he was saying. Or, rather, he didn't know why he was saying it. A short time ago, in England, he hadn't even wanted to come to Peru. But since then, everything had changed. Every fiber of his being told him that he couldn't let the Incas take on his fight alone. "I'm coming with you, Atoc. I started this and I want to be there at the end."

"Yo también," Pedro said.

Atoc hesitated for a moment. But he could see something in Matt's eyes that hadn't been there before, and slowly he nodded. "We will obey you," he said. "For it is true, as the Inca said. You were sent to lead. . . ."

"Then it looks like I'm coming, too," Richard said.

Matt turned to him. "You don't have to, Richard. You can stay with the professor."

"You're not getting rid of me that easily." Richard sighed. "I told you back in York. My job is to look after you, and that's what I'm going to do. All the way to the bitter end."

"Then let's do it," Matt said.

He raised a hand. And at that moment he was in command, the head of an army that had assembled to do what he asked.

As one, they set off to do battle.

The night of Inti Raymi had arrived.

Salamanda's compound lay ahead.

NINETEEN
Control Center

Darkness had already fallen as the Incas took their positions around the compound, stretching out in a long line across the sand. Matt couldn't believe he was with them. A thousand years before, the Inca army had swept across South America: fast, merciless, and unstoppable. Now their descendants were at war again and they were here because he and Pedro had called them. Pedro was right in the middle of them, next to Atoc. He didn't look afraid. Anyone watching might have thought he was in command. Matt hardly recognized him as the beggar boy he had met in the streets of Lima. With every minute that passed, he was becoming more like the figure he had seen on the gold disc. Manco Capac, the first lord of the Incas.

The razor-tipped wire of the perimeter fence loomed in front of them. Atoc gave a signal, lowering his palm toward the sand. At once everyone dropped to his knees. It was ten o'clock at night but the compound was still active with lights burning in many of the buildings and the occasional vehicle crossing from one side to the other, its engine whining like an oversize mosquito.

Atoc pointed at the radio mast and spoke quietly in his own language. Matt understood what he was saying. This was the primary target. Once the transmitter had fallen, Salamanda would be unable to control his satellite — his silver swan. Matt glanced upward. Already the stars were appearing in the night sky. He could see them twinkling over the mountains, falling into positions that had been dictated for them twenty-six thousand years ago. But one of them was a fake, a ton of aluminum and steel, sneaking in to complete a deadly combination. Which one of them was it? Matt thought he could see a pinprick of light moving faster than the others — but he couldn't be sure. All he knew was that the swan was up there, just as it had been in his dreams, and that unless they stopped it, it would soon be in place.

Two of the Incas shuffled forward and took up positions closer to the wire, crouching on one knee. They were each holding a spear, a three-meter length of wood whose point had been hardened in flames. Silently, they waited. Atoc took one last look around, then nodded. The two Incas ran a few paces and threw the spears, aiming upward. Matt was astonished by their strength and precision. The spears flew into the night, rising above the compound. There were two soft thuds and, high up in the watchtowers, two guards turned and crumpled. One disappeared from sight. The other slumped forward and lay still, with his head and arms hanging toward the ground. The spear had gone straight through him.

The attack had begun — but they still had to get inside the compound and that meant passing through the electronic gates. Atoc signaled a second time and a low, open-backed truck covered in a tarpaulin rolled up to the

276

security barrier. The driver — bored and unshaven — leaned out of the window and hooted as if he didn't want to be in here and was in a hurry to get home. Three guards, all of them armed, came out to meet him. They were moving warily. Matt guessed that they would have been told to allow nobody in. Not tonight. The entire compound would be on a state of alert.

"¿Quiénes usted? ¿Qué quiere?"

The words sounded faint and distant. The driver muttered something, but so quietly that the first of the guards had to lean into the cabin to hear what he said. It was a mistake. Matt saw a hand lash out, clutching the guard around the neck. At the same time, the tarpaulin was thrown back and two figures leaped out, each swinging a club with a star-shaped head. A second later, all three guards were unconscious. The driver raised a hand toward Atoc.

"Here we go," Richard whispered.

Matt nodded. It was incredible to think of these age-old weapons being used to storm a twenty-first-century research center. But so far the Incas had proved themselves to be deadly effective.

The entire line of men rose up from the desert floor and began to move forward. At the same time, the men from the truck had slipped into the guard house and the electronic gates slid open to let them in. Matt's mouth was dry. It seemed almost too easy. Was there nobody in the compound watching out? But the guards in the watchtowers were already dealt with and — he reminded himself — the Incas were all wearing dark clothes. Even if anyone did happen to be looking, they would blend into the gray emptiness of the desert. They were silent and just about invisible.

Pedro was the first in. Then came Atoc and the others, spreading out across the roads and walkways, finding shelter next to the nearest walls. The compound lay ahead of them, and for a moment there was nobody in sight. Only the lights behind the windows and the distant hum of machinery warned them that they were not alone. Richard and Matt were among the last to enter. So they had the clearest view of what happened next.

A group of four Incas ran over to the radio mast and began to climb it. Atoc and the others were covering them, looking out for anyone who might approach. Still nobody knew they were there. But then, at the very last minute, a dead man gave them away. It was the guard in the watchtower. He had been killed instantly — but since he had died, the blood had run into the top part of his body and his weight had shifted. Quite suddenly, he fell forward, plunged through the air, and hit a corrugated roof with a thunderous crash. Nobody moved. Nobody even breathed. Was it possible that such a loud noise could have gone unheard?

An alarm rang out, shattering the still of the night. At the same time, searchlights exploded into life, and what had a few moments before been no more than a gathering of dark shadows and half-seen shapes was instantly blazing white. Every one of the Incas was exposed. Matt and Richard, crouching together in a flat, open area of asphalt and rubble, were in the worst position of all. Doors crashed open. Guards appeared. A machine gun began to chatter. Pieces of brickwork were blown out of the walls. A whole group of Incas were sent flying to the ground, rolling in a hail of bullets. Richard grabbed hold of Matt and pulled him across to a pile of fuel drums. Part of him knew that it was insane to hide behind gallons of petrol during a gun fight. Another part of him said that surely Salamanda's men wouldn't be mad enough to fire in this direction.

The Incas were scattering, trying to find cover. More shots were being fired. There were guards on the roofs. The door of the largest building opened and a man stepped out, a pistol clasped in one hand. Seemingly unconcerned by the chaos all around him, he took careful aim and fired. One of the climbers who had made it halfway up the radio mast cried out and fell to the ground. Matt felt his blood go cold. He knew the man who had just fired the shot. It was Rodriguez, the police captain he had first met in Lima. As Matt watched, he took cover in the doorway, at the same time barking out an order to someone behind him. What was the police chief doing in the compound? It was no surprise that he was working for Salamanda. But it seemed he had now abandoned his normal duties completely to take over security here.

Something glinted in the hard light and a spear hurtled past Rodriguez, burying itself in the door. Rodriguez laughed, showing animal teeth, and fired a second shot. Matt saw something go whirling across the empty space in front of a building: three copper balls, tied together with cords. They vanished into the darkness and a moment later a guard stepped off the roof, half strangled, the cords wrapped around his throat. He crashed down in front of the police chief and lay twitching on the ground.

More machine-gun fire. There seemed to be guards everywhere, pouring out of doors and taking up positions across the compound. Matt's heart sank. They were obviously outnumbered. And where was Pedro? Matt was beginning to regret coming here with the Incas. He couldn't help them. There was nothing he could do. Unless . . .

He and Richard were in front of a small, brick building with a skull and crossbones painted on the side and the same word he had seen at the airport. *Peligro.* Danger. There was some sort of machinery humming inside.

"Richard!" he called out.

Richard understood. He drew back his foot and, using all his strength, kicked open the door. Matt hurried in. The building was filled with machines and heavy-duty fuse boxes, each one with silver handles set in the ON position. Together, Richard and Matt began to turn them off. If they could cut the power supply running into the compound, perhaps they could interrupt the signals being sent into outer space.

There was a buzz and a crackle of electricity. The Klaxon fell silent and darkness returned to the compound. Richard and Matt had managed to disconnect the security system and this gave the Incas the advantage they needed. Spending their lives high up in the mountains, they were accustomed to the darkness. Now they used it, flitting in and out of their hiding places, taking out Salamanda's men one by one.

"Let's get inside," Matt said. Without waiting for Richard to reply, he ducked out of the generator room, underneath the radio mast, and into the building on the other side.

It had to be the main control center. It was right next to the radio mast, connected to the various satellite dishes by thick cables that looped through the air. Matt didn't know what he was going to find inside. He wasn't armed and knew that he was taking a terrible risk. But he couldn't just watch as the Incas fought his battle for him. Somewhere in his mind it had occurred to him that if he and Richard could find the controls, they might be able to redirect the satellite, send it flying off into a different orbit. Or he might find Salamanda. There had been no sign of him so far, but surely he would want to be here now. This was meant to be the night of his triumph. He wasn't just going to stay at home.

Trying to make as little noise as possible, Matt made his way into a large, fully enclosed chamber. He looked up and took in the glass dome that he had seen from outside. On the other side he could make out the night sky and the radio mast with its satellites towering above.

All the walls were covered with plasma screens, some filled with digital readouts, some showing what must surely be live footage of the night sky. Mainframe computers stood beneath them and there were twenty or more workstations set out on a shelf that curved the whole way around. There were about a dozen tables and chairs in the center, arranged like a classroom. They were covered in charts and other papers, some of which had been scattered onto the floor. Most of the staff must have left when the fighting began. The whole place had been abandoned. But one man had remained behind. He was sitting alone at one of the tables, busily scribbling away at a pile of papers. As Matt approached, he turned slowly round.

It was Fabian.

For a moment, neither of them spoke.

Then Fabian broke the silence. "Matthew!" he exclaimed. "Mr. Cole! What are you doing here?"

"I think we should be asking you that," Richard said.

But it was obvious, really, when Matt thought about it. A driver — Alberto — had been sent to the airport to pick him up and deliver him to the police at the Hotel Europa. He had always assumed that the driver had worked for Captain Rodriguez. In fact, he had been working for Fabian — and Fabian had admitted as much the last time they had spoken, on the telephone in Cuzco. And that telephone call had almost been Matt's undoing. The moment he had told Fabian where he was, the information had been passed on to Salamanda and the police.

Fabian was the traitor. He always had been.

Fabian seemed to have shrunk since they had last seen him. As always, he was wearing an expensive suit — but this time he had no tie. His clothes hung loose off him and he hadn't shaved. He had been drinking. There was a half-empty bottle on the table and his eyes were glazed. Staring at Richard and Matt, he blinked nervously — more embarrassed than scared or surprised.

"You . . ." Richard swore viciously.

Fabian looked around him. "Where is everyone?" he asked. "There were a whole lot of people here a few minutes ago."

"When did you start working for Salamanda?" Matt asked.

"Oh — a long time ago. Before Raven's Gate. As a matter of fact, he's my publisher. He published two of my books and

282

he asked me to meet him. He said he was very interested in some of the things I was writing about. Ancient history. Nazca. The Nexus was interested in me, too. They asked me to join them. But I'd already made my choice. . . ."

"Why?"

"Because I want to be on the winning side. The world's going to change, you see. Everything's going to change. And the question you have to ask yourself is — do you want to spend the rest of your life in misery and pain or do you want to be with the winners? That was how Mr. Salamanda put it to me. He persuaded me that the Nexus didn't have a chance. I mean, it had always been predicted that the Old Ones would return. So what was the point of trying to fight against it?"

"You gave him the diary."

"I told him about the meeting at the church . . . St. Meredith's. And I told him where you were, when you called in from Cuzco. I'm sorry about that. I didn't want you to get hurt — but it was all or nothing."

Fabian stood up, took a drink from the bottle, then went over to one of the largest screens. Matt had noticed it when they came in. It seemed to be showing some sort of radar signals. There were about a hundred dots, black on white, all of them static. But high up in the left-hand corner, a single dot was moving slowly across, traveling about a centimeter every few minutes.

"There it is," Fabian said. "Cygnus. The swan. You have to admire Salamanda's genius. I mean, there's a guy with a head on his shoulders!" He laughed briefly to himself. "He's using an artificial star to unlock the gate." There was a time code at the bottom of the screen. It showed 22:19:58 for an instant; the numbers were rapidly changing as the seconds ticked away. "It'll be in place in less than two hours from now and there's absolutely nothing you can do," he mumbled. "Then it'll all be over. . . ."

"We can still stop it," Matt said.

"No. You see . . ."

But before he could say any more, there was a crash as a door burst inward and a man reeled into the room. It was Rodriguez. He had obviously been in the thick of the fighting. His face was gray, streaked with dirt and sweat. He had a gun in one hand. His other hand was clutching his arm. He had been wounded. There was blood seeping through the jacket of his uniform. Matt would never know if he had come in here to hide or to look for him. Either way, Rodriguez had found him.

"You!" The single word was spat out with a mixture of hatred and amusement. Rodriguez straightened himself and raised the gun, aiming at Matt.

Matt said nothing. He was standing just a few meters away. The appearance of Captain Rodriguez had changed everything. He and Richard were defenseless. Fabian wasn't going to help them. There was nobody else in the room. What could he do? A thought flashed through his mind. Forrest Hill. The bully — Gavin Taylor — holding a glass in his hand. Matt had used his power. It had been an accident, but still it had been unforgettable. He had made the glass and the chandelier explode, simply by thinking about it.

Could he do the same now?

"You got away from me in Lima," Rodriguez said. "And again in Cuzco. But there will be no third time. This is where it ends."

"Leave him alone!" It was Richard who had spoken, and for a moment the gun turned on him.

"You are . . . the journalist?" Somehow the policeman had recognized him. "Do you want to die first or do you want to die second? Tell me! I can arrange it. . . ."

Desperately, Matt tried to focus on the gun. Why couldn't he do it? What was the point of having some sort of hidden power if he didn't know how to use it? It should have been easy. A single blast of energy and the gun should have been spinning over to the other side of the room. Along with the man who held it.

But it wasn't happening.

Rodriguez was aiming the gun at his heart. Matt could almost feel the policeman's finger tightening on the trigger.

And then Fabian stepped into the line of fire.

"You don't have to kill them," he said.

"Get out of the way!" Rodriguez commanded.

Fabian was walking toward him. "No, no, no," he was saying. "There's no need for this. You don't have to kill anyone. We've won! It's what Salamanda always said. In an hour, the Old Ones will be here and the whole world will be ours. I'm sorry, Captain Rodriguez. I don't care what you say. I'm not going to stand here and watch you shoot a child."

"Get out of my way!"

"No!" Fabian had reached him. He was unsteady on his feet . . . from the drink, from exhaustion. But he was between Rodriguez and Matt, his hand pressing down on the policeman's arm. "Salamanda promised me the boy wouldn't be hurt," he said.

"Salamanda lied!" Rodriguez laughed and pulled the trigger. Matt flinched. Fabian was thrown backward but somehow remained standing. He looked down at his stomach. Blood was gushing out of him. His shirt and his trousers were already saturated. He took a step back and collapsed quite suddenly, as if every nerve in his body had suddenly been whipped out of him.

Rodriguez took aim at Matt a second time.

And then there was an explosion, much louder than the gunshot, but outside the room. Matt looked up.

The Incas had blown up the radio mast. How they had done it he would never know, but it was clear that they had come to the compound with more than bolas, spears, and the rest of it. One of them must have brought a quantity of plastic explosives. Matt saw it quite clearly through the glass dome. There was a great flash of light as the steel mast was cut in half. Flames leaped up. And then the top of the mast came loose, separating from the bottom. Taking three of the satellite dishes with it, it keeled over to one side. And suddenly the very top of the mast, where it tapered to a point, was traveling down like a spear thrown from the sky. As Richard and Matt dived to one side, it smashed through the glass and kept coming. All of Rodriguez's concentration had been on Matt. He had been perhaps half a second away from shooting him. He hadn't seen what was happening until it was too late.

Half a ton of steel girders, cables, and satellite dishes crashed into the room. Rodriguez was directly underneath the dome. He didn't even have time to scream as a massive pile of metal and glass slammed into him, obliterating him utterly. Matt hit the floor and kept sliding. It seemed to him that the whole room had exploded. The noise was deafening. A hundred splinters sprayed into his shoulders and back. He could smell burning. Everything had gone dark.

Silence.

Weakly, he tried to stand up and found that his leg wouldn't obey him. For a moment he was terrified. Had he been crushed under the weight of the radio mast?

"Richard . . . !" he shouted.

"Over here!" Richard sounded a long way away.

Matt slowly picked himself up. Apart from a few superficial cuts and scratches, he hadn't been hurt. Richard was also getting to his feet. He was covered in glass. It was in his hair and on his shoulders and there was a cut on his forehead. But he was all right, too.

The door opened and Pedro came running in. He had his slingshot in one hand. There was a ferociousness in his face that Matt had never seen before. Atoc was with him. Matt was relieved to see that both of them were uninjured.

"It is over," Atoc said. "Salamanda's people have run. The mast is down. There is no more they can do from here."

"Then we did it!" Matt said.

"We have won!" Atoc smiled tiredly.

"You're wrong. . . ."

The voice came from the middle of the wreckage. Matt looked past the dead body of the police captain and saw Fabian, painfully trying to ease himself into a sitting position. He was very pale. It was impossible to say how much blood he had lost, but most of his suit was crimson.

"I was trying to tell you," Fabian said. It was as if he were talking to a very young child. The words came out very simply. Perhaps he knew that he had only moments to live. "You were wrong from the start," he went on. "The swan . . ." He gulped for breath. "They controlled it from here to start with. But when it came in range . . . Salamanda took over."

"Where is he?" Matt demanded.

"At the place of Qolqa. He has a mobile laboratory. He's in control. Look. . . ."

Miraculously, although the plasma screen had been damaged, the black dots were still there. And the single dot was still moving. It had traveled almost halfway across the screen. Soon it would be at the bottom. The digital clock showed 22:24:00. Ninety-six minutes until midnight.

"I'm sorry," Fabian whispered. "But I told you. It was always true. You could never win."

His head fell sideways, and Matt knew that he had died.

"What does he mean?" Atoc asked.

"It's not over yet," Matt said. "Salamanda is in the desert. He's controlling the satellite." He pointed. The dot had only half a meter to travel. How many miles? Matt could imagine it edging ever closer to its destination between the mountains.

"We must be able to stop it," Richard said. "We can't have done all this for nothing. . . ."

"How far is he from here?" Atoc demanded.

"I don't know. A hundred miles. Not more than that . . ."

"There's a helicopter. . . ."

The helicopter was a two-seater.

Richard, Matt, Pedro, and Atoc had emerged from the control center to find that a new sort of silence had descended on the compound. It was the silence of death. There were bodies everywhere, some of them Inca, but the majority were Salamanda's men. The smell of burning hung in the air. Above them, the radio mast had been blown in half, the bent and broken steelwork shrouded in smoke. There were loose bricks and broken pieces of metal everywhere. The walls were pitted with bullet holes. All the lights had been extinguished, but the Incas had brought oil lamps and were using them to examine the wounded and the dead.

Forcing themselves to ignore the devastation, they had run over to the launchpad only to discover the bad news. The keys were in the ignition. Atoc knew how to fly it. But it could only take one passenger. Atoc and one other would face Salamanda at the place of Qolqa. Which one of them would it be? There was no time for negotiation.

"I'll go," Matt said.

"Matt . . ." Richard began.

"This is my fight, Richard. I began this. It's all because of me. I'll go with Atoc."

"I go, too." Pedro stepped forward. He was still holding his slingshot. He reminded Richard of a Peruvian David, about to take on Goliath.

Matt nodded. "The two of us can fit into one seat," he said. "Pedro's right. He must come, too."

"But you're just kids!" Richard cried. His voice was

hoarse. The smoke seemed to have gotten into his throat. "You can't do this on your own."

"We've always been on our own," Matt said. He smiled tiredly. "It has to be this way, Richard. The *amauta* said it would happen like this. It seems he was right."

"We have no time," Atoc said.

It was twenty to eleven. Very soon, the satellite would be in position. Matt nodded. He and Pedro moved forward.

The helicopter took almost five minutes to achieve full power. By the end, the rotors were whipping up the sand and the whole thing had disappeared in a cloud of dust. Richard tried to watch but his eyes were raw. His arm was folded across his face. He could hardly breathe.

The engine increased in volume. The helicopter rose clumsily off the ground. Squinting, Richard could just make out Matt with Pedro squeezed next to him. Matt looked more serious, more determined than Richard had ever seen him look before. The helicopter rocked on its axis, once, then again.

Then suddenly it rose and soared over the wire.

There was only one hour left.

TWENTY
The Gate Opens

It was Pedro who saw it first. From the air it looked like a silver matchbox, glinting in the moonlight, sitting on its own in the great emptiness of the Nazca plain. It could have been a trailer or some sort of mobile home. But it had been driven into the middle of the desert, its tires gouging out a track in the soft earth, and parked in front of the place of Qolqa. There could be no doubt at all who was inside it. This was the laboratory that Fabian had warned them about. Salamanda was controlling the satellite from here.

The journey had taken half an hour. There were just thirty minutes until midnight.

"Something wrong . . ." Atoc said.

The words were no sooner out of his mouth than Matt felt it. The helicopter shuddered and seemed to come to a halt in midair. They were twelve thousand feet above the ground and suddenly Matt was horribly aware of every single one of them. His stomach churned as they dropped. Pedro, squeezed into the seat beside him, cried out in alarm. Atoc pulled desperately at the controls, and the helicopter recovered, tottering in the air like a drunken man.

"What is it?" Matt demanded.

"I don't know . . . !"

A single, stray bullet had done the damage. It had slammed into the side of the helicopter, severing one of the main hydraulic cables, and although it had held for a while, the truth was that they should never have taken off. The power to the rotors had been cut and now the helicopter went into free fall. It was like being sucked into a black hole. The entire universe seemed to twist around them and — in a blur of silver and yellow and black — Matt caught sight of the desert floor rushing toward them. Atoc was shouting in his own language, perhaps a final prayer. All the instruments on the dashboard had gone mad, needles spinning, counters turning, warning lights flashing uselessly. Pedro grabbed hold of him. The entire cabin was vibrating crazily. Matt was seeing three of everything. His eyeballs felt as if they were being torn out of his head.

Atoc did the best that he could. Even without power, there was enough energy left in the spinning blades to bring the helicopter down in some sort of controlled landing. At the last moment, he shouted out something but he had spoken in his own language — Matt would never find out what he meant. The helicopter, traveling far too fast, slammed into the ground at an angle and began to topple over. Matt was thrown on top of Pedro. Then the rotors came into contact with the ground. There was a hideous screaming sound as metal stanchions were ripped apart and one of the blades shattered. Matt wasn't quite sure what happened next. The air was full of spinning pieces of metal and one of them must have hit the cockpit, because the glass disintegrated. He could smell burning. Sparks were leaping out of the control panel and there was a brilliant light, just above his head, flashing on and off. He thought he was falling forward. It was as if the helicopter were somersaulting. But then it lurched back again. There was a crash as the tail hit the ground. At last everything was still.

Matt looked around him and saw nothing. They were surrounded by dust; it hung over them like a shroud. Part of the cockpit had buried itself in the desert floor. The helicopter was lying on its side. He couldn't move! For a few, horrible seconds, he thought he was paralyzed. Then he realized it was the seat belt, pinning him down. Slowly, he forced his hand down and released it. He could smell petrol, and somewhere in the back of his mind he had to fight back a murmur of pure terror. The helicopter was about to blow up. He and Pedro were going to be burned alive.

"Pedro . . . ?" he called out, suddenly wondering if the other boy *was* still alive.

"Matt . . ."

Pedro dragged himself from underneath Matt and wriggled out of the cockpit, onto the desert floor. Matt followed him.

His entire body was in pain. He knew that he must have suffered whiplash injuries to his neck and spine. It was a miracle he could still move. He pushed with his feet and felt the cool earth underneath him. The rotors, mangled and broken, hung over him. The tail of the helicopter had been snapped in half.

He dragged himself over to Pedro. "We need to move away," he said. He sniffed the air. "The helicopter could still blow up. The fuel . . ."

"Atoc . . . ?" Pedro asked.

Atoc was slumped in the front seat, and Matt saw at once that he was dead. The Inca had fought hard to save the two boys, but he hadn't been able to save himself. Looking at him, Matt felt a great wave of sadness descend on him. First there had been Micos, killed at the hacienda at Ica. And now Atoc. Two brothers, both in their twenties and both of them dead. Why? Did they really believe that Matt and Pedro were so important that it was worth giving up their lives to help them? Matt felt his eyes watering — but at the same time, with the sadness came a sense of anger and hatred for Salamanda, for Fabian, for Rodriguez and all the other adults with their greed and their ambition . . . their desire to change the world. They were the ones who had drawn him into this. Why couldn't they have just lived their lives and left him alone?

Pedro glanced at him questioningly. The look in his eyes was obvious. *What now?*

"We find Salamanda," Matt said. "We stop him."

But Pedro wasn't going anywhere. Matt looked down and saw the horrid truth. Pedro hadn't complained and he hadn't shown any sign of pain, but his leg was stretched out and his ankle was obviously broken. The foot was turned at a dreadful angle and there was already a massive swelling that went halfway up his leg.

For a long minute, Matt didn't say anything.

One boy will stand against the Old Ones and alone he will fall.

The words of the *amauta* seemed to whisper back to him in the midnight breeze. So this was how it was meant to happen. It had all been neatly arranged. A helicopter crash. Atoc killed. Pedro too injured to move. Matt on his own. Just as predicted.

Matt smiled grimly. *"Adiós,"* he said.

"No. Matteo . . ."

"I have to go." Matt stood up. The wreckage of the helicopter had begun to cool down. There wasn't going to be a fire or an explosion. He could leave Pedro here. "Richard and the others will be on their way," he said. "You won't have to wait too long."

He didn't know how much Pedro understood. It didn't matter anymore.

He turned and walked away.

He felt nothing. He might have done some damage to his neck and his back, but otherwise he hadn't been injured in the crash. It was late, but he wasn't tired. He didn't run but walked quickly, listening to the soft contact of his feet with the earth. It seemed to him that the breeze had died down. There was an extraordinary stillness in the desert, as if the whole world were holding its breath. He looked up. The sky was very black and littered with stars. He could make out the rise and fall of the mountains in the distance, nothing more than a single brushstroke on the great canvas that was this night. Briefly, he wondered about the condors that had attacked him the last time he was here. Well, let them come. He was ready for them. He could feel the power welling up inside him. He hadn't been chosen for this because he was an ordinary boy. He had been chosen because he was one of the five. He knew what he had to do.

The mobile laboratory was in front of him. The

helicopter had come down less than a quarter of a mile away. What time was it? He still had no watch and he wondered if he was too late, if midnight had already passed. In that case, somewhere in the Nazca desert or perhaps even in another part of Peru, the gate would have opened. The Old Ones would already be walking, once again, on the face of the Earth.

The laboratory was part truck, part container, part mobile home. It had been driven here on eight fat rubber tires but once it had arrived, it had been jacked up on steel legs so that the wheels were about twenty centimeters off the ground. There was a driving cabin at the front — empty — and a door with a couple of steps leading down the side. Matt's eyes were drawn to the roof. Another satellite dish, about three meters wide, pointed upward, connected to the main body of the vehicle by a series of thick wires. There were other machines surrounding it. A ladder led up at the very back. This was going to be easier than Matt had thought.

He stopped.

He remembered how he had to do it. The key was the smell of burning. Somehow, all this had begun with the death of his parents in a car accident when he was eight years old. That morning, his mother had burned the toast. And whenever his power came back to him, so did the memory of that single, defining moment in his life. When Gavin Taylor had tripped him up at Forrest Hill, he had smelled burning. A moment later, the chandelier had exploded. And the next day, in class, as Gwenda prepared to drive a petrol tanker into the school . . . the same thing.

He smelled it now. He closed his eyes and let it happen. His arms were loosely folded in front of him. He could feel the cool of the evening on the back of his neck. With a sense of calm, he waited for it to happen. He wasn't in any hurry. At last he was in control.

He opened his eyes.

In front of him, the satellite began to shimmer and bend, as if caught in a heat haze. Matt concentrated. It was as if he were pushing himself, or some part of himself, forward. Something invisible was flowing out of him. He heard a shot but he knew that nobody had fired at him. He had torn one of the bolts out of the roof. He smiled to himself and at once another bolt snapped, then two more. If there had been four men standing on the truck, they would have been unable to move the satellite dish. But Matt was ripping it out as if it were paper.

The entire dish rattled as if it were trying to jerk itself free of the metal roof. Matt helped it. He merely flicked his eyes and the dish came free, the cables and supports snapping, the whole thing spinning away into the night. And that was it. It was over. Whoever was inside the trailer would no longer have control of the satellite. Matt was astonished that, after all he had been through, the whole thing had ended so quickly.

The door of the mobile laboratory opened and a figure stepped out.

It was Salamanda. Matt had only ever seen him once, but of course the elongated head, the tiny eyes and mouth, and the colorless skin were unforgettable. He was wearing black trousers and a white shirt, the sleeves open and loose.

Carefully, he stepped down from the trailer. Even the three steps were a challenge for him. All his attention was focused on keeping his head upright. It was the same task that had occupied him throughout his life. Behind him, through the open door, Matt saw other men and a woman wearing a white coat. Miss Klein. He remembered her from the hacienda and wondered why she was here. But Salamanda wouldn't have been able to track the satellite on his own. He had brought along his technicians to help.

Almost idly, Matt wondered what would happen next. Salamanda reached the ground and stood, staring at him. He had something in his hand. A gun — of course. Did he really think he could use that against Matt?

"Why are you here?" Salamanda screamed in fury. His face would have been contorted in anger except that it was contorted already and always had been. His eyes blazed. "How did you get here?"

"What time is it?" Matt asked.

Salamanda stopped. It was as if he had been slapped. "What . . . ?"

"What time is it?"

The man understood the question and why Matt had asked it. "It's five minutes to twelve!" he replied. "Five minutes . . . that's all I need! Five minutes more!"

He raised the gun and fired.

The bullet exploded out of the barrel and began to travel toward Matt, aiming for his head. It didn't get anywhere near it. Matt simply stopped it in midair and sent it spinning away into the night. And at the same time, he pushed a little harder. Salamanda felt the waves of pure energy shimmer past him. He wasn't touched himself, but behind him, it was as if the truck with its mobile laboratory had been hit by a nuclear blast. The whole thing was picked up and flung away like a toy in the hands of an angry child, somersaulting over and over again as it bounced across the sand. It traveled for a hundred meters and at last came to a stop, crumpled in on itself, and lay still.

Salamanda stood where he was, out in the open, exposed. He had nothing to support him. The gun hung limp in his hand.

"You think you've won," he said. "But you haven't. The world belonged to the Old Ones and it will belong to them again. It said so in the diary. . . ."

"Maybe the diary was wrong."

"It can't be."

Matt gazed at the man who had caused him so much torment, who had tried to kill him and who had been responsible for the deaths of his friends. "Why did you do it?" he asked. "You're rich. You've got all these houses. You've got a huge business. Why wasn't it enough?"

Salamanda laughed. "You're a child!" he said dismissively. "Or you'd understand. There's no such thing as enough." He fell silent. Nothing moved. The people inside the laboratory were either unconscious or dead. Still there wasn't a hint of a breeze. "Do you have any idea how much I hate you?" Salamanda asked.

"Hate is all you have," Matt replied.

Salamanda lifted the gun and fired the five remaining shots.

Once again, Matt turned the bullets around and

scattered them. But this time, there were too many of them. He couldn't control where they all went. Three of them spun away into the night, but the two others smashed into Salamanda's chest. Salamanda was thrown off his feet and onto his back. Matt heard his neck break. The huge head rolled to the side. The eyes stared blankly up at the night.

It was over.

Matt let out a deep breath. He would go back to the helicopter and stay with Pedro until the morning if he had to. By then, Richard and the others would have arrived. They would probably be on their way even now. He shivered. It seemed to him that it had gotten very cold. And there was something else. He hadn't noticed it before, but there was the smell of decay in the air. Rotten meat. He looked up, remembering the condors. There was no sign of them. But the sky had changed color. There was something pulsating inside the blackness. A sort of dark mauve light. The stars seemed more intense than ever, unnaturally so. They were like lightbulbs that were about to fuse. Matt's head was aching. He looked over to the mountains. And there it was.

A single, brilliant light was traveling horizontally across, making for a point between two peaks. It was very low in the sky. From where Matt was standing, it looked as if it were just meters above the ground. He knew at once that it wasn't a star. Nor was it a plane. It was the satellite. It had to be. With a terrible sense of emptiness, Matt thought back over what had just happened. Salamanda had lined up the satellite. He had been guiding it into position. Then Matt had arrived and destroyed the laboratory.

But he'd been too late. It was as if he had destroyed a gun after the bullet had been fired. He hadn't had time to change the trajectory of the satellite, and even without guidance it had continued moving, making for its final resting point. Of course, it wouldn't stop. Perhaps it would end up crashing into the Earth. But that didn't matter. At the very instant that it reached its correct position, the alignment of the stars would be complete, the combination lock would be forced, and the gate would open.

And that was what was happening.

The gate was opening after all.

Matt felt something tremble underneath his feet. He looked down and saw a crack appear in the sand. It began quite close to where he was standing and then twisted and zigzagged into the distance. Another crack ran across it. Several more began to spread in every direction. It was as if the entire desert were breaking up. At the same time, some sort of liquid began to ooze out from below, spilling onto the sand. It was dark in color, somewhere between brown and red, with the consistency of glue or treacle — except that it was obviously blood, because Matt could smell it everywhere in the air, sweet and sickly. The cracks widened. Matt actually felt himself moving. It was as if he had been caught in an earthquake, except that this was somehow slower and more deliberate. The mauve light in the sky was pulsing harder than ever. Something somewhere began to scream. The sound came from everywhere, thin and high-pitched. Matt wanted to put his hands over his ears but he knew it would do no good.

He understood something now that he hadn't understood before. He had come to Peru looking for a second gate and had thought that it would be found somewhere in the Nazca desert. But he had been wrong. They had all been wrong. Because the Nazca desert *was* the gate. The whole thing. He could actually see the famous lines from where he was standing, even though it should have been impossible. They were glowing. There were circles and triangles, rectangles and squares, drawings on a vast scale, activated and ready after a wait of more than twenty thousand years.

The ground was rumbling. He could feel the vibrations traveling through him. He tried to refocus, to gather in his own power, but it was hopeless. He was as completely alone as he had been told he would be. There was nothing more he could do. The rumbling grew louder, and at the same time an icy wind sprang up all around him, throwing the sand into his eyes and sending his hair flapping against his forehead. Matt lost his balance and staggered. He heard laughter echoing across the plain. His vision shimmered and then there was the sound of what could have been a huge whiplash, so loud that it almost threw him off his feet. Light burst out of the desert floor, slicing through the air, lancing up into the sky. Blinded and battered, Matt fell to his knees.

Silence. Everything had stopped.

Then the creatures began to appear.

There was an eruption as if from a volcano. A huge bird exploded out of the ground in front of Matt and hung, static in the air, its wings beating so fast that they were barely visible. The earth boiled all around it. Matt felt the air buffeting against him and covered his face with his arms, afraid of being blinded. It was a hummingbird. Its eyes

302

were black and brilliant and full of wickedness. Its beak was half open, and Matt knew that if it chose to, it could swallow him whole.

Four massive, hairy legs suddenly appeared, reaching out over the edge of the desert, and a gigantic spider pulled itself up from below. Matt saw the poison sac hanging under its belly. Two glistening fangs jutted out of its neck. It paused for a moment, twitching, then scurried away.

There was a screech, and a monkey leaped out of nowhere, its tail curling and uncurling, its teeth stretched in a grotesque smile. One by one, the pictures that he had once seen from the air sprang to life. Matt stayed where he was, on his knees, waiting for his own death to come.

For perhaps twenty seconds, nothing more happened. Matt heard a buzzing sound. It started low and distant, then rose, getting louder and louder until it was as if there was a chain saw trying to cut the world apart. Matt pressed his hands against his ears, and the next moment a vast cloud of insects burst out of the cracks in the ground and twisted into the air. They were flies with fat, black bodies and beating wings. They flew out of the cracks in an endless swarm — thousands of them, then millions, then thousands of millions, a plague of flies thicker than the air, filling the entire sky. Then, as Matt watched in horror, they began to re-form themselves. They flew together, forming the shapes of men, armed soldiers. Each man was made up of perhaps ten thousand flies and in an instant there was a whole army of them, standing at attention in long lines that stretched all the way back to the mountains.

They were the advance guard. But there were still more creatures climbing out of the bowels of the Earth, finally breaking free from the world where they had been held captive for so many centuries.

The ones that came now were like no recognizable life-forms. They were just strange, freakish shapes with the beginnings of arms and legs stretching out of them. Some had horns, some teeth, some gleeful, bulging eyes. Some were part animal and part human, an alligator on legs, a pig the size of a horse, a huge toad with the head of a bird. Each one was more deformed, more horrible than the one before, and they continued to pour out of the ground until the entire desert floor was covered by them. Some were black. Some were gray. Occasionally there were bursts of color: green feathers, glistening white teeth, the dirty yellow of pus dripping from an open wound. They stood there, breathing the air of the world they had come to destroy with the fly soldiers stretching out behind them, waiting for their first command.

But their true commander was still to come.

A fork of lighting splintered through the night sky and the rumbling deepened. One after the other, thirteen more figures in the form of men appeared on horseback, dressed in rusting armor and rags. Each one of them was a giant, ten feet tall. There was a flash of lightning — the entire sky blazed — and in that instant their shapes changed. Now they were skeletons, on skeleton animals. Another flash and they were ghosts, creatures made up of smoke and air. They made no sound and moved like shadows, rippling across the desert surface. Once again they seemed to shimmer and become solid and stood in a semicircle, waiting. It was colder than ever. Their breath was turning white, curling around their lips.

At last the King of the Old Ones rose out of the desert floor.

Matt trembled. The king was larger than any of the creatures that had appeared so far. If he had wanted to, he could surely have stretched up and touched the clouds. Each one of his fingernails would have been larger than Matt himself. It was difficult to see very much of him. Darkness clung to the terrible creature like a cloak, hiding him. The King of the Old Ones was too gigantic to be seen, too horrible to be understood.

Very slowly, he became aware of Matt, sensing him in the same way that a poisonous snake might sense its prey. Matt felt the creature turn its eyes on him. He began to search for any of the power that might still be inside him even though he knew he would never have enough. There had to be five of them.

Matt got to his feet.

"Go back!" he shouted. His voice was tiny. He was nothing more than an insect. "You have no place here."

The King of the Old Ones laughed. It was a hideous sound, deep and deathly, like thunder, echoing all around.

A quarter of a mile away, lying beside the helicopter, Pedro heard the sound and turned to where he knew Matt must be standing.

"Matt . . ." he whispered.

Matt heard him. The prophecy had been wrong. He wasn't quite alone after all. Pedro was nearby, and if there were two them, that doubled his power. With renewed strength, he got to his feet and lashed out, sending all the energy that he had left toward the huge creature that was standing in front of him. The whole desert rippled. The

305

King of the Old Ones screamed and fell back a step. All the other creatures, feeling his pain, screamed, too. Later it would be said that the sound had been heard all over Peru, though nobody had been able to say what it was or from where it had come. It seemed to Matt that he was winning. The Old Ones were withering in front of him, shriveling like scraps of paper in a bonfire. Pedro was with him and if the two of them could just continue a few seconds more . . .

But Matt had taken his power to its limit, and it was burning him up. He saw two suns, searing his eyes. Something huge and black, bigger than the night itself, rushed in on him and struck him down. He was thrown backward, crashing into the ground. Blood trickled from his nose and out of the corners of his eyes.

The King of the Old Ones, badly wounded and weakened, took one last look at the limp body. Then, calling his hordes around him, he folded himself into the night.

TWENTY-ONE
The Healer

The doctor was a small, neat man with light brown hair and glasses. He was holding a scratched and battered leather case that was too full to close properly. His name was Christian Nourry and he wasn't Peruvian, but French, working with the Red Cross in some of the country's poorest towns.

"I'm sorry, Professor Chambers," he said. "There's nothing more that I can do."

"Is the boy dying?"

The doctor shrugged. "I've already told you — this is outside my experience. Matthew is in a deep coma. His heartbeat is far too slow and there seems to be very little activity in his brain. My guess would be that he is unlikely to recover. It would help me if you could explain how he got himself into this state."

Chambers shrugged.

"Well, in that case, I can't say for sure what's going to happen. There is one thing I am sure about, though: He'd be a lot better off in a local hospital."

"I don't agree. There's nothing a hospital can do for him that we can't do here. And we prefer to keep an eye on him."

"You mentioned another boy. What about him?"

307

"Pedro? He *is* in hospital. He broke his ankle and they had to put it in a cast. We're expecting him back this afternoon."

"What have these two young people been doing? Fighting a war?"

"Thank you for coming, Dr. Nourry."

"Well, call me day or night. I'll come immediately." The doctor sighed. "I think you should prepare yourself. It seems to me that he's hanging on to life by a thread, and that thread could snap at any time."

Professor Chambers waited until the doctor had gone, then went back into the house. Inside, everything was cool, the air circulated by fans in every room. Slowly, she climbed a polished wooden staircase and went into a large, square room with rush mats on the floor and bright plaster walls. Two open windows looked out over the garden. There was a sprinkler just outside, rhythmically pumping water out over the lawn.

Matt was lying in bed with his eyes closed, covered by a single sheet. There was an oxygen mask strapped to his face, and a plastic bag hung over him with a saline drip connected to his arm. He was very pale. The rise and fall of his chest as he breathed was so slight as to be almost imperceptible. Professor Chambers thought about what the doctor had just said. Matt didn't just look close to death. For all intents and purposes, he looked dead already.

"What did the doctor say?" Richard asked.

The journalist had been sitting beside the bed for the past thirty-six hours, apart from a few hours in the early morning when the professor had forcibly sent him to get some rest himself. He had aged ten years since the two of them had driven out to the desert and found Pedro, lying in the wreckage of the helicopter with a broken ankle and the beginnings of a fever, and then Matt, sprawled facedown in the dust. There were deep lines in his face and his eyes were bloodshot. Nobody knew what had happened in the desert but it was obvious to Chambers that Richard blamed himself for allowing the two boys to set off on their own.

"It's not good news," Chambers said. "He doesn't think Matt's going to make it."

Richard let out a single breath. He could see Matt's condition for himself but he had been hoping against hope for good news. "I should never have let him come to Peru," he said. "He didn't want to come. He didn't want any of this."

"You should get some lunch. It's not going to help Matt, making yourself ill."

"I can't eat. I don't have any appetite." Richard looked down at the silent boy. "What happened to him out there, Professor? What did they do to him?"

"Maybe Pedro will be able to tell us." Chambers glanced at her watch. "I'm going to the hospital to pick him up this afternoon."

"I'll stay with Matt." Richard ran a hand across his cheek. He hadn't shaved for two days and he had the beginnings of a beard. "When I first met him, you know, I didn't even believe him. I thought he was just a kid with an overactive imagination. So much has happened since then. And now this . . ."

There was a commotion outside in the garden. While

the two of them had been speaking, a car had drawn up and the driver was unhappy about something. He was shouting and one of the gardeners was trying to calm him down. Professor Chambers went over to the window and looked out. The car was a taxi. The driver was demanding payment. She frowned.

"It's Pedro," she said.

The two of them hurried out of the room, reaching the stairs just as Pedro came in through the front door, support-ing himself on crutches. He was still wearing hospital pajamas. There was a brand-new plaster cast on his left foot.

"*¿Qué tú estás haciendo aquí?*" Professor Chambers exclaimed. She spoke fluent Spanish. "What are you doing here? I was coming for you this afternoon. . . ."

"*¿Dondé está Matteo?*" Pedro demanded.

It seemed to Richard that Pedro, too, had been changed by whatever had taken place in the desert. The boy had always been quiet; he had no choice when so much of the conversation had been in English. But he had also seemed detached, somehow on the edge of events. Now, for the first time, he was in command. He knew exactly what he was doing. He had marched out of the hospital and into a taxi. He had persuaded the driver to bring him here. He knew what he wanted, and he wasn't going to let anyone stand in his way.

Professor Chambers must have sensed this, too. "*Matt está aquí,*" she said, pointing at the stairs. Then, realizing that Pedro would never make it on his own, she held out an arm. Pedro gathered up his crutches, and the two of them began to climb up awkwardly together. As he went, Pedro turned and glanced briefly at Richard, and in that moment Richard felt a sense of relief that he couldn't begin to understand. Suddenly, he was sure that Matt was going to be all right.

Pedro rested briefly against the door of Matt's room. He took everything in very quickly. Professor Chambers wanted to go in with him but Pedro shook his head, then muttered a single word in English, "Alone."

Chambers hesitated. But there was no point arguing. She watched as Pedro dragged himself into the room. The door closed behind him.

•   •   •

Pedro didn't move.

He still wasn't sure what had brought him here, and now that he had arrived, he didn't know what he was meant to do. The English boy looked dead. No. That wasn't quite true. His chest was moving, and Pedro could hear the rasp of his breath behind the oxygen mask. Aside from the last day and a half, Pedro had never been in a hospital in his life and the sight of the medical equipment unnerved him: the metal cylinder pumping out its carefully measured quantities of air, the liquid dripping down the plastic tube into Matt's arm.

He knew that he had to be here. The two of them had spoken, of course. Pedro asleep in the hospital. Matt unconscious here. They had met one last time, and Matt had urged him to come.

"I need you, Pedro."

311

But why? What could he possibly do?

Pedro limped over to the bed and sat down on the edge, letting his crutches slide gently onto the floor. Now he was leaning over Matt, who was spread out beneath him, underneath the white sheet. The oxygen hissed. The plastic mask briefly misted. Otherwise everything was silent and still.

Pedro reached out.

He knew. It was as if someone had given him a book of his entire life and he was reading it and understanding it for the first time. He had once told Matt that he had no special powers . . . but he knew it wasn't true. After the flood, when his parents and entire family had been killed, he had been aware of something inside him. A new strength. And over the years it had grown.

He was a healer.

Living in Poison Town, there were so many diseases. People were getting ill and dying all the time. But not those who lived close to him. They were never sick, and Sebastian had often remarked upon it. He had said as much when Matt was there.

"There is no illness in this house or in this street. Nobody understands why. . . ."

And he had been aware of it again when Matt had been brutally beaten up by the policemen at the hotel in Lima. After just one day together, all of Matt's bruises had gone. The cracked ribs had somehow healed themselves. Pedro hadn't done anything. He hadn't needed to. Just being there was enough.

Gently, Pedro placed a hand on Matt's chest. At last he was fully aware of his power. Now he was going to use it.

But would it work? Had he left it too late?

Pedro closed his eyes and let the energy flow.

• • •

A week later.

The sun was beginning to set over the town of Nazca, and the air was heavy and warm. Professor Chambers came out of the house, carrying a jug of iced lime juice and four glasses. She had lit a barbecue and the flames were leaping up, filling the garden with smoke and the smell of charcoal.

Richard, Matt, and Pedro were waiting for her, sitting around the table in wicker chairs. Pedro's crutches were lying on the grass. He would need them for a couple more weeks, though his ankle was already on the mend. But it was Matt's recovery that had been all the more remarkable. He had woken up just a few hours after Pedro's return. A day later he had been eating and drinking. And now, here he was, sitting as if nothing had happened.

Richard found it impossible to believe, even though Professor Chambers had tried to explain it to him. "Thaumaturgy," she had said, as if it had been something she had been expecting all along.

"What's that?"

"Faith healing. Of course, in this day and age, few people believe in it anymore. But ancient civilizations relied on it. The Incas, for example. They used it all the time. Thaumaturgy is the ability to treat sickness using some sort of inner, psychic ability."

"And Pedro . . . ?"

"Well, the Incas seemed to think he was one of their own. So I suppose it's no surprise he has the ability." She shook her head. "What does it matter how it happened?" she exclaimed. "He saved Matt's life. That's all we need to know."

Now Richard watched as Professor Chambers put down the tray and went over to the barbecue. The coals had begun to glow. She spread four steaks over the grill and went back to the table.

Nobody spoke while the meat cooked. In the days that had passed since Matt's recovery, they had all gotten used to his long silences. Matt still hadn't told them what had happened at the place of Qolqa, and they knew not to ask. Everything would be said in its own time. Sometimes, still, Richard worried about him. Matt wasn't quite his old self. The pain had changed him, and now and then Richard could see it; the evidence was in his eyes.

Matt was reading a newspaper. It was several days out of date, but Susan Ashwood had sent it to them from England with an article highlighted on page five.

CHURCH DISPUTES DISAPPEARING BOY

Was it a miracle, as some are suggesting, or is there a rational explanation for the disappearing boy of San Galgano, as he has come to be known in the ancient Tuscan city of Lucca?

The facts are these. San Galgano is an ancient abbey just outside Lucca, dating back to the twelfth century. It is occupied by a devout order of Cistercian

314

monks who are unused to the glare of modern publicity. But earlier this week, in the cloisters, one of these monks encountered a young boy who spoke to him in English. The boy picked a flower and then walked through a door and disappeared.

The story may seem ordinary enough until you examine the facts. First of all, the abbey is not open to the public, and it would be impossible to enter without being noticed. But more bizarre is the door which the boy used to enter the cloister. This door is not only kept locked — it was actually bricked up a hundred years ago by the abbot.

It seems also that the door has a curse attached to it. According to local legend, the appearance of the boy signals nothing less than the beginning of the Last Judgment! However, a church spokesman, speaking at the Vatican today, insisted that this was more likely to be simply the case of a tourist who had lost his way. . . .

As the professor sat down, Matt folded the paper away. He knew that he was the boy the monk had seen. He had gone through a door in London and it now seemed that he had come out of one in Lucca, somewhere in Italy. William Morton, the antique dealer who had briefly owned the diary, must have learned about the passageway. That much was clear to him. He had tested Matt by making him walk through the door at St. Meredith's. By returning with a flower plucked in another country, Matt would have proved that he was indeed one of the five.

But how had the doorway worked? Had it been constructed

by the same people who had built the gates — and if so, why? These were things that Matt still didn't understand.

The steaks finished cooking. Professor Chambers served them with salad greens that she had grown herself. It was only when they had eaten that Matt began to speak.

"We have to talk about what's happened," he began. His voice was soft and somehow didn't sound like him. Richard glanced at him, trying to conceal a sense of sadness. Matt's childhood had ended. He could see it. It was as simple as that.

"The Incas told me that the gate would open and that the Old Ones would come into the world," he said. "It was their prophecy. And they were right. Salamanda knew it, too. I suppose it was written in the diary. . . ."

"Where is the diary?" Richard asked.

"Salamanda had it. Now that he's dead, perhaps we'll never find it."

"Were the Incas really right?" Chambers asked.

Matt nodded. "I thought Pedro and I could stop the gate from opening, but I see now that some things can't be changed. They'll always happen the way they were supposed to."

He drew a breath.

"We won the first time, in England," he said. "We managed to close Raven's Gate. But this time we lost."

"No . . ." Richard began.

"Yes. I'm sorry, but it's the truth. I saw the Old Ones and although I tried to fight them, even with Pedro helping me, I didn't have enough strength. We have to face the fact that the Old Ones are here, in the world."

"Then where are they?" Richard couldn't believe what he was hearing. He didn't want to believe it. "It's been a week now. But the world is still the same. Nothing has happened. You must have beaten them!"

"I *wounded* them. Maybe they're resting, waiting until they regain their strength. But I can feel them, Richard. There's a coldness in the air. They're already spreading out, making their plans. They're everywhere. And soon it will begin. . . ."

"Well, that's great!" Richard couldn't keep the bitterness out of his voice. "So why did we come here? What's this all been about?"

"We had to come here, Richard. It's all so difficult, but I think I'm beginning to understand things a bit now."

Matt took a breath, then continued.

"There are five of us. Four boys and a girl. We're all the same age and we've all been born for the same reason. Somehow, we have to find each other. Once there are five of us, that's when the real fight will begin."

"But where are the others?" Richard asked. "They could be anywhere in the world."

"Pedro is the second of them," Matt said. "That's why I had to come to Peru. To find him. And I've seen the others — but only when I've been asleep. We have dreams which help us. They're not like ordinary dreams. They're part of how it all works. And it's not going to be as hard as you think. Pedro and I came together even though we had completely different lives, thousands of miles apart. I think the others are already looking for us. It's just a matter of time. . . ."

"But the Old Ones are already here," Chambers said. "How much time do we have?"

Matt didn't answer.

A cloud passed in front of the sun, and a shadow fell across the garden. And elsewhere, all around the world, the shadows were stretching out, too.

Evil star had risen.

The darkness was drawing in.

**The story continues
in NIGHTRISE.**